Praise for Eli...

The Winds of Fate Reviews:

"...captivating romance that takes us to the world of seventeenth-century London...Sexual tension and legal and familial intrigue ensue with the reader cheering on the lovely pair." – *Publishers Weekly*

"has everything...full of passion, betrayal, mystery and all the good stuff readers love." – *ABNA Reviewer*

"Original...strong-willed heroine...I love all of it...the unlikely premise of a female member of the aristocracy visiting a man who is condemned to die and asking him to marry her."– *ABNA Reviewer*

Surrender the Wind Reviews:

Surrender the Wind won the National Excellence in Romance Fiction Award and a prestigious Holt Medallion Finalist. "The lush descriptions of the southern countryside, the witty repartee between the characters, the factual descriptions of battles woven into the storylines, and the rich characters kept me glued to the pages." – *Alwyztrouble's Romance Reviews*

Surrender the Wind received the "Crowned Heart" and National "RONE AWARD" finalist for excellence. "With twists and turns...and several related subplots woven in, no emotional stone is left unturned in this romance." – *InD'tale Magazine*

Sweet Vengeance: Duke of Rutland Series I Reviews:

Sweet Vengeance received the International Book Award. "A historical romantic masterpiece...sizzling sensuality, touching emotions, and great historical detail. – *International Book Award*

Surrender to Honor

Surrender Series II

Elizabeth St. Michel

Surrender to Honor
Surrender Series II

Copyright © 2019R by Elizabeth St. Michel

ISBN: 978-1-9500160-02-0
ISBN: 1-950016-02-1
Library of Congress Control Number: 2019914267

For Stephanie

A daughter to laugh with, dream with, and cherish with all my heart.

Forgotten and worn, but strongly forward,
The warrior's province, war and labor;
Roves along a burdened life;
Tactics, strategies, campaigns still pursuing;
With confidence of Hercules to slay the Hydra;
Ares rages, raucously roaring;
Rulings made by Attila's sword;
With stealth the war-lust, coarse and wild;
Surrender honor to the noble warrior.

~Elizabeth St. Michel

Chapter 1

Midnight September 1864
Richmond, Virginia

Night clutched the city with its treacherous dark talons. Inside an empty warehouse, Rachel Pierce pushed a wobbly cart that teetered then jolted over uneven brick. Farther and farther down a labyrinth of ill-lit corridors, she searched for the one she had come to free.

Her legs leaden, she stopped at a narrow window and pried it open. A shower of coal dust settled on her head. She peered out. Acrid smoke belched from the fiery forges of the Tredegar Iron Works, stinging her nostrils and throat. Down below violent rapids thundered on the James River while soot rose and fell from a slight breeze before falling as a filmy veil that coated every surface.

Rachel glanced at her hands, rubbed with butternut to darken her skin. Appearances did not concern her. Stooped in darkness and dressed in tatters, she masqueraded well disguised as a male slave.

She rattled her cart into a cavernous wing, jutting from the main building like the claw of a crab thrown on its side. Windows were broken and blocked with wooden boards. Ceiling moisture pattered onto the floor and dripped on her shoulder. Her nose twitched with the stink of ancient tobacco bales soured with mold. A rat scurried across her foot, and she squelched a scream. Bile rose to her throat. A second later, the crack of a whip ripped the air, followed by agonized moans. She wanted to run, to breathe the damp air of freedom. If caught, she would be hanged.

To improvise at the last minute? No time to plan implied high risk and greater odds of failure. She had eavesdropped on a conversation, had learned that the Rebs had secured someone of great importance and were interrogating him at the Oak Street warehouse.

Her quicksand feet refused to move. Seared memories of her father taunted her, beckoned her to go farther, to drown her fears, to do her God-given duty.

Rachel dragged her feet. Hot tears stung her eyes.

The moans rose louder. She followed flickering yellow lantern lights smudged by coal dust. She bundled the growing panic in her chest, took a deep breath and entered a large room. Two guards, too busy with their card play, ignored the slave who had come to clean and empty chamber pots. Her hands clammy, she pulled a broom from her cart and swept, making her way into the room opposite the groans.

A hole in the wall allowed her to spy. Two men loomed about their captive. His hands were tied above him and the ropes had cut the skin from his wrists. His toes barely grazed the floor. His dark hair lay matted to his nape and he was stripped of his clothing. Ugly welts across his muscular back and arms gleamed in the lantern light. Blood oozed from his wounds and ran down his buttocks. The whip sang through the air and slashed his flesh. The prisoner jerked and moaned aloud.

Rachel wiped beads of sweat from her forehead. She had to save him. He couldn't end up like her father.

A Confederate officer, his back to her, raised his whip again and said grimly, "You'll tell us soon enough. It might as well be now while you can talk sensibly."

"You'll roast in hell first," his victim said in a deep vibrant voice that carried easily to Rachel's ears. She did not recognize the voice or him. Under the circumstances, the prisoner's demeanor astonished her, but his underlying stress touched her heart. His southern accent, she noted, seemed incongruous with the Union uniform on the floor. But then again, many in the south wanted the nation whole.

"You realize my skill," boasted the one with the whip. "You screamed before. You dare test me further?"

The prisoner's muscles clenched. *Snap*. The lash descended. The man's cry of agony pierced the air. Rachel shuddered.

"I admire your courage so much I have ordered one hundred lashes. Half of that will kill a man," boasted the captain.

"Do your worst. You won't get anywhere," the captive growled.

"There won't be any flesh on your bones when I'm done with you. However, I have the power to make your stay more comfortable. Just give us the names of all the spies in your network."

When the prisoner remained mute, the officer ordered him

dropped to the floor. They pushed his head into a bucket of water until Rachel thought he'd drown. She bit her knuckles to keep from screaming. Three separate times she counted. The officer kicked him. The captive retched. They pulled him up.

"Are you going to give us the names? The Saint says you have them all. He's the one who helped us trap you."

Rachel's breath burned from the lie.

Again, they let the lash fly. The prisoner crumbled.

"He's unconscious. Give it up for now, Captain. Go out and get some air, free from this stinking Yankee. We'll revive him when we return. I've never seen a body take so much."

"He'll die by inches if I have my way about it," the captain said and pushed out the door.

She waited until their footsteps fell away to distant echoes and disappeared altogether. Rachel shifted into the hallway. She tried the rusty handle on the prisoner's cell. Locked.

"Hold on there. Where do you think you're going?" With angry stares, both guards turned from their cards. These were not the best of the Confederacy. Straw-haired and shaggy faces like unshorn sheep, they glared, fleshy mottled brutes in filthy uniforms with large bloodshot eyes.

She held back in the shadows. Ice shot through her veins. Her legs shook. Attempting to sound nonchalant and in her best imitation of a slave boy's dialect, she said, "Captain ordered me to clean out this here cell. I have to hurry 'cause master wants me home."

Rachel kept her head bowed, still had them in her line of vision. The saw-toothed guard swore and threw down his cards. He hit her with his bulk, throwing her against the wall. "Serves you right, nigga, for getting in the way." He growled a strange raspy noise that imitated laughter and set his key into the lock.

Her hat fell to the floor and her hair tumbled down her shoulders. She stuffed her hair under her hat, clamping it to her head, a heartbeat before either guard noticed. Once inside the prisoner's cell, she listened as the guard locked the door and settled down to his cards. Rachel breathed a sigh of relief. How easy to manipulate the foolish guards, but how could she help an unconscious man escape through a locked door?

She touched him lightly on the shoulder so as not to hurt or frighten him. He did not respond. When she cut him down, he slumped to the floor. She thrust a vial of ammonia beneath his nose. He reared his head.

"I've come to free you," she whispered.

He shook his head, unsteady but conscious. She knelt beside him and rubbed his hands to restore circulation. "There are two guards out there. I'll create a diversion to get them in here. Are you able to help me incapacitate them?"

He nodded.

Rachel searched the room, grabbed a wooden rod left on the floor and handed it to him. She snatched up a metal baton, stood to one side of the door, motioned the captive behind the door on the other side and started screaming. "Glory be Almighty! Da man is dead. I'm scared of the dead. The devil gonna get me. Please let me out!" Keys jangled; the door swept wide. The two guards rushed in. With lightning speed and using all her strength, Rachel hauled the rod back and whacked the first guard on the head. He fell to the floor like an oak. Almost simultaneously, the prisoner sprang from behind the door and cracked the club down on the second guard and he fell as quickly as the first.

"Take his clothes off and put them on," Rachel ordered. "Hurry!"

Despite his lacerated back, the man needed no prodding. She helped him remove the guard's clothes. With great care, she assisted him into the filthy shirt. He winced from the pain. The clothes were a little baggy, but his wide shoulders and tall frame took in the excess. He bobbed and weaved, and she urged him to a chair, then tied and gagged the jailers.

"Get my ring and watch hidden in my trousers."

She rifled through his pants, thrust the items in her pockets, and then placed the prisoner's arm around her shoulder and forced him to rise.

"Stay with me." Every inch of her body protested under the additional weight. She locked the door and tossed the keys in a chamber pot. He staggered with the effort to keep up. Where he got the strength, she did not know, but with certainty, the fortune of securing the damp air of freedom motivated him. "If we encounter anyone, just look official."

His voice, though quiet, cut through the silence. "Why is it your speech has changed so?"

Damn. She had slipped from her practiced resonance and pitch. No time to think about the slip. Must find a way out. Were they followed? She peered over her shoulder. No one. She exhaled, and then crisscrossed several rooms to a door that led to the street. She hesitated, peeked through the window and reared back. A guard strolled on the walk. She squeezed the prisoner's hand to warn him. God he was hot. The guard ambled past, and then disappeared around the corner. The prisoner slumped more, his energy ebbing. She scrunched her eyes shut, pushed up with her knees.

"Don't pass out on me. I can't carry you." Rachel shoved the door open and, together, they stepped onto the street. Walking as fast as possible under the circumstances, they passed the charred remains of Crenshaw Woolen Company, then she pulled him into the shadows of the next vacant building and propped him against what was left of the door.

"I'll make it, and if providence prevails," he grated out in heavy breaths, "I vow to wrap my fingers around the Saint's throat and wring the life from him for every traitorous thing he's done."

Rachel stiffened. A shout shattered the night's calm. An alarm had been raised. Out of the darkness came a clatter of hooves and the snorting of horses. A covered funeral wagon with black sides and black plumes pulled up.

"Get in," she snapped. The wagon's boards bowed and creaked with the additional weight. The outcry came from the next street over. Feet pounded the boardwalk. Lots of feet. Her blood rushed. Only seconds before they were discovered.

She thrust herself inside as the gaudy wagon took off, and she dropped directly on top of the injured man. Rachel jammed a hand over his mouth, quelling his scream. "Shhh. Quiet," she hissed. "I'm sorry I caused you pain," she said, sliding to the side. "Now close your eyes. I have to change my clothes."

Nervous, undressing in front of a man present, a total stranger, she glanced over her shoulder. In the shadows, she could not see his countenance and assumed he obeyed her request. And she had not time to worry about it if he didn't.

Sitting on the floor with barely enough room to move, Rachel pulled off her shirt and tossed it aside. She loosened the tie that belted her pants then slipped from them.

Moving swiftly, she plucked off her cap and shook her head. Her long hair tumbled down her back. She smoothed back an errant curl, then unwrapped the material that bound her breasts, stripping off everything down to her pantalets and chemise. Noticing the interior, lined in black velvet with enough room to hold a coffin, she shivered.

Rounding the corner, the wagon lurched. She tumbled against him again, bringing her in contact with his lean frame. Her blood pounded. Her face burned. Mercifully, the darkness hid the extent of her embarrassment. Then Rachel felt the hard boldness of his hands as they moved over her breasts. She gasped and scrambled to her feet. In the meager light, she saw his jaw drop.

"Why, you're a woman."

She all but suffered a fatal apoplexy. "As a gentleman, I'd assumed you were looking the other way."

She heard a chuckle from deep inside his chest. "Am I being rescued by a woman, or am I dreaming?"

"You are hallucinating." She let out a long exasperated breath and made a grab for her hoops, hidden under a blanket on the seat with the rest of her clothing. Her fingers shook, making it impossible to tie them. She began to doubt the wisdom of saving a man she couldn't yet identify.

"There are certain...attributes...of yours that make my hallucination...delightful." His voice, though a bare whisper, seemed to fill the very corners of the wagon.

"I should throw you out for such insult. It would be wise to thank your benefactor, or perhaps you are more inclined to entertain your Confederate friends who plan to make short work of you." Rachel knotted her hoops then flung her dress over her head.

Just then, from north, east and west, the bellows of men grew near. Had the whole city been drawn to the chase?

Sitting, she gritted her teeth with the rocking movement of the wagon and fumbled with the buttons at the back of her dress. To ask him for assistance nettled her. "You are a scoundrel, but pray help me. There's no time to lose." She dropped down beside him, presenting her back. "Hurry!" Scarcely breathing, Rachel waited, feeling the stranger's nearness, yet not daring to move. His hands hovered above her back. She braced herself then felt his hands sweep her hair over her shoulder in what felt like a caress.

"It's like silk…" he rasped.

Rachel snatched her hair from his grasp and piled it on her head. Every fiber in her body warned her as his warm fingers brushed against her back and buttoned her dress. Had her cause been less dire, she would have fled in disgust. Indeed, she had to fight the urge to do so now. He seemed to take his time. "Is your delay deliberate or are you addled?"

She heard him draw a ragged breath. "I enjoy this feast so much I would not like to see it end."

Unable to bear it longer, she sprung away from him. "You're a fool."

Apparently unaffected by her pronouncement, his eyes stayed riveted on her as she rubbed the brown off her face, then brushed and pinned her hair.

"No fool…growing weaker. If I'm to die now, I am fulfilled with the most wonderful fantasy." His voice was hushed but sounded hollow.

"More like delirium." The wagon stopped in an alley. Men shouted over the hill. "Get out," she ordered with efficiency.

He did not answer.

"Simon!" she called to her servant. "He's losing consciousness. Help me."

Using all their strength, they transferred the prisoner to her open carriage and dropped him onto the floor.

"Ditching the funeral wagon and switching to my carriage will throw the Rebs off our trail." She sat in the rear seat, her back pressed to the squabs and fluffed out her hooped skirts to conceal the prisoner. Simon hopped in the front and snapped the whip. As the horses broke off at a clipped pace, the prisoner lurched against her legs. Her face heated to the roots of her hair.

She glanced over her shoulder. A legion of men on horses with torches crested the hill blocks behind them. "Simon, turn right past the Episcopal Church, left at the capitol building…" She knew Richmond like the back of her hand, having memorized every street and alley with her photographic memory. The carriage rounded a corner on two wheels, flying past Marshall's house, then slammed down on four wheels. Rachel smoothed her skirts and jerked white gloves over her stained hands. Where could they go?

No doubt the Confederates had a chokehold on every street. "Stop at Jefferson Davis' house." She hated deviating from her original plan, but it had taken precious time to load the captive into her vehicle. Seconds she could ill-afford to lose.

They parked their vehicle in front of the elegant façade of the Confederacy's presidential mansion. Soldiers on horseback drew up beside them. *Were they caught?* In chest-squeezing panic, logic dictated her wits held all the power.

"I do declare, you startled me, Lieutenant Washburn. Is it truly you?" asked Rachel. The lieutenant was a stringy, middle-sized man with a froglike face and jerky movements. His whiskers did not hide his jutting front teeth.

"Yes, ma'am." He held his head up like a woodpecker ready to strike.

"Are you just arriving at President Davis' ball? I daresay you're a little late. All evening I pined for your tender arms to escort me onto the dance floor, but instead I shall have to cry all night long." She fluttered her lashes at him with practiced ease.

"Miss Rachel, I'm on military business."

"Indeed. You never care about my tender feelings, and to think the handsomest man in all Richmond denies me. I shall never forgive you."

"Beg pardon, Miss Rachel." The lieutenant flushed. "You know I have great care for your feelings, but I'm looking for a dangerous spy."

"Oh, my! A dangerous spy? I'm frightened." She placed a gloved hand over her heart.

"Someone said they saw a carriage like yours near the wagon the spy used to get away. About a half-mile from here."

Rachel tasted fear. "Oh, my goodness. I would have fainted if I knew he was even close to me." She waved a hand to fan her face and leaned over, letting her shawl fall away to expose a delicate amount of bosom. His muttonchops worked up and down. She smiled, her impact well made. "Look there." She wagged a finger at the carriages parked in front of a line of stately oaks. "Perhaps your spy is in one of those."

It was risky business she was about. All Lieutenant Washburn had to do was question someone at the ball to find out she had left early.

"Your genius gives me pause, Miss Rachel."

"You know President Davis dances wonderfully, and Varina appeared so lovely in her rose silk gown," she breathed wistfully. "The whole evening was absolutely divine, but now I've a headache, and I'm going home."

The lieutenant straightened in his saddle, then frowned at her. "By yourself?"

"I have Simon, my servant, to drive me, but you could make up for your lack of attentions and be kind enough to escort us."

That earned her a scornful glance from Simon. The man under her skirts moaned.

Lieutenant Washburn looked sharply at her. "What's that noise?"

"Why, that's Simon." She leaned over and whispered confidingly, her feminine weapons fully primed. "He has intestinal upset at times, purely an agony for him. If I don't get home soon…" She held a hand to her head, capturing a dramatic pose. "I may swoon myself."

"Yes, ma'am. I'll do the honors of escorting you personally. Men, fan out and search those carriages. Leave no stone unturned." This time Simon genuinely moaned.

As they traveled to her home, Rachel noticed the lieutenant swatting at numerous flies buzzing about his face.

"You do have problems with loop flies," she offered sympathetically as he rode his quarter horse abreast of her carriage.

"I never heard of loop flies."

"Simon is an expert. Do tell Lieutenant Washburn what loop flies are."

Simon bent his head with earnest and humble admission. "Loop flies are common on farms as they are almost always found loopin' around a horse's rear."

After a full minute, Lieutenant Washburn snapped at her. "Is your boy calling me a horse's rear?"

"Oh no," she chided the lieutenant sweetly. "Simon has complete respect for all Confederate officers. He would never think of calling one a horse's rear."

Simon snapped the reins and she was jerked back, leaving Lieutenant Washburn in their dust.

Chapter 2

"Can you hear me, Simon?" Rachel demanded.

He pulled his ears out from his head at right angles. "I got ears. You ain't goin' in that room with that man no more. He's awake now, and I don't trust him. I smell a rat, and you're goin' to find yourself bound in a trap."

"I can only be hanged once," she sniffed, fingering the satin fringe on the drapes. A full week had passed since they rescued the prisoner and gambled bringing him to her home.

While gazing out her window, she shivered with the dust and odor of desolation. Seton Plantation, her ancestral home once rose imposing, but with years of war, it lay in ruin, a pale shadow of its former majesty. The lawns and gardens lay unkempt, the fields rioted with weeds, the fences were torn down for firewood, and the tumbledown slave cabins sat empty.

Not one penny would she put into repairs of an unholy edifice that symbolized cruelty and misery, and stood, shrunken from the world, hoping to be invisible, a crumbling ghastly silhouette of some previous existence she wanted no part. Grandfather, if he were alive, would have been in a temper.

Rachel didn't care one bit.

"That's a fine thing. I must protect you with every ounce of my backside. And you invitin' that Lieutenant Washburn to follow us home. Pure craziness."

Used to the devotion of her servant, Rachel smiled. He was still angry from the episode a week ago. "It happened to be the best I could improvise. Besides, Lieutenant Washburn practically swooned when I fainted into his arms."

"And if I didn't whip them horses around the house, he would have swooned some more if he caught that spy he was lookin' for in the bottom of your carriage."

Rachel laughed and ruffled his jet-black hair. They were united in their goals of ending the evil of southern slaveholders and over the years had developed an extraordinary bond.

"It ain't proper," he pouted. "If anyone were to find out you're the Saint, they'd hang us higher than the moon."

"No one's going to find out. There are only two Union officials who have that knowledge. I promise it's going to stay that way. Furthermore, I'm too careful."

Simon stuck his lower lip out, like he always did when he swelled with stubbornness. "Lately, you've been takin' too many risks for my blood to warm."

"We've important work to do. The Union needs us. We exercise a small role but an important one. You know it's the only way we can get things changed. We can't lose our perspective." She moved to hug him, but he put his hand up, not in the mood to be cajoled.

"What if he's spy-workin' for the South to find out who the Saint is?"

Why would anyone go to such lengths? "The only way to find out is by what we're doing. I'll simply use my instincts. They haven't failed me yet."

He swatted the air. "There's always a first time."

She laughed to cover her fear. As the Confederacy teetered from General Grant's hammering blows, the South grew increasingly desperate. Each mission she undertook bore a more dangerous struggle. At Jefferson Davis' ball, she had learned about the "Big Fish" whom the Confederates interrogated. She had snatched him from beneath their noses. All of Richmond rose in a blistering fury.

That "Big Fish" currently resided in the bedroom next to hers. Many nights, she had cared for him, dressing his wounds, and forcing laudanum down his throat to ease his pain. With her captive conscious now, she held a frantic sliver of hope to obtain information from him. Simon's warning rang. If he worked as a double agent, he'd sell her to the Confederacy for the highest bid.

Hadn't he vowed to kill the Saint? If he worked for the North and felt betrayed by the Saint, by being caught by Confederates, then his distrust would hold them at odds. A dark chill ran down her spine.

His stamina in disabling the guard when he was so weak and his terrific strength of mind, regardless of the tortures he endured was admirable. He did not break. One of those rare men who walked the earth honor bound.

Would he overpower her? She patted a knife hidden in her pocket. Oh, she'd make use of her strongest assets…wit and

making the pain of his wounds disappear. Her fingers massaged in circles, working deftly and easing the tenderness so well.

"You are healing nicely. You've come a long way from near death. A very lucky man to have escaped the Grim Reaper. Next time you may not be as lucky."

Lucas peeked at his abdomen, purple and lumpy where it should have been smooth. He clenched his hands into fists. He'd remember the Saint's minion who lived to beat and kick him.

Remarkably, he felt better. She replaced the bandages, plumped the pillows and helped him into a sitting position.

"Yet...I'm still a prisoner."

"Is it so bad?" She played a game with him, waiting for his reaction.

"My mind can barely absorb so much splendor. After the torture I received, I have another to take its place. Will you tell me your name, or are you going to keep it a secret?"

Her golden eyes flickered with interest. His words trite to her ear. She shook her head, tossing the curling tresses enticingly, and laughed somewhat ruefully. "Rachel," she said, her voice washing over him like a warm wave upon the sand. How adept she was, saying as little as possible.

"I am at a loss, sir," she murmured. "For I do not know your name."

"I guess we are at an impasse," Lucas fenced. He'd be frugal with information as well.

"We are going to need a level of trust if I'm to help you. My late departed mama said all Yankees are rogues. Are you a rogue?"

He admired her eloquent wordplay. All good liars were quick-witted. "I imagine I've done a few roguish things." He waved his hand over his surroundings. "I apologize if I have little to offer you. Since my departure from my last accommodations…my hosts have left me little to recommend."

Her eyes slid to where a Bible lay open on an end table. She gritted her teeth, and then rolled her shoulders back, as if forcing herself to relax. What was significant about the Bible that she dropped her emotional camouflage?

"The worst of sinners can have the best of intentions. So, there is hope for you…" She let her words fall, no doubt hoping to have him divulge his identity.

He smiled at her cleverness. "I gather you Rebels know my name if you took the trouble to kidnap me. What is it you want?"

She continued to assess him, her amber eyes skimmed over him, from his toes all the way to his face, her gaze ending on his mouth.

The hair rose on his neck. Instead of torture, was the Confederacy using the ruse of a beautiful woman to extort information from him? So, he followed her lead, assessing her from the toes to her tiny waist and elegant bosom to her sensuous, full lips.

She didn't flinch, obviously used to having men admire her.

"Am I so ugly that words are stricken from your tongue?"

"On the contrary," Lucas answered with a casual ease he little felt. "If this is to be my prison, then I will accept all terms of *your* punishment."

She laughed, her features composed.

A talented actress? "What are your opinions on the war?" Lucas asked, a question most women would brush off.

She stood haloed in shafts of late afternoon light. Her shadow stretched over him, caressing him. "I don't know. I don't think I have an opinion. I'm a woman after all."

Lucas' amusement died. Well-prepared, an original thinker. "I believe I have met my match."

"Whatever do you mean?" She lowered her voice, being purposefully mysterious.

She was the epitome of womanhood, exquisite and elegant. Though lacking trimming and hoops, the threadbare calico gown enhanced her loveliness. A rare jewel, she complemented the simple dress, making the mere garment a work of art. The lace at her throat parted, and the hollow of her neck filled with soft shadows.

Lucas sat transfixed. Time slipped past, and still he did not respond, all his senses involved with her. He failed the test. Although he gave it his best effort, he was powerless to control his own reaction to her. His gaze clung to hers, analyzing what lay beneath the surface. There appeared a puzzling glimpse to which he could not lay a finger, a hint of independence, a brief flash of impudence, and a surreptitious touch of guarded intelligence.

He dragged his attention from her and glanced out the window. There stood a barn in the distance, and in the paddock, horses curved their hooves, digging up bowls of dust. Despite his condition, he could and would, if necessary, overpower her to escape. How many Rebs guarded him outside the room?

With the grace of an angel, she fanned out her skirts and settled in a chair facing him. She folded her hands demurely together, appearing to be relaxed unlike moments before when she viewed the Bible he'd been reading. How white her fingers were clasped together, whether from fear or anxiousness, he couldn't tell. Her vulnerability was unexpected, and he found himself searching to find a way to put her at ease.

"I'm Colonel Lucas Rourke, Army of the Potomac," he said, hoping he wouldn't regret revealing his identity.

Her mouth dropped open. "You're Colonel Rourke? With great fortune, you have been rescued by the Saint."

Her words snapped him to attention.

"The Saint works without conscience for his personal gain. When I'm done with him, he'll wish he never inhabited the earth."

Her eyes scorched amber fire. "Perhaps you remain addled from the laudanum I dosed you with this week. The Saint can move through southern latitudes like an Indian savage with no trace of his footsteps and defy every one of his enemies without the slightest hint of their knowledge." She snapped her fingers in the air. "Just like a ghost."

Lucas had received an emergency missive to meet the Saint in Washington. He'd trusted the spy and went to meet him at an inlet on the Potomac. Ambushed by great numbers, he had been rendered unconscious, and then woke to the crack of a whip scoring his back in the capitol of the Confederacy.

Lucas lowered his voice. "The Saint has taught me a grievous lesson in betrayal. I'll see he is hunted down like the cur of a dog he is and have him hanged from the nearest tree for his crimes."

Her lips drew back in a snarl. "The Saint has employed every capacity that God has endowed him with. He's been far more successful than anyone might imagine, netting the North's most accurate information from politicians high in council as well as ubiquitous War Department clerks, military officers and a network that extends over most of Virginia." She yanked a note from her pocket and dropped it on his lap. "The Saint gave me this to convey to you."

Lucas opened the missive, signed by the Saint, flourished with his signature "S". He told him to trust Rachel Pierce. How could he trust her? He didn't trust the Saint. Caution was his best friend.

The Saint. The fabled agent who made a high art of spying. Lucas had never met the Saint, nor had anyone in his office, and no one had been able to provide a description. Up until now, the Saint had achieved a revered status of epic proportions. He astonished Union officials in Washington and generals on the line with maps of detailed troop numbers and movements, sketches of military arsenals and blueprints of weaponry. Repeatedly, information filtered through the lines like fish through a wide-meshed net. With confidence, he surfaced a genius, breaking many a rule, living on the edge of danger.

Lucas remained bitter, his most trusted spy had double-crossed him. "Of late, the Saint has discovered dishonesty is more profitable than honesty. How much gold does he require?"

"The Saint has always been loyal to the Union." Cold and lashing, her voice ripped at him. "Never once has he wavered from his task. I am sure he would be disappointed over your lack of appreciation for his heroic endeavors. Perhaps you have endured a head injury during your incarceration and suffer from circumstances of which you have no control. I am sure the Saint will understand your reluctance to put him in the best possible light. He would never dream that you would say disparaging things about him, and that your faith in him actually lays unbounded."

Her accent was unusual, more clipped when she was excited than the imperfect drawl she attempted to imitate. Where was her place of birth? Definitely not Virginia. "Why is your faith in the man so solid?"

She clapped her hands together in supplication to mock him. "The Saint is so romantic, don't you think? It makes me swoon to think of him. Has he not sent you Richmond's fortifications and other vital information?"

How would she know of Richmond's critical defenses the Saint had sent to his office? How close was her relationship with the Saint?

Lucas crossed his arms. What the Saint had accomplished over the past three years was legendary. But after what he'd been through, a part of Lucas remained wary of those operating in the shadows. "A season of war will teach you that mankind is not honest."

She glared holes in him. "Your character thus far demonstrates your painful lack of indiscretion. Might it be a better part of valor to treat your liberator with…more benevolence?"

Was lying natural as breathing for her? Words itched to get free. "I become obtuse when the Confederacy plays games. Brilliant, the use of a beautiful woman. You can ply your wares elsewhere. I've lived long enough to look a second time into things I am most certain of after the first instant."

She inhaled. "If you desire to seek additional comforts, I suggest you have a care to further remarks."

"I take great delight with you well-bred southern ladies,

notwithstanding the thunder of your treason." With purpose, he made his responses difficult. She had to be tested. He had to make sure she didn't work for the South. He remained responsible for far too many people.

"I find most men…incompetent, sir. Your presence perseveres that notion. On this, I am most sincere."

"I have learned a little sincerity is a dangerous thing. A great deal of it is absolutely fatal." He grabbed her wrist, refused to let go. "Where am I and why did you help me?"

"It was the Saint who rescued you. Dare you inflame him by besmirching his character?" She scowled at him, as if she would shoot him if he spoke one more insult. "I understand your hesitancy to trust. The Saint said to use the phrase, "day and night". Does this help?"

His muscles eased. The coded phrase she offered was designed for him. There was also the signed letter from the Saint and his baiting of her. He had weighed her reactions. No one could be so defensive unless legitimate.

His job lay heavy with risk. He'd take that gamble and trust one more time. Slowly he released her wrist. "My apologies, madam, but one can never be too sure in this endgame. How do you propose I get back to Washington?"

She inhaled. Her bosom rose, pressed high enough where the tops of her breasts caught the fading light underneath a soft shadow. He swallowed.

"All of Richmond is up in arms, seeking the great Yankee spy who has escaped. They are searching homes, barns, railroad depots and fields for you. I am afraid, Colonel Rourke, you are bigger news than General Lee."

The soft purr of her voice melted him further. Like she'd said, *welcome to temptation*. He shook his head. "I'm sorry…the laudanum. Could you repeat the last part?"

"I said, you must resist the temptation to leave before things die down."

He raked his fingers through his hair. He'd been a brute, knew it, but was unable to erase the hours of torture he endured. "Then I'll continue to appreciate your hospitality?" How long might he endure being in this close proximity?

A knock at the door caught both of their attentions. Lucas froze.

"It's me, Simon. I've come with dinner."

"Please enter," she said, rising and taking a tray from a willowy boy. The slave stood at the foot of Lucas' bed. Intense brown eyes stared at him with such arrogance, and cool disapproval, that he suspected the boy would take extreme pleasure in sticking splinters of oak into his eyeballs.

"All is well, Simon. This is Colonel Rourke. He is a friend. You may leave and rest well."

The boy dragged his feet. Lucas caught him muttering something about loop flies. He heard Rachel laugh. Until this moment, he never realized a human voice could mimic that of angels singing. He accepted a plate from her hand, and their fingers touched during the interchange. His were warm and hers were chilled. He raised a brow.

"Surely, you're not cold, Miss Rachel?" A gleam of satisfaction grew with her uneasiness she'd tried so hard to hide. He enjoyed her discomfort.

"I have a million things I must attend…" She turned and

gazed out the window. A touch of sadness covered her countenance. Black smoke billowed out of the chimneys of the ironworks to the west, and blanketed the fields of uncut, knee-high timothy hay. Chickens scratched around a broken-down coop. Menacing spikes of a burned-out barn exposed a forbidding rectangular foundation. The sun sank, diminishing to a thin amethyst line on the horizon with somber fingers of orange and magenta.

"Pray tell, would I be first and foremost on your mind?" he teased.

She narrowed her eyes. Though a gentle amber, they seemed unusually penetrating, as if they had witnessed a profundity of experience seldom met by a person her age. "Rest assured there will be no enjoyment found at my expense."

Lucas had been properly and deservedly chastised like a boy before the schoolmarm. "Truce?" he grinned.

"Done. Now eat your dinner."

Chicken soup. He hated chicken soup. "I'm not hungry."

"With all the people starving in Richmond, it seems a sin not to eat."

"I wouldn't know. I'm a stranger to sin." That earned him a smile. What else could he do to make this creature smile?

"If it makes you happy, I'll eat it." That earned him another smile. "Do you always get your way?"

"Always," she said as she bent to tuck a napkin under his neck. Lucas' head filled with the delicious scent of roses. He had to work harder on what he was saying. "Your boy seems less reserved than most slaves."

Her chin lifted a notch. "Simon is not a slave. I freed him."

She was fond of Simon, and her voice reflected that affection. "There is more?"

"Simon and his mother were escapees. They were caught and herded into a barn with other escaped slaves. Their masters decided a lesson must be learned. The barn was locked and torched. In the confusion, Simon's mother pushed him through a hole in the back wall. He escaped. However, his mother was not so lucky. Simon was captured and resold."

Lucas raised a brow. "From his attachment to you, I sense the history goes further."

"Simon was to be hobbled by his new master who tired of him running away. I happened to be visiting and bought him right then and there. Of course, his master extracted an exorbitant price. Simon's worth every penny and has been with me ever since."

She rose and walked to the door, the sway of hips and soft swish of her skirts mesmerized him. Good Lord, the woman possessed weapons to scourge his backside all over again.

She stopped, pulled items from her pocket, then dropped his ring and pocket watch in his palm. "I forgot to return these to you."

"My father's pocket watch. He gave it to me before I left…the one item that reminds me of home. Thank you." He saw her gaze drift to his gold West Point ring he placed on his finger. He said nothing.

"I must go about my errands."

"One more question before you leave. Do you love the Saint?" For some insane reason Lucas had to know.

"I would hope so," she said, bestowing a sly secretive smile that confirmed his suspicion. "Tell me, Colonel Rourke, will you miss me when I am gone?"

She teased him now. Yet, he hated any thought of her affections for the Saint, a man who used her for his schemes. Rachel presented a rare picture of a woman, a breath of fresh air, far from the dowdy women who inhabited Washington, especially the annoying general's daughter who was trying to trap him into marriage.

Her amusement swiftly died as if she sought to erect a wall of defense against him. "I apologize, Colonel Rourke, but I have to lock you in here for your own protection. Good night."

Lucas might have entertained the notion of annoyance for the locking of his door. Her footsteps fell softly into the room next to his. He smiled. She slept one wall away. "No apologies, Miss Rachel. But perhaps you should lock your door...*for your protection*."

The irony struck deep.

She lay safe.

He was an honorable man.

Chapter 3

"Miss Rachel, you got callers," Simon yelled from the bottom of the stairs.

She hesitated before the mirror. Black circles shadowed beneath her eyes. Unaccustomed to someone sleeping in her home, she had not slept well and had risen late. The annoying Colonel Rourke had paced her father's room during the long night hours, and she'd been aware of his every movement.

The Confederates had pulled off a brilliant coup capturing Colonel Rourke. He was one of the top commanders of the Office of Civilian Spying, an asset owning dangerous and vital information for the North that the Rebels would seize upon. Netting Colonel Rourke was almost as bad as apprehending President Lincoln.

She had studied Colonel Rourke while he was unconscious, reclined like a warrior taking his rest, and it did not quell the rioting in her stomach. Regardless of his wretched state, he was the most beautiful man she'd ever seen. His face was shockingly handsome with high cheekbones and full lips. His thick wildly unkempt hair, dark in the sunlight, waved over his temple. His bearded jaw spoke of determination and…stubbornness. Or did it shroud a delicate, feminine chin?

While he'd been out cold, she had cut off his clothes and checked for bone breaks. His arms and legs were sound, but his back had been a bloodied pulp. She had worked tirelessly cleaning the wounds. How shameless she had been smoothing a healing balm on his back, lingering her fingers over his sides and applying the unguent over his buttocks. Her cheeks reddened from the memory.

She buttoned the buttons on her frock, her fingers lingering on her bodice. The man oozed masculinity, probably made every girl a conquest. His dark good looks and excellent physique would make any girl's heart hammer double time. Except Rachel's.

Yet, engaging the irascible Colonel Rourke stimulated a diversion, a game she had to win. Competitive by nature, she enjoyed setting goals and achieving them, and there was little doubt she was dealing with no ordinary man. He exuded confidence and an air of command. Power clung to him. Men would follow without question. How she looked forward to provoking him.

She had developed the art and power of the unspoken, scrutinizing his body language as closely as his speech, noticing the slightest gesture, a twitch of his jaw, a dip of the brow, anything that could betray doubt, weakness or subterfuge. He had exceeded her assessment.

Yet, why did she feel like she was the one being provoked?

Do not allow yourself to become comfortable with him. Remember what you are about. One small error in judgment could land an appointment with the hangman.

Her fingers clenched tightly to her hairbrush. Her father's Bible had been tucked in a drawer never to be read again. How dare Colonel Rourke touch her most cherished possession?

"Miss Rachel! You hear me? You got callers." Simon stretched his vocal cords, yanking her from her woolgathering. On rare occasions when a visitor happened to be someone Simon tolerated, he'd be polite and knock on her door. Given his tone, it had to be someone he didn't like.

Rachel leaned over the balcony to get a peek at her guests. Lieutenant Washburn. Her eyes narrowed on Captain James Johnson. Now she understood Simon's antagonism. Her hands clamped the railing. If she had power enough, she'd snap it in two.

She vowed before the war ended, she'd settle a score with Captain Johnson whose presence erupted a violent memory. Her father's death two years before had been a giant crack that had fractured and ruptured her soul. She had lain in bed for days lulled into an opium-like listlessness where the rest of the world didn't exist. A part of her had died, but by God, she rose from the ashes, fueled with a rage to overthrow tyrants and free prisoners and slaves.

No more did she fall to despair and pity, choosing the life of a recluse. A social stigma had been bestowed on her by the gossipmongers of Richmond. She didn't care. Being alone afforded her the freedom to move about and accumulate information without being suspect.

She rounded the balcony. A hand shot out and yanked her into a bedroom, pressed her hard against the back of the door. Awake and rested, Colonel Rourke was a ferocious man. Oh, how those blue eyes of his belayed a lethal calmness that sent shivers up her spine. Heat flooded her with the awareness of his attire. Nothing more than a thin sheet wrapped around his hips. She dipped her eyes and cleared her throat. "I see you picked the lock."

"Did you expect anything else?"

She gritted her teeth. Attila the Hun might be cowed under that stare.

"Colonel Rourke, you need to let me go." His nostrils flared with his fury and she understood his fear.

"Who are they? Why are they here?"

"If you were to be handed over, don't you think it would have been done before? One is a neighbor and the other is Lieutenant Washburn. I must attend business for the Saint."

"Whatever information the Saint needs, let him get it for himself. Send them away."

"I'm sorry, Colonel. There's no other way. You must understand it is a means to an end."

"Is the Saint so cowardly he hides behind a woman's skirts?" he jeered, sharp as scissor blades.

She looked heavenward, thinking of Colonel Rourke beneath her skirts. Had he no recollection? But his sharp eyes missed nothing, and then his jaw dropped in disbelief. "You were the one who freed me. The Saint put you in terrible danger. It ends here. Is that clear?"

There emerged a maddening glimpse of arrogance about Colonel Rourke that endeared him to her. Months of secrets, hiding truths weighed on her shoulders with backbreaking force. Rachel closed her eyes, imagining the luxury of letting someone else take over for a while. Too heady to consider.

She looked down to where his hands squeezed her arms. So it was to be a test of wills. "Colonel Rourke, my goal is the same as the Saint's and yours. I cannot do my duty while being manhandled by you."

"Make up an excuse."

He did not let her go. No one countermanded Colonel Rourke's orders. Gathering all her strength, Rachel thrust him off. Losing balance, he clawed at the air, grabbed her, pulling her with him. They sprawled across the floor. *Oof.* His hands grazed across her breast and she felt heat rise from the tips of her toes to the roots of her hair.

Twisting in his arms, she crawled off him, jumped to her feet and smoothed down her gown. "Damn you. You've made a mess of your wounds and I have no time to dress them."

Like a ghost, Simon appeared, kicked the door shut and moved in between them. "Stay right there, Colonel Rourke," Simon said, leveling a gun at Lucas' heart. "We got more important fish to fry."

Rising, Lucas winced, his face murderous.

Simon gestured with his pistol for the colonel to get back in bed. "You goin' to keep me good company while Miss Rachel goes about her business."

"The younger man, without the sideburns," Lucas said, "he's the one who whipped me."

Rachel darted a glance at Simon, the boy's look of disdain calculated by Lucas.

"Be careful, Miss Rachel. You playin' too close."

"Keep Colonel Rourke quiet even if you have to shoot him," Rachel ordered.

Simon cocked his pistol. "It's a repeater."

Rachel patted her hair into place, collected a cool composure, stepped from the room and slammed the door. Colonel Rourke remained in good hands.

"Lieutenant Washburn, it is so good to see you again." She took his hands and gave them a squeeze and released them.

"And you of course, Captain Johnson," she inclined her head.

"It is a pleasure." He took her hand and kissed it.

She shuddered. "Shall we?" She waved the men to her side parlor and fluttered to a single chair. "Do sit down, gentlemen."

Captain Johnson leaned against the white mantel of a brick fireplace. How like an animal he looked, not a bold lion, nor graceful like a deer or a decent horse, but sly, cruel and shifty. He was an animal for certain, but what kind?

"What honor do I have of receiving both of you today?" Her face tightened. She suffered Captain Johnson gazing down her bodice. Rising, she crossed the room and pulled back the velvet drapes and then chose a chair opposite him. What were his vague responsibilities, his unexplained disappearance, and sudden reappearances? She licked her lips. Why had he been in the warehouse interrogating Colonel Rourke?

"Do tell me news of Richmond. Have they caught the spy?"

Captain Johnson ran his finger over the neck of a china figurine of a woman. With one flick of his finger he could decapitate the valuable piece. "What was that noise upstairs?"

"Noise? Yes, of course, the noise. I lost my brush and turned a chair over in my search for it." She twirled a frond of hair around her finger to reinforce her plausible explanation and wished Colonel Rourke to perdition for placing her under suspicion. She turned her full attention to Lieutenant Washburn. "You were saying, Lieutenant?"

"I came to call on you and ran into Captain Johnson a quarter-mile up the road," said Washburn. He did nothing to hide his irritation.

To play the enmity between the two men came to light as a healthy strategy. "You don't think the spy is in the vicinity, do you?" She clutched her throat in horror.

"No, ma'am. We have reliable reports he's been seen in Stafford County."

"Thank goodness. To think of Yankees loose in Richmond. How dreadful!" Rachel smiled inwardly. Her people covered her tracks well, spreading eyewitness accounts of Colonel Rourke's description over northern Virginia. A gun exploded upstairs. Her heart in her throat, Rachel flew to the stairway, blocking the lieutenant and Captain Johnson before they could ascend. Simon arrived at the top of the stairs, a revolver smoking in his hands.

"Miss Rachel, I sorry to give you a fright. I was cleanin' the gun like you told me, and it went off. I promise it won't happen again." Simon went back into the room and slammed the door. Rachel cursed beneath her breath. There was not a hell hot enough for Colonel Rourke.

She turned to her guests. "Good heavens, I should hope so. I swear it is by sheer providence I do not swoon."

"I'll catch you, Miss Rachel, if you do," offered Lieutenant Washburn, his arms ready.

"This reminds me of the time…" Her voice dropped to the

low admonition she used to tell one of her fearful stories as she maneuvered both men away from the stairs, and then stopped. "Oh dear! In all the excitement, I forgot my manners. Would you like some lemonade?"

"No, Miss Rachel," Lieutenant Washburn said, again pained by Johnson's presence. He cleared his throat. "Could I have a private moment?" Rachel darted a glance at Captain Johnson who glared at his competitor.

"If you don't mind, Captain, could you wait in the parlor?" she asked sweetly. His eyes narrowed, his lips thinned as he removed himself. She smiled even as his expression chilled her.

Lieutenant Washburn quickly said, "I must return to my duties posthaste. Would you be so kind as to honor me with your attendance at the Rutherford ball in two weeks?"

"Why, of course. How could I reject a hero of the Confederacy?" Rachel linked her arm in his and led him to the door. How fortuitous to receive an invitation to the Rutherfords'. To worm her way into Rutherford's office. Everyone knew how close he was to President Davis. To study war documents? She smiled prettily for Lieutenant Washburn, his muttonchops working up and down.

Emboldened by her acceptance, the lieutenant said, "There is something more pressing."

Rachel knew what was coming and could only imagine Colonel Rourke and Simon, listening to every word. Washburn knelt and took her hand. "Miss Rachel, you are the most wonderful, endearing and beautiful creature upon this earth. My cup runneth over with love. I must tender a proposal of marriage."

"You impress me with your gravity, sir. You are so brave." She brought him to his feet. "I shall have to think it over."

"It must be very soon, Miss Rachel, for I'm suffering for want of you," he said, disappointed.

Rachel gave her tale of rejection with drama and color. As her story climaxed on a high point, she added a dash of guile and flattery, overwhelming the dull-witted lieutenant with promises of possibilities.

She had become accustomed to proposals and had become so swift and sincere in her refusals that half of Richmond still stood in line. At times, she felt pricklings of remorse, like she did now. Still, Rachel reminded herself of her goal where circumventing southern slaveholders had become the passionate fabric of her life. No one would stand in her way.

Standing in the doorway, she said her farewells and good wishes that would have done a snake oil salesman proud. Mollified for the time being, Lieutenant Washburn mounted his horse. She waved goodbye, wishing Captain Johnson was gone as well. Her fingers dug into the folds of her skirts, thinking of how she'd deal with him.

When she turned around, he trapped her between his arms. Apparently Johnson was no fool to the games she played.

A pain shot to her jaw from clenching her teeth. Revolting in every way a cockroach of a man could be, she wanted to beat his face with her bare hands until his eyes swelled shut and bloody spit drooled from his slack jaws, until he lay foul in his own fluids. She prayed she'd not betray her fury. "I declare, Captain Johnson. You will remove yourself promptly from the premises, before I hail Lieutenant Washburn."

Her knees shook. Washburn was long gone.

A ferret! He's a true ferret with the pointed face of the crafty animal, the stunted ears, and the long sharp nose and shifty eyes.

"Why don't you let me make a decent woman out of you, and marry me?"

"Decent? I already have those traits, Captain Johnson. I take exception to your slurs on my reputation." Visions of a rope blurred in front of her eyes…what had happened to her father. "Are you interested in my reputation or are you more interested in my plantation that borders yours?"

"You're letting this place run to ruin like your worthless father did."

A true animal he was. Without warning, he lunged for her and seized her roughly by the upper arms. Surprised by the attack, she screamed but the muscles in her throat were taut with fear and she barely uttered a sound.

Simon sauntered down the stairs, polishing the pistol in his hand. "Miss Rachel? I believe there is one more bullet left in this gun. What should I do with it?" His face belied a mask of innocence.

"You shouldn't let your darkie have a gun," Johnson said.

Rachel twisted free of his hold, refusing to be cut down by this brute. "I'm most comfortable with Simon holding a gun for me. Good day, Captain Johnson." She swung the door open and he strolled through it like he owned the place. She locked the door and sagged against the wall.

Chapter 4

Colonel Rourke's antics had sent her into screaming fits. Earlier that day, Rachel rode her stallion, forcing the animal over hedgerows, driving him across meadows, plunging through trampled cornfields until the mount lathered and foamed, and she was drenched in sweat. To think all three of them might be swinging from the nearest tree.

When she stalked by his bedroom and found him struggling to shave with no mirror, she drew back and leaned against the doorframe. He wasn't to blame, it was Johnson.

"Would you like some help?" she offered.

He arched a brow. "Promise you won't slit my throat."

"You deserve worse for putting us in jeopardy when you grabbed me into this room when Johnson and Washburn came to call." She placed the bowl on his lap, took the razor from him, and then glanced at his face, obscured with shaving soap. Rachel smiled. He looked like a little boy.

"What do you find entertaining?" His eyes warmed and danced with merriment, and on closer inspection revealed an unusual blue flecked with brighter sapphire highlights.

He dipped his eyes to the razor in her hand. "I hope you have experience at this."

"We'll have to find out," she said, and commenced shaving. When her father's eyesight had begun to fail, she had enjoyed the familial pastime, but this was different. She willed her hands to stop shaking, and carefully scraped along his chin, rinsed the blade in the basin of water and scraped again. From time to time, she stepped back to see what sort of delicate, feminine face had been hidden by his thick beard.

Far from her musings, she was quick to modify her earlier assessment. As his face cleared of soap, his square jaw with proper cleft revealed an air of obstinacy and strength.

"What do you think?" he asked when he caught her studying his profile.

She had been leaning so far back, she could not recover her balance quickly enough to pretend she had been doing exactly that. Stumbling, she dropped the razor into the basin, splashing the contents on his chest.

Devoid of beard, the beauty of his pure, classical bone structure reminded her of a painting of Sandro Botticelli, the Italian Renaissance painter whom she venerated. Maybe his jawline was almost perfect, but just enough off to have character. Below the ridge of his brow, intelligent, probing eyes raked her...and those sculpted lips? Her cheeks heated, his face so designed would make a nun whisper with lust.

Why wasn't she surprised by his obvious smugness? Too handsome for his own good, she said, "I could be cruel."

"Be candid."

If beauty was power, his smile was a sword. "Tolerable, I suppose."

"Your flattery is hardly charitable. Do you think I'd have a chance with the females of Richmond?"

Rachel picked up the blade again. "I imagine, Colonel Rourke, you fascinate and dominate women until they surrender all with blissful pleasure, sacrifice and servitude."

"And of course, you are immune?"

Was the self-assured Colonel Rourke flirting with her? With imperious formality, she inclined her head. "Be assured, I will not add purpose to your vanity."

"That, Miss Rachel…is a very interesting theory."

"Do not under any circumstance attempt to dazzle me with silver-tongued flattery, Colonel Rourke, for you haven't a prayer of success."

"I'll warn you about demolishing a man's confidence. Of course, I suppose you'd find that notion amusing."

"That bad?"

"Worse. I listened how you puppeted those yokels on your strings. Two proposals in one morning and the day not over yet."

She pulled hard on a swipe.

"Ouch. Do you tear the wings off grasshoppers?"

She finished shaving and wiped the blade, and then taking a towel, patted his face clean of soap. To Rachel, most men seemed stupid or selfish. Colonel Rourke evoked a camaraderie and intelligence that cut through her pretenses, and he treated her as a peer. To spar with someone on equal footing proved stimulating.

"How is it a southern belle has knowledge of an insignificant Union officer?" His lips parted in a dazzling display of white teeth.

He referred to her recognition of his name when he had told her who he was. She carried the bowl of soapy water across the room, placing it on the dresser. "I make it my business to know." As a rogue spy, she memorized all of those in the Northern command, never knowing when she would have to employ their services.

She turned and smoothed her chestnut hair. "And you are significant. You are one of the three Chiefs of Civilian Spying working under General Grenville Dodge. A West Pointer, graduated top of your class, excelling in tactics, and later won distinction in an Indian fight where you were wounded. You come from a well-respected Virginia family. Despite your family's loyalty to the Confederacy, you have chosen to throw in your allegiance with the Union. Your courage at Manassas and Antietam earned you respect, but it remained your stealth in scouting and ferreting vital information that earned you admiration and trust of your superiors which precipitated your ascension to a high office in Washington."

"Bravo," he drawled, studying her as if he could read her every thought.

Had she blundered? Did he suspect she and the Saint were one and the same? *Stupid.*

He leaned back on the pillows, his expression as cunning as a fox. If he learned of her true identity all may lay in ruin. No man could take that amount of torture for long and not crack. The Confederates in their wrath would come straight for her. She closed her eyes. The people who worked for her…she must not fear. Fear was the mind killer…let it pass over her…through her. When the fear was gone, she opened her eyes, and seeing a clearer path, settled in a chair opposite him.

"Enlighten me, Colonel Rourke. How did you find yourself in this precarious situation? Picking the capital of the Confederacy to dally is not good for your health. I'd think Washington a better climate for a man with…Union sympathies."

"On my desk, I received a message from the Saint assigning an immediate meeting place and time, citing important information that only he could give me and, of course, with his signature "S". I trusted him. Traveled alone, at night, to the Potomac, and then was seized by a group of ruffians, obviously Confederate sympathizers. Fought them off, but their sheer numbers overwhelmed me. I can only guess, but I believe I was drugged and smuggled through the lines."

She shifted, thinking of all he'd endured. "Via information I overheard at Jefferson Davis' ball, I was lucky to locate you before they transferred you to Castle Thunder. Into the 'Mouth of Hell' they call the impossibly guarded behemoth. Even southerners cross themselves when they pass."

"I owe you a great debt."

Rachel tapped her finger on her lips. *Who sent the note? Who was close enough to copy the Saint's inscription?* Six possibilities came to mind. Three she ruled out—two high level officials who would never betray the Union and Lucas. The other three were his superior, General Grenville Dodge and his immediate subordinates. "Do you have any idea—"

"If I knew who betrayed me—" He turned his head, giving her his fierce profile. The remaining light etched his cheekbone and the line of his jaw, his expression lost in gloomy shadow. With certainty, his clever mind probed the acts and motivations of men he suspected.

"I gather there are no servants other than Simon."

She flinched. Why the abrupt change in subject? Why the accusatory tone? "You are correct." There was no point lying. He had plenty of opportunity to free range her home when she was gone to know the truth. She didn't need servants around to complicate her activities. "I prefer to live alone."

"And your parents?" he asked.

She steeled her reserves. But inside, her chest ached with buried grief until she thought she might bleed to death from the pain of it. "My mother died with the influenza, and my father passed on...two years later."

"I'm sorry for your loss," he said, and seeming restless, he flexed his cramped arms, and eased from the bed and rose. The sheets, he kept around his midsection, and the rest trailed across the floor. Time to get him proper attire.

He gazed out the window and despite the bars of red scars, his back muscles were a masterpiece of movement. "And what prompted you to get into the spy business?" he asked.

She tightened her fingers around the arms of her chair. "My father was a staunch abolitionist and made no secret of his dislike of slavery. Upon my grandfather's death, my father freed the slaves. Hearing that the children or relatives of neighboring plantation slaves were to be sold by their owners, he bought and liberated them. When he ran low on funds, he helped them escape."

"A hazardous activity."

"Very." The memories dug their claws into her soul. The memories of slavery, the cruelties she'd seen some men inflict upon others gave her nightmares. Daymares, too. The horror of her father's death that stayed with her forever, playing over and over for the rest of her life. It didn't go away; it became a part of her, step for step, breath for breath. "Slavery is cruel, tyrannical, not only over the slave, but mankind itself. I want it destroyed. And you? Were you riding at the head of the column, gathering the bouquets the ladies threw at soldiers?"

He turned toward her. "I could see the war coming and looked on it with detached inevitability. How it possessed every mechanization to make it occur...arrogance with an ample amount of flint and steel to strike a spark. My sad privilege to differ in many things disdained by the opinions and principles of my locality, where fighting against Virginia deigned an unnatural act. For myself, to uphold the Union came at all costs...a country united in infinite strength. A vision of what it could be."

Like a stump orator, he bristled with his dogma.

"Your profession is paramount to you?"

"Very. Hopefully with recognition through promotion."

"Is it your pride, Colonel Rourke, where you must be recognized for your martial genius, manifested in a career singularly original and romantic; in the forceful fluency of your record of history made by yourself for the Union? Or is it your endowed diligence and honor that will win the approval and subsequent elevation you seek from General Grant and President Lincoln?"

He ignored her mockery. "The thought has crossed my mind."

"Like walking downstairs to get to heaven." And because she had to know, she asked, "And your family?"

"The greatest of all costs," he said, the sharpness in his voice betraying his unwillingness to discuss the matter further. Yet there had been a flash in his eyes, too complex to indicate a particular sentiment. Anger? Hurt? Despair?

What was it that drove him to be head of Civilian Spying when his family's sympathies lay with the South? To go up against his family must have been a difficult decision. Did rejection spur his desire to succeed? Might there be more to Colonel Rourke than pride, promotion and career?

He meandered about the room, taking in the disregarded, overlooked, and ignored furnishings—brown plaster on the ceiling from water damage, a stretch of drooping wallpaper, a chipped marble washstand, worn expensive area rugs, bricks in the fireplace that lacked mortar, and scuffed wainscoting. "You did not finish how you arrived in the venture of espionage," he said.

She smoothed her skirts, inclined to point out that he was the one who had changed the subject. Regardless of his belligerent mien, she needed someone to communicate with as much as the air she breathed. "Of course, the Confederacy espoused that their ideology was far superior. When the mess over Fort Sumter occurred, nobody cared whether it was a constitutional right they were exercising, or an act of revolution. In the delirium of the hour, reason was silent, and passion prevailed. The people of Virginia could barely suppress the war cry, 'To arms!' they all shouted, and their hubris resounded throughout the land. So then came secession and the boilerplate of war. The chaos freed me to begin my activities with the Saint."

Rachel had emerged as the notorious Saint. Dressed in a multitude of disguises, the Saint's destinations pinpointed army camps near sites of military importance, crossroads settlements, and small towns filled with new recruits.

Sometimes she had set out as a humble civilian, an Irish peddler of notions clothed in a butternut suit, a broad-brimmed hat, beard with a stick and pack over her shoulder. To everyone she met, she played the part of a moron salesman, a contrived fool of nature. Other times, she adopted the costume of a slave or ancient prostitute.

She developed a vast underground network of slaves, abolitionists and others sympathetic to the Union. Notes were sent northward by folding them lengthwise and stuffing them into the craw of a chicken, boot heels or emptied eggs carried by an innocent farmwife or slave. Her genius was infinite.

If she was ever suspect, she had a back-up plan to escape to Washington where she kept a home.

"What type of activities?" Colonel Rourke prompted her out of her silence.

To give him a little information seemed plausible. "Once, I learned a much larger submarine had approached near completion at the Tredegar Iron Works. Of course, Captain Stanton was delighted to escort me there, attuned to my every desire. At Tredegar, he pointed out equipment and devices, and I listened and permitted myself a few questions. After I feigned a headache, the good captain escorted me home where I spent two whole days in seclusion. I labored over notes and sketches, putting down everything I committed to memory. I included the trivial or important sounding, what was clear or vaguely understood. Despite my lack of engineering background, I have been congratulated on my detailed specifications."

Colonel Rourke strode across the room, towered over her. "The Saint has overused you, and your idea that a lone woman can abolish slavery for the South is foolishly mistaken."

"Then wallow in your ignorance!"

He scoffed. "My intentions are honorable and meant to keep you out of harm's way...I do not encourage the use of young unprotected women. For that, I consider the Saint the worst of scoundrels."

"You never know when the Saint will be listening," she taunted.

"You are confident of that, are you?" He glanced at the wall, separating their rooms.

"Yes."

Their gazes locked, his guarded, always mindful of impending danger.

"Am I to assume he is in the bedroom next to mine?"

It was her room, and he knew it. If he believed she slept with the fictitious Saint, then so be it. What end would it serve to supply him with her innocence when her identity needed to be protected?

"Perhaps."

She cringed beneath his hot scrutiny. For once, she did not want to engage in the role she played. But she'd have to provide him with the truth instead of allowing him to think her...a harlot.

"You don't have any fears, do you?"

She clenched her hands into fists. Her nails bit into her palms as she translated his words...*you don't have any morals, do you?* The fool. He did not realize his greatest asset was right in front of him. His greatest ally was her.

She forced a coolness in her voice. "I fear drowning. I fear fire. It haunts me sometimes. Do you have any fears, Colonel Rourke?"

His cobalt eyes bored into her. "Not being able to protect the people working under me."

She rose, stood her ground. "I suppose you have no flaws?"

"There are times, I think before I act. You're flawed because of your undying loyalty to the Saint."

The mockery in his voice set her teeth on edge. *Stubborn, arrogant man.* "Are you jealous?"

"Of a gutless man that uses a woman? No. What else do you offer him?"

Hot coals of anger burst into fiery flame inside Rachel. She slapped him across the face.

They stared at each other in the deafening silence, his face a bright red where her hand made contact.

His eyes darkened. "My apologies," he said. "I deserved that."

He took her hand. Her breath hitched. His fingers were tapered, conveying warmth in the strength of his grip. An electric sensation passed between them, from his hand to hers. She tugged her hand away, but he held fast, gazing at her, eyes narrowed, unsmiling, and then glancing at their clasped hands, cleared his throat.

Rachel studied their joined fingers, too. He was a man of contradictions. Harsh, yet gentle. Smart and yet not entirely aware. At least not where she was concerned. Or maybe he was too aware?

"What does the Saint look like?"

"Tall, handsome, blue eyes."

He narrowed his eyes, as if distrusting the truth of her words. "Could be half the men in the north."

"Colonel Rourke, it is important we keep affairs on a professional basis."

"Your affairs are my business."

He rubbed his thumb over the back of her hand. The contact sizzled…as if he'd trickled hot oil there and rubbed it in.

Rachel snatched back her hand, determined to guide their association to a semblance of propriety. "We need to discuss getting you back to Washington…once the manhunt dies down." The sooner she delivered him behind Union lines, the sooner she'd get back her sanity.

Chapter 5

Rachel had seized upon Lieutenant Washburn's invitation to the Rutherford ball and had easily slipped away unnoticed into the Confederate's private office. Footsteps rained down the hall. So close. She darted her eyes around the room. Where could she hide?

On the table, she smoothed the papers into their original placement and dashed to a cupboard, her ladies fan swinging from her wrist. Pushing aside coats, she crawled in the cramped space, crushed in her hoops and tugged in the remainder of her gown. Damn. The door would not close all the way. No time to get out and reconfigure. She used the hooked end of a hanger to keep it shut. A half-inch crack was exposed. If anyone looked closely, they'd be capable of seeing her.

Several men filed into Rutherford's office, the strains of a *La Dorset* quadrille played in the outer ballroom followed. The men were an eclectic mix, some she identified as high-ranking Confederate officers, government officials and some civilians she didn't recognize.

A light-haired man entered the room and closed the door.

Her hands fisted around the hanger keeping the door shut…and keeping *her* safe. Shadows fell on the sharp angles of the ferret-faced man. Oh, how he'd be forever stamped in her memory.

"Captain Johnson, an honor to see you again," said Secretary of War Seddon.

The men surrounding him stood in awe. Or was it fear? Accustomed to the platitudes, Johnson moved to the table and began to orate. "We must be responsible as the choice of our target will not be an easy matter and our collective responsibility is a heavy one. It is not the question of blowing up a building or kidnapping a general, such horseplay is not significant enough. We must be delicate, refined and aimed at the heart of the Union. It must be grave damage done and so loud it will create a hue and cry across the north. They will marvel at our cleverness," he boasted.

Johnson took a proffered cigar, lighted it, and puffed until a fiery red appeared. "They will tremble. Traitors and possible defectors will change their minds. The heartbeat of the South will be stimulated and encouraged to greater efforts by our strength and genius. But of course, our plans must be kept top secret. It is of paramount importance that the Union is in complete ignorance of our arrangements."

"Hear, hear," the men cried, stirred by his fervor. Johnson preached a baptism of blood to purge the evil. Wasn't his blood, that was for sure. The men listened with the penitence of little children before the pulpit to embrace the truth.

Rachel's foot cramped. The cupboard grew hot and stuffy, and her stomach churned with the cigar smoke and expensive liquor permeating the air.

"I must have your opinion," said Seddon. "What do you think is the most dangerous? What will do the most damage?"

"As leader, I have been in New York for the past eight months, doing reconnaissance and became well-acknowledged with our Copperhead strengths."

Rachel's grip on the hanger slipped, but she caught herself and held even tighter. Johnson, head of the Copperheads? His status explained so many things about him, his long absences, civilian attire at times. No regular assignments in the army when every available male yielded to enlistment.

Her fan stabbed into her hip. He commanded the biggest spy operation of the Confederacy, conspiring to secretly organize and disseminate the government of the United States. How powerful he'd risen with an alliance of dangerous and anonymous Rebel collaborators in the north ready to wreak destruction.

"I narrowly escaped capture returning on a blockade runner," said Johnson. He gritted the cigar between his teeth and unrolled maps across the table.

The men bent their heads low over the maps, whispering. Rachel strained to hear.

"Get us another whiskey," said Rutherford, angling his bushy head to her cupboard. "In yonder cabinet is my inventory."

A man had his hand on the doorknob. She held her breath, sweat trickled beneath her arms.

"Hold there," said Johnson. A tense silence enveloped the ornate room. "We need to keep clear our heads."

The man released the door. Rachel breathed a sigh of relief, thanking a higher power.

"We need men to serve with devotion. It is dangerous work

and not to be considered an adventure, as the business is serious. It should be noted that under the auspices of a special agent in Washington, a further plot will end the Lincoln tyranny."

"Here, here," the men echoed their approval.

A young officer cleared his throat, nervous, pinned down by all eyes upon him. Rachel strained to catch every word.

"In this matter, one must not confuse seizing power and overthrowing the Lincoln government without being aware of outside forces at work. The Union spies are a great nuisance to us. The Saint and the embarrassment of losing Colonel Rourke have proved a great humiliation."

Rutherford slammed down his glass, the contents spattered the table. "The myth of Northern intelligence is exactly that. It is a fable," blustered Rutherford.

"Do not discount the Northern agents. They are crafty and with the Saint still about we are at peril," said the young officer.

General Alexander scoffed. "You speak of this Saint as if he were the bogeyman, seeing through walls, shadowing every breath we take."

"I do not take the Saint lightly. It would be unfortunate to do so," said Johnson, the hard bitterness in his voice evident.

"Next, you'll be saying General Grant is smarter than our General Lee. The Northern agents have not the enthusiasm for their work as we do," said Rutherford.

Johnson pointed his cigar at the men, no doubt having enough of their trifling stupidity. "You underestimate them. They have successes. They can sow a million seeds and reap at least one potato. Do not fail to believe the northern agents will try to engage us. In reflection, I have decided to make a modest proposition."

The men bent their heads low, allowing her to hear bits and pieces of their conversation. Her core froze. What was to occur was of utmost importance to the Union. She had to look at those maps.

"Our Trojan Horse will lie in the loyal northern states," said Johnson. "With this war of attrition, President Davis will be fortunate to drive Lincoln to the bargaining table."

"It is ambitious," an officer remarked, followed by the nods of men around the table.

Johnson flicked a hand in front of his nose as if to get rid of a bad smell, and said, "If I should ever get my hands upon Colonel Rourke again, or my hands on the Saint," he drawled, "I promise...I will take great pleasure in making them talk before they die."

Rachel licked her lips, well aware of the evil Johnson reaped.

"With your permission," said Rutherford, "leave the maps until President Davis arrives and has a chance to look them over."

"One hour," said Johnson.

After everyone left the room, Rachel slipped from the cupboard, massaged her foot to release the cramp and limped to the maps.

New York. Chicago. Baltimore. Several other northern cities lay detailed, charts on stored munitions and lists of names and addresses of those friendly to the Confederacy. The information was so voluminous, it made a gold mine look like a dump. Captain Johnson plotted revolution in the north.

Rachel had been born with a photographic memory. As a young girl, her father had seized upon this talent and drilled facts to expand her memory. Little did he realize the valuable resource her memory would support.

But what was the plot in Washington? A clock chimed in the hall. *Hurry.* Rachel scanned the pieces of information for names and dates. Nothing hinted at Washington. She lifted the maps and grasped every layout, absorbing every detail, leaving no possible information behind. One drawing of the new Capitol building caught her eye. Twenty-four Elm Street printed in barely visible letters.

The orchestra stopped. Loud applause discharged from people in the ballroom. President Davis had arrived.

She smoothed her dress over her hoops, hoping she didn't look like she was pressed inside a cupboard. Opening the door a crack, she peered out. Her heart gave a lurch. No one guarded the long passageway, a wing of the house dedicated to Rutherford's private office. Rachel closed the door behind her and moved down the hall, taking one soft step at a time.

Damn. A knot of men stood at the far end, the same group in Rutherford's office. A lump clogged her throat, yet with the President's entrance, they were distracted. If she hugged the wall she might slink by without being noticed.

One. Two. Three. She counted her steps. Captain Johnson stood four feet away. He swung to her, narrowed his eyes into dark slits.

"What are you doing here?" he demanded.

All eyes fastened on her. Rachel froze. Jefferson Davis approached, halted next to Johnson. The room grew smaller and smaller. Ignoring Johnson, she moved forward to address the President.

"President Davis." She bowed and touched the tip of her fan with her finger. "It's so good to see you. Is Varina with you tonight?" The casualness in her voice veiled the nerves roiling in her stomach.

Jefferson Davis played with his beard, pulling it down to a point. "Varina is home attending one of the children taken ill."

"I'm sorry to hear that. I hope it isn't anything serious," she said. "If there is any way, I can help—"

"Forgive me for interrupting these civilities," Captain Johnson's scathing voice cut in. "Miss Pierce has not answered my question. What are you doing here?"

Rachel leaned forward, taking her time to look him up and down, tracking him from the brim of his protruding brow to his folded arms to the scuffed tips of his boots. She then met his gaze with a cool evenness; withstood the blazing anger that echoed in the hostility of his voice. "I believe it is bad manners for a gentleman to inquire of such activity. I'll be delicate...I wished to find a retiring room. It's...been a long evening."

His eyes flashed. "I don't recall seeing you enter the hallway."

She drew her closed fan through her hand. "Mr. Rutherford's home is so vast, and I am a female with no compass."

Davis sighed. "Gentlemen, we have more important things to discuss than to detain a good and noble daughter of the Confederacy" He stood firm in his remark, tolerating no argument from the men.

Rachel smiled prettily for Captain Johnson and skirted around him.

He grabbed her arm. "One more question."

Do not create a scene. Her gaze flicked to where he dared to hold her arm. How she clamped an iron control on the bottled-up hatred of the man. To her, he was more than just a spy and what he'd done to her father was unspeakable.

She spoke slowly, enunciating each syllable as if speaking to a child. "My remarks were addressed to President Davis and not to you. If I did not discover by your language and abuse of my person that you must be ignorant of all laws of good breeding, I should suggest here and now to have you punished for your impertinence."

President Davis moved to her side. "Miss Pierce—"

Rachel jerked her arm from Johnson's grasp. "Oh, never mind, he is too ignorant to know what he has done."

"I've been waiting to dance with you in the ballroom." Lieutenant Washburn swooped down on her like a condor. "Where have you been?" Then observing Jefferson Davis and other dignitaries, he flushed and saluted. "Excuse me, Mr. President."

Rachel hooked her arm with the lieutenant's and swept him to the far side of the ballroom. "I've been dancing the night away, but now I've a headache, and wish to retire," she complained.

"Those headaches, Miss Rachel, are an anathema. I have not had one dance with you all evening."

Poor Lieutenant Washburn. He had a face like three rainy days, but Rachel needed to get home and write down every detail while it stayed fresh in her head.

Chapter 6

Rachel pressed her fingers to her temples, her mind reeling with all she absorbed. She'd spent hours writing everything down she remembered from Rutherford's office that evening. While making a final cursory inspection of her charts and maps, she sipped a cup of tea. The activity relaxed her, as did the cozy environment of her father's study. She dipped her nib pen in an inkwell, jotted down a few more details, and finished, glad she did not to have to deal with the wandering Colonel Rourke who had dogged her every step for the past two weeks. She reached beneath the desk, pushed a button and with a twang, a spring released, and a hidden compartment popped out. When the ink dried, she folded the documents and secreted her recordings in a concealed partition, snapping the panel shut.

As a rogue agent accustomed to operating on her own, Rachel had developed a personal annoyance with the interfering colonel. They had words earlier in the evening, escalating into a heated argument concerning her dangerous business with the Saint until Lieutenant Washburn landed on her doorstep and ended the debate.

Now, she wished she had not placed her father's Bible in the guest room where the colonel lay sleeping. For the first time in two years, she wanted to smell the leather, feel the pages with her fingers, to read and find comfort. Was she doing the right thing? Doubts about her activities occurred rarely. The Saint succeeded under terrible pressure, but there were times like tonight when she became afraid, well-aware Confederate agents wove a rope, strand by strand to capture her.

She placed her pens and inkwell in the cubby and turned the wick down low in the oil lamp. Forlorn shadows filled the walls with gloom. She stretched to smooth an aching muscle in her back and with her teacup in hand, rose and sat on the settee. Into the cushions, she pushed her hand, her fingers touching the Colt revolver she'd hidden there.

How she loved her father's study. It was the one room she cared to maintain because of the fond memories shared in that part of the house. Her gaze shifted over rows of leather-bound books lining the shelves, an ancient globe, armchairs and a polished carved black walnut table. How many hours, when the winter blew its wrath, had she spent reading before the hearth while her father worked at his desk? How she basked in those times of shared silence when her mind could reflect.

She congratulated herself on being serene and comfortable in solitude. Oh, how that boast was an unsuccessful illusion. Loneliness and fear filled the emptiness within her as if it might spread wide and vanish her.

Oh, to have a solid presence beside her, fingertips light at the nape of the neck, and whispers entangling hers in the night. Someone who'd smile at her like a million rainbows when he saw her coming. Who'd dance with her beneath a starlit night, share promises and know her secrets, and make a little world with just the two of them.

Silence shrouded her in its tentacles. No confidante, no confessor, only the beat of her heart for company.

The door swung open, and she jumped.

"I see you've returned."

"As you can see, I'm busy, Colonel Rourke."

"I can see real well."

He leaned against the doorframe. He was there for the long haul.

Maybe she'd show him her newest cache of information, maybe she wouldn't. "You don't trust me to do my job, do you?"

"At the ball, I suppose you kept all the men tight on your strings, your mind weaving strategies to overwhelm them."

She smiled over her teacup. "I rely on a hidden weapon— male gallantry."

One eyebrow raised, Lucas said, "I'll be reminded not to succumb to your methods."

She gestured for him to have a seat which he ignored. "Why there was one time, I reminded Senator Jackson how his stirring discourse on the Old Testament moved me to tears, my heart in deepest rapture. His face beamed like a full moon and he gave me a note to the Provost."

Lucas scoffed, moved to the sideboard and poured a glass of her father's brandy. The clothes she had procured fit as if tailored specifically for him, and she could not, nor had the desire to tear her eyes away. The butternut shirt clung to his wide shoulders and the pants fit snugly, outlining his long, lean frame.

On a long, deep breath she pulled her gaze away and continued, "In any case, as the wagons rolled into Richmond with Northern prisoners, I discovered the appalling conditions of Libby Prison. They would not allow me to visit the prisoners, claiming the venture unfit for a lady, and forcing me to employ other approaches."

He pivoted. "Such as?"

"Manipulation, guile and cunning with a liberal dose of flattery."

He threw back the contents of his glass and wiped his mouth with his sleeve. "Really, you don't strike me as someone who is the least insincere."

She took a sip of tea and returned the cup to its saucer with a deliberate clink. "I secured an invitation to meet with Secretary of War Seddon, with whom I had prior acquaintance. A bit overbearing, stuffy, behaves exactly how a baboon does when looking into a mirror and admiring the charm of his own reflection. Typical man, don't you see?"

Lucas picked up the decanter and flopped beside her on the settee. He had healed extraordinarily well. No longer could his restlessness be contained, and like a caged beast, he prowled her home, waiting for her to give him the go ahead to return to Washington when her sources indicated the noose had slackened. She had evaded him whenever possible. Except tonight, engaging him relieved her stress.

"Then there is Old Winder. I can flatter almost anything out of him. I would smile and tell him his glorious white head of hair would adorn the Temple of Janus. I was even bold enough to liken his form to Michelangelo's *David*. I had all the passes I wanted."

He poured another glass, lifted it high, looking triumphant although there remained a coldness in his eyes. No doubt, his reflections were on the Saint. "To the toast of Richmond." How he watched her like a fox snaring a rabbit in its jaws.

With the looming Copperhead plot, the Union teetered on the edge of disaster, and all he could do was pine away about her mythical lover. The excitement of showing him the information procured at the Rutherford ball evaporated. "Your suspicions have clouded your judgment. If it were as easy to arouse your trust as it is your cynicism, just think what could be accomplished."

He took out his pocket watch clicked it open and snapped it shut. "It's my business not to trust."

"That's a rare and fine sentiment. There is a reward for you, preferably alive, though a dead Colonel Rourke would also be acceptable."

He rose, skulked about the room, examining gilt-framed portraits on the wall, one with her stern-faced grandfather scowling down from his position of honor.

"Your family?" Without waiting for her to respond, he said, "You have a close resemblance to your mother, a beauty who probably broke many a heart. Your stubborn traits must yield from your father."

With his glass in hand, he sauntered to within inches of her, his eyes thoughtful, and his astute regard unraveling her nerves. "No pictures of the Saint? Why not a picture of a paramour?"

She tilted her head. "Have you ever battled with humility?"

"Humility?"

"Yes, humility. Is it difficult for you? Did you travel by boat or simply walk across the James River?"

He caught her chin in his hand and, smiling at her, stroked the curve of her jaw with his thumb. Her skin grew hot, her mouth went dry.

"No telltale signs of a male visitor, despite your constant avowals of communication with the Saint…strikes me as an odd relationship."

She was unable to breathe. *Steady now.* But when he smiled like that, it was as if the sun had come out. Was it the unexpected tenderness that smile conveyed, that shared moment of intimacy that made her breath hitch?

She smelled the brandy on his breath.

"I'm suffering for want of you," he mocked her. "The tormented, Lieutenant Washburn. I feel sorry for those poor souls lolling at your feet like lap dogs. Your amber eyes could trap the devil. Almost any man alive could make that mistake."

"Even you?"

The fireplace snapped and spit with a newly laid log. He let his hand fall away. "I make myself the exception. Poor Washburn, his heartfelt desire the size of Texas. You blindside him with all the punishment of a steaming locomotive. I must admit, your beauty gives you a unique advantage, a desirable woman can manipulate so well. But then again many men are ignorant that beauty does not necessarily ring true with honesty and virtue."

She pulled away, raised her chin. His words stung…her damaged ego the price of her belief that she could help change things. "Oh, we are at that again. You play the high-handed Washington bureaucrat, toasting away your life while the rest of us roll up our sleeves and do the dirty work. Tell me about your quiet safe little existence in Washington. Was the horror of your imprisonment in Richmond a reality for you?"

He flopped on the sofa next to her. "You're right, I don't see it up close, but every agent I have in the field, I would die a thousand deaths for. I deal with the reality of Yankee bullets fired at my brothers, General John Rourke and Colonel Ryan Rourke daily. And too many of our brethren in blue, face Confederate bullets. The Rebels will have no mercy if they discover who has revealed their best-laid plans to the Northern armies. It's not a pretty picture—a shovelful of dirt over your eyes."

She flourished her handkerchief and fluttered her eyes. "Do you not think I am good at what I do?" Why did she require his approval?

He set his glass down, looked at her with unflinching directness. "I cannot think of anyone more suited to the task. You are intelligent, resourceful, and an excellent actress. Do you laugh at me while the Saint has you in his arms?"

"Get out."

He did not leave. He moved his arm around her. Her pulse beat wildly like a hummingbird whose wings never stop and would die if caged.

"Need I remind you that you are in my home and under my protection? I demand you reciprocate and act your part as a gentleman."

"But I'm not a gentleman."

Silence loomed like a heavy mist. The grandfather clock ticked.

"I could scream."

In the shadowed lantern light, the colonel's eyes fixed upon her, predatory, a physical threat. She had not the slightest wish to embrace that threat, or to cultivate it. "You won't."

He raised a hand and tipped her face up to meet his. He lowered his head, his lips hovering above her. Was he going to kiss her? She had never been kissed, had pushed away those girlish inclinations. What would it feel like? Luscious anticipation and the slow burn of curiosity and desire curled through her.

He took her in his arms, crushed his mouth to hers, kissed her longingly and deeply, igniting a bone-melting fire that spread through her blood, consuming her. His fingers splayed through her hair, making her scalp tingle. Unable to halt the overwhelming stirrings ensnaring her heart, she moaned into his mouth.

From the time she clapped her eyes on him, her fascination for him knew no bounds. And touching him now, she was incapable of resisting the growing tenderness she held for him as a man.

Control. Take control. *Stop now!* It was all wrong. He was punishing her. Was it his anger with the Saint? The war? Rachel shoved against his chest. Grabbed the Colt. Pointed the long, steel barrel at him.

He stopped cold.

He could have slapped the gun away by brute force. Instead, he sat quietly, breathing as hard as she was.

"I'm sorry, Rachel. I'm truly sorry." He raked his fingers through his hair. "This war has made us all a little crazy."

"I don't understand—" Her hands shook holding the gun. Her emotions swung like a wild pendulum between the irony of his behavior and her shameful response.

"I don't expect you to," Lucas said. "May I?" He took the gun from her trembling hands and placed it on the table. "Despite your assumptions, I do not take advantage of unwilling women, and I assure you, I do not need to do so."

An unaccustomed pain settled in her breast along with a stripe of jealousy. "You must be inured with women throwing themselves at you, Colonel Rourke. Is this a new experience for you to have a woman say no?"

He shrugged, rose and halted in the doorway, his back to her. "I'll leave tomorrow."

She listened to his footsteps thud up the stairs, kick his door shut and settle on his bed. She did the same, then punched a pillow and covered her face to muffle her sobs. She cried for all the months of isolation and loneliness. She cried for living on the edge of danger. No…she could not hold him responsible for what happened. The war in its infinite idiocy had raked death and ruin and madness everywhere. No one was unaffected.

She touched her lips where his mouth had been. Was it so wrong? How would it feel to sleep comforted by him, to have his arms around her…

Chapter 7

Lucas lay in the darkness. Peace, he knew, could be shattered in a million variations, a rain of ashes, a disease borne on the wind, a cannon blast, the firing of a thousand devil Rebels, the sun dying like a candle snuffed out. In smaller ways, the hushed whispers and moans in the dark. Rachel and the dratted Saint. Images beyond the wall broke into blisters and dripped like acid. He paid attention, listening to his uneven breathing, his hands curled into fists, letting the night sink in, allowing the loneliness to fester.

He counted the hours chiming on the clock in the hall and, with it, the hoot of an owl retired to the coos of mourning doves. The sun did not rise, it overflowed in a blaze of glory in brutal contrast to his mood. He ripped the sheets back, crawled from the bed and stared out the window. The day stayed silent except for an occasional snort from the horses in the barn. The stallion smelled the heat of the mare. Simon hummed a tune as he fed them, but both seemed to come from far away.

On the other side of the wall, she moved about, and he listened to her every footstep, had grown to know every nuance of her, every movement, every gesture, every touch, even her scent. The heavier footsteps of a man, he did not hear. Had the Saint departed during the wee hours or had Lucas imagined his presence?

Over the past two weeks, Lucas had wandered through her rambling home. He imagined visitors admiring the chandeliered parlors with their walls covered with brocaded silk, mantels of imported marble, the lengthy hallway, elegant stairway and polished oak floors. In better days, the plantation boasted a charm of its own with terraced gardens lined with boxwood, and the summerhouse at the edge of the James. Wealth, mingled with superb elegance and class, were suggested everywhere, making it obvious no allowable desire or requirement would be left wanting.

Now, the ornate silver candelabras lay tarnished in the hall, the decorative plaster corbels in the doorframes crumbled like stale gingerbread. The dark, wooden floors no longer polished to a brilliant gleam, lay dull and neglected. Like so many southern plantations at present, sagging forgotten, neglected and abandoned. Why didn't the home fit the image he had of the mysterious Miss Pierce?

He allowed his thoughts to drift back to when he helped create the Division of Civilian Spying, and where he encouraged iron discipline, shrewd tactics and utmost secrecy. He orchestrated a world populated with scavengers, thieves, and an extensive slave network, abandoning distinction to obtain information of value. Some did it for profit. Others like Rachel, for the cause they believed.

His hand came to rest on the Bible. He opened the well-thumbed book, carefully flipping through the pages. What value did the item hold for her? A paper fell out and floated to his feet. He stooped to pick up the missive.

To Rachel, my beloved daughter, and the many wonderful hours we shared reading.

Of all her grand possessions, Lucas' instincts identified the Bible as her most cherished. He couldn't help but picture Rachel in a different light. Conflicting with her guarded, impertinent, worldly-wise manner rose a simple girl with heartfelt compassion. At once he saw through her pretenses—a girl who stood lonely and vulnerable against a world turned upside-down. He tucked the note inside the book and placed it on the table.

Without a doubt, Rachel Pierce was a paradox. In his arms, she had responded to his kiss, the experience incredibly extraordinary. Despite her supposed affairs with the Saint, she didn't seem to know what she was doing. Lucas felt her innocence in his bones.

Do not get involved. There was nothing on earth more likely to steal a man's common sense than a woman.

Last night, he stepped over the line. Every coherent thought had gone out of his mind.

In his thirty-two years, he had never felt an unbearable need for someone…just to be in the same proximity as her. Even now, he longed to take her in his arms and kiss her. He was her superior and remained responsible for her.

He stared through the trees as the sun reached its zenith, the towers of Richmond clouded, the smoke, mottling and blotching the capital as if charcoal soup had been dumped on the surface. A mind-numbing disgust rose inside him. There remained one answer to the problem.

He strode to the door. Why the fool woman locked him in at all remained a mystery to him. He picked the lock and moved into the hall.

"Where do you think you're going?"

"Stay out of this, Rachel, I'm leaving."

"You have a predilection for the undertaker? He can bring you back from the place where you caught the bullet as lifelike as if you were asleep. Your casket…rosewood? Pine? Or something in-between?"

How she possessed a terrible knack of unraveling him with her parrying of words. Words tinged with pointed barbs, significant to aggravate the devil.

"I won't get caught." Amber pools beneath thick dark lashes stared back at him. There was no denying the gravity and emotion he saw there. She had rescued and cared for him. He owed her his life. His insides twisted, and he chafed at the moral code in which he'd been raised…and too well…the Colt revolver that had been pointed at his heart the evening before.

She stood inches away.

"Unless you can fly, I'd say your chances are like snow in August for I've never seen the Confederacy weave a web so tight."

Did she care about him? God help him.

"I must go." He dared to graze his knuckles across her cheek. A clock chimed in the hall. He wanted to forget the war, wanted to pretend none of it existed, to erase the reality surrounding them. He dropped his hand.

"If it's about last night," she said.

The silence lengthened between them. Never would he forget the softness of her voice. The way she looked at him, the denial in her eyes that said yes. Her magnetism tore through his veins like the moon pulling the tides.

"It's not about last night, and you know it. It's about tonight and the next and the next. I can't make any promises…"

"I've asked for no apologies—"

He couldn't get it out of his head that she didn't love the Saint—never did. Not in the way a man was meant for a woman. Then what? Did she fear the Saint?

Lucas knew life didn't work that way.

"Imbibe on my infinite wisdom. Wait 'til things cool down. There's no sense in getting killed or risking my people." She caught his hand and drew him away.

He'd vowed not to touch her, and here she was, leading him like a dimwitted child. When he didn't move, she looked at him, the implications dawning on her innocent gesture. She tugged her hand free, blushing. He liked the color rising in her cheeks.

"I have something vital to share with you, Colonel Rourke. I attempted last night…but you were…difficult."

No way to escape her. She led the way to her study. The soft sway of her backside put his mind on other things. Unlocking her desk, she tripped open a secret compartment, and withdrew several papers.

"Were you aware of the imminent threat to the United States of America, emerging as a grave and gathering danger by Copperheads in the north?"

"They're always scheming. We have them closely surveyed, but Southern agents are elusive."

She spread the sheets and detailed maps. The minutiae immediately commanded his attention. He smoothed back his hair under his collar and pored over the information, grasping the seriousness of the situation. The Copperheads were bringing revolution to the northeast.

"It starts in New York," Rachel began. "The United States Sub-Treasury on Wall Street is to be apprehended, City Hall turned into a fortress, Broadway to reverberate with the march of twenty thousand traitors. Policemen who are associates of the Copperheads will take possession of Police Headquarters on Worth Street. The Federal Courthouse and all government buildings are to be taken. Six cans of gunpowder will be buried under the central gate of Fort Lafayette in the Narrows off Brooklyn to blow a hole through the thick stone walls. General John Dix will be taken hostage. All Confederate prisoners will be released, on the rampage and armed. The Stars and Bars of the Confederacy will fly over City Hall in twilight's purple light. By nightfall, all New York City will be a sea of flames.

"At the same hour, the U.S. Government will be up to its eyeballs. Chicago will be ransacked, set ablaze, plundered and turned into an enemy city. Fifteen thousand howling Rebel prisoners will be released from neighboring prison camps, armed with bayonets and Navy Colts smuggled to them. State and municipal officials will be slain and substituted with puppets. There will be twenty thousand battle-experienced Copperhead and Rebel prisoners ransacking the state. Baltimore and Washington, they are also targeting. I have names and addresses of Southern agents and those aligned with them, also stashes of weapons and munitions." Rachel tossed her hair back.

Lucas stood spellbound. "How did you get this information?"

"At the Rutherford ball. I hid in a closet and eavesdropped."

Lucas' blood ran cold. "You little fool. You might have been caught." Beneath gritted teeth, he asked, "Where did you get the maps and other information?"

She had the audacity to stand there with a mutinous expression on her face that sent his temper soaring.

Lucas narrowed his eyes. "The Saint. How do I know I can trust this information?"

"I would know."

"I don't echo your sentiment." That was the rub. He had to depend on the Saint to return to Washington and…for the valuable information. "How does the Saint maintain his anonymity?"

She plunked her hands on her hips. "It's very simple, Colonel Rourke. The Saint does not get caught because he never trusts anyone until he is absolutely sure of their loyalty."

"Does the Saint trust me?"

She snorted. "Probably trusts you more than he should."

"Sit down," he ordered. "As your commanding officer, I order you not to get involved ever again."

She sank into a chair and tapped her toe on the carpet. Yielding to his authority had struck a nerve. He could care less.

Yet, little did he feel his rank altered her inclinations to take matters into her own hands or curb her rebellious attitude. He leaned against the desk and folded his arms in front of him, silently amused, and pondering the problems facing him. Keeping a tight rein on her maddening independent streak would be a challenge well met.

Why was it then, that instead of feeling like he was in charge, he felt like a pawn under a tiger's paw?

Chapter 8

Rachel sat dwarfed by the four massive, cathedral-like columns that accentuated the front porch. Peeling from lack of paint and now fodder for termites, the pilasters once welcomed guests with great stateliness.

In the distance, a lone rider approached her home, the horse kicking up little ploughs of dust with its hooves. Via a trusted courier, she had sent a coded message to the one man in Washington who could stop the Copperhead plot. The courier was captured crossing the James River and arrested. Fortunately, he sank the dispatch in the river and claimed he was catfishing, the story buying his release. She had to try again to get the valuable information through but the search for Colonel Rourke had the area bottled up tight.

She shrugged and breathed deep, enjoying the warmth of the noonday sun until a dark cloud swept overhead. The rider rode through a bevy of chickens, sending them clucking and skittering to the safety of their coop before he halted.

"Captain Johnson." *Why was he here?*

With so many people to insulate her there was no way could

she have been implicated in sending the message…or had she been?

Rachel did not offer any well-wishes or formal greeting. Nor did she stir herself. Instead she concealed a black rage boiling in her blood. *Play the game, Rachel. Stay above suspicion.*

He tied his horse to the hitching post, keeping his eyes on her at all times.

They had been neighbors for years. His assumption that she'd marry him. In fact, the entire county speculated on the banns, confident of an obvious match that linked two leading families. His, from the wealthiest plantation, and a perfect complement to Rachel's, a prominent Virginia family, as old and well-renowned as the Lees.

Strong rumors indicated deep financial woes for Captain Johnson, and with the advent of bankruptcy looming, he grew desperate.

Because of his supposed wealth, most women fell at his feet. Not much taller than Lucas, he wore his uniform nice and clean, pressed to sharp flat edges. His lips were taut like the flesh of a dead animal dried in the sun, and when he smiled, it solidified an assertion of uncurbed evil.

Rachel had put him off with her well-extended and obligatory mourning period, mindful to tread careful where Captain Johnson was concerned. She was well-acquainted with his history, and the horror stories of his youth. When he wanted something, he'd acquire it with his fists or bullying. The bloodthirsty rage of his fighting and slyness made him win over peers. Despite having the advantages of a good education, he didn't apply himself, more interested in terrorizing the boy in the desk next to him. At home, he beat his slaves for any infraction and bragged about the thrashing.

Was it the result of his father hating him? Or the result of his mother's infidelity? She waved her palm fan, convinced his conduct went beyond the accident of his birth, and believed his behavior was inherent in the cruelty of his nature.

He stood by the railing, in front of her, his shadow engulfing her, a tactic on his part to intimidate—a perfect monster for the Confederacy.

Rachel ignored him, waiting for him to break the silence, but his attention was directed on a fly which he had been trying to catch. Suddenly, with animal-like swiftness, he closed his hand and trapped it. Then he bent over to pull off the wings, one at a time. When the mutilated fly tried to escape, he reached out a thick, wide thumb, holding it over the fly for some moments, moving it about as the insect twisted. Then, grinning, he dropped his thumb heavily and crushed the fly. Only then did he look up at her.

He took off his gloves, one by one, and then drew her to her feet, holding her hands. Her skin crawled. Like a rat in the sewers, he worked behind the scenes, a Copperhead, dissolving and disappearing at a moment's notice, emerging crafty and cunning enough to fool his staunchest enemy.

"You are a beautiful woman, Rachel. You need a strong hand," he drawled.

Rachel snorted. "I suppose you are the only one to guide me."

"I've come to demand your hand in marriage. I promise it will be the last time I offer you this proposal." His dark eyes shifted over her, insulting, and unveiled his underlying menace.

Apparently, he chose to forget his conduct at the Rutherfords'. "I am overcome by your consideration for my tender heart. I promise you, I will never forget, nor will I accept."

He hovered close to her ear. "At the Rutherfords', you pricked my suspicions. Have a care—"

Rachel tugged her hands from him, thanking providence for the lemony scent of a blooming magnolia to wipe away the smell of foul whiskey.

"I don't know what you are talking about."

How she loathed this man. She flicked her eyes to the foundation of what remained of the barn, and a vision of smoke swirled before her, choking her, fire singeing her hair, torching her skin. The image gave sudden rise to the night her father died, and to hot, angry, impotent tears. Never would she be vulnerable again.

"You may fool most, but not me. You bear watching."

She glared at him. "Are you threatening me?" She kept her voice low, prayed Lucas wasn't listening, prayed he'd have the common sense not to intervene if he was.

"As for marriage to me, it is your only way out. I can overlook the blemish of your father's sins, since your mother's southern blood runs in your veins."

Was he damning her father as a northerner or for freeing slaves or both?

He grabbed her then, kissing her, bruising her lips, his wet tongue stabbing into her mouth. She pushed at him, but his fingers dug into her arms. Nausea heaved in her stomach and rolled in her throat. The cicadas sang louder and louder. How she wished they would swarm together and devour him. With all her might, she thrust him away.

"I will never stoop to marry the likes of you."

Simon appeared, carrying a tray with tall glasses of lemonade. "I thought you all might want some refreshment on a warm day." Simon ducked his head.

"Thank you, Simon." She wiped her hand across her mouth and sank into a chair. Simon's timing was perfect. She reached for a glass and he warned her with his eyes. With a slight nod, she chose the other glass.

Johnson cracked his neck from side to side, picked up his proffered drink, and took a long draw, finishing the contents to the last drop. "Your darkie doesn't seem to know when not to intrude on important conversation. He should be taught to know his place."

Simon laid the tray on a table, and stood at Rachel's side, staring daggers at Johnson.

"What I do with my people is my business and none of your affair. You may leave," she said.

He stomped off her porch, his boot heels making half-moon marks in her yard. "I guarantee you'll regret turning down my offer."

"The only regret I'll have, Captain Johnson is you not leaving my property soon enough."

Johnson mounted his horse, yanked the bit so hard the horse reared, and then whipped the animal.

When he was gone, Simon slapped his hat on his knee and cackled. "I'm afraid Captain Johnson will regret drinkin' that lemonade long before he arrives home."

Rachel widened her eyes. "You didn't."

"I certainly did. Colonel Rourke suggested it." Simon produced a bottle filled with a vile purgative. "A good dose too. And unless that horse starts gallopin', Captain Johnson will be a hurtin' Rebel."

Chapter 9

Moonlight spilled through the window, casting her father's study in a luminous glow. In a haze of sleep, Rachel reclined on the settee, murmured, and then bolted upright. An obscure figure rose out of the gloom, and a wave of awareness raised her above the reign of slumber.

"Lucas?"

"Why are you crying?" He struck a match and lit a candle, emitting an arc of brilliant gold in the blackness.

She wiped away tears. Had she really cried? "It's nothing."

"I heard your screams—"

"I did not ask you to come."

"No, you did not. I am here despite your objections." He eased onto the settee and placed a worn pillow on the other side of her.

Rachel hugged her knees beneath her knitted shawl, twisting a strand of loose hair around her fingers. He leaned back on the sofa, tucking her head beneath his chin. No, she should not allow the intimacy.

But for now, she felt safe.

"Was it the purgative given Johnson that has you weeping?" he teased.

Rachel shook her head and wiped a tear. "On the contrary, if it had been me, I might have emptied the entire bottle in his glass."

Lucas produced a handkerchief and she blew her nose.

"Tell me what's troubling you."

Her heart gave an unswerving leap from the genuine warmth of his deep baritone voice.

Infinitely patient.

Memories boiled and churned and surged. Most of what had been bottled up inside had been there too long. Trembling, she sat there silently, and like a fallen leaf caught in a whirlpool, drowning in all the sadness and sorrows, and sinking her farther into the muck. Couldn't breathe. No...far too agonizing to resurrect. Talk. She had to talk...about anything else.

With fingers as light as a feather, he lifted her chin to meet his gaze. Candlelight glimmered over his handsome face...so strong and confident and reassuring. But to expose the most vulnerable part of her life?

To share the yoke of her guilt.

Rachel released a ragged breath. "To me, my father stood a giant, a great and noble man. I loved him dearly. He was a wonderful father, and my life was rich and full because of him. He was my best friend and was to be admired, ready to sacrifice his world against a horrible wrong. He hated the tyranny of the slavrocracy, it was so against his grain to see men bought and sold...beaten and worked to death. He grew bolder with each success in helping slaves escape."

Rachel swallowed the lump in her throat. Lucas did not

speak. He did not seem to judge. He waited for her to continue and the telling came easier.

"One night, Father had helped a group of slaves cross the river. We were in the barn when a group of horsemen rode into the yard. My father told me to flee. I refused and hid in the haymow. I watched everything. I watched Captain Johnson with other men…" Rachel wrapped her arms tighter around herself. "Unspeakable things," she whispered.

She tore her gaze from his, swiped her cheeks with the back of her hand. She didn't want him to see her cry. To see how weak she really was. "They tied him to a timber and whipped him. I can still hear his screams. Before they left, they threw a rope over a beam and hanged him. I inched across the beam…tried to cut him down…the barn had been fired…I was unable to reach him… there was nothing left for me to bury."

Lucas cursed and yanked her into his arms while she wet his shirt with her tears. A knot grew in his chest, and he felt the heat of her tear roll down his hand from her cheek. "There was nothing you could do to save him. It was an act of violence against a loved one. You should never have witnessed it."

At last, he understood why this lovely woman with outward steely confidence stood so brazen against a hostile world. To have kept all the years of loneliness, grief and isolation locked inside? Most men crumbled to what she had endured.

Standing up against a society so wrong and championing her cause the best way she could, astounded him. The fact she cared more for others less fortunate than herself and risked her life, slammed into his heart.

For lack of knowing what to do, Lucas sat there for a long time, cradling her, and unable to get her revelations from his mind. "Never-ending remorse is a detrimental reaction. You should not feel guilt."

At a loss of what more he could offer, he allowed the stillness of the night to garner all her burdens and sufferings like so many moonbeams painted across the floor. The War Between the States still raged but in the tiny nucleus of her home they contented themselves with a peace cut off from the misery and bloodshed.

When she was able to get her grief under control, her body relaxed against him. He smoothed her long auburn hair, and an urge to protect her washed over him. Determined to talk about anything that might take her mind from her troubles, he said, "Tell me about your family."

She sighed and warmed to the subject. "My mother happened to be the most beautiful girl in the county. My grandfather had orchestrated a brilliant match with the son on a neighboring plantation. The engagement was heralded as the wedding of the season. My father happened to be visiting a friend in Richmond. With all the balls given, it seemed inevitable that they would meet. When they locked gazes on each other, it was as if Cupid's arrow had hit them. Since my grandfather did not sanction a marriage to a no-account Yankee lawyer, they eloped. Enraged, Grandfather disowned my mother, and they moved to Illinois."

Lucas let out a low whistle. "I detected a northern accent from you at times, but I considered it to be Ohioan with the way you roll down on your R's and your I's are short vowels."

Rachel bumped her head on his chin, turned and stared at

him, her amber eyes flickering with interest. "I'm surprised by your perception. I have taken great lengths to eradicate my northern accent. Everyone I encounter never guesses of my time in the north."

"You forget, I'm head of Civilian Spying. You're in company with the best." The fragrance of roses clung to her. When she nestled her head against him and innocently stroked the hair on the back of his neck, a spike of heat hit him low in the gut.

"At first it was hard for my mother to adapt to the wilderness since she was accustomed to a life of leisure with many servants to wait on her. But my mother was deeply in love with Father and both remained tremendously happy regardless of the hardships. The most difficult thing for my mother to adjust to was my father's long absences. He rode the circuit with another lawyer and a judge, and since it encompassed an expansive area, his work took him far away from home. Due to my father's brilliance, he prospered and provided a larger cabin with a servant to lessen her load."

"When I came into the world, they both lavished their love on me. Father refused to send me to a boarding school in the east and insisted on a generous education, bringing many books home from his journeys. At a young age, I acquired a voracious appetite to read, and then my father discovered my talent—a photographic memory. I possess the rare ability to memorize everything put before me.

"Father said I should have been a boy, claiming my mind bright enough to debate a favored colleague of his. I loved his associate. He was tall and would set me up on his lap, telling me amusing stories and let me pull on his beard.

"Despite not having worldly amenities, I couldn't have had a happier childhood…except for once when I almost drowned and for that I have a terrible fear of water."

She became so wrapped up in her story that she pushed back from him to see if he remained listening. "Confidences shared at this time…I expect will remain confidences?"

Not only was she hinting at the intimate details of her history, but at the closeness they were now sharing, an act which society ordained scandalous and branded an unmarried woman forever. "I'll take your secrets to my grave."

With his assurance, she continued. "There were no other children in our settlement, so I played with the Indian children of the Illini tribe, where competing in the woods provided a challenge and indoctrination for survival. Like the rest of them, I grew up to run fast, hunt, and track. Are you horrified, Colonel Rourke?"

"I'm intrigued." The indisputable truth of her history fascinated him, and pieces of a puzzle started to fit together by her extraordinary upbringing. Living in the harshness of the wilderness, and with Indians as companions accounted for a lot about her and gave her an inner strength that in no way allowed her to fail. It also explained her lack of material need and strong conviction in what she was doing. She triumphed, smarter and more sophisticated than any woman he'd ever encountered.

"Mother practically had a heart attack as soon as I started blossoming, and the chief's son declared his love for me. Every day a haunch of deer hung on our front porch. Horrified, Mother cried to my father that her daughter would never learn the refinements of a lady growing up in the wilderness with Indians.

"Yet, providence had its hand in the matter. On my grandfather's deathbed, he had a change of heart about his only child, heir to his home and fortune. We moved to Virginia, and my mother made me trade in my buckskins for corsets and dresses." She pulled back to look at him. "Are you shocked yet?"

Lucas chuckled. "Not at all…do go on."

She leaned back and, in thoughtful silence, she struggled to remember where she was in her story. After a short pause, she began again.

"Richmond happened to be a very different and difficult world for a girl accustomed to living as a tomboy. Mother insisted I learn every nuance of becoming a lady." Rachel made a study of her hands, folded in her lap. "I have failed her."

"She would have been very proud." Distracted by the myriad of emotions playing across her lovely face, Lucas suppressed a grin, smoothing his expression into an admirable imitation of earnest gravity.

"The sad part is that I have to pretend to be meek, unintelligible and weak. Can you imagine the chagrin of male suitors of the county if they knew I could outshoot and outgun them?"

"I imagine their mamas would grieve and take to their hartshorn, fainting away at the mere suggestion," said Lucas.

Rachel burst out laughing and Lucas' mood buoyed like a million warm sunny days rolled into one.

"I haven't laughed like that for a long time. Thank you, Lucas," she said huskily, and toyed with the wooden button on his shirt, driving him mad.

"I want to get back to the night you were kidnapped. Do you remember anything unusual about anyone, peer or supervisor, who had knowledge of the Saint? Anyone who would possibly set you up?"

"Other than waking up in a cell with the sadistic Johnson debriding every inch of my skin, there is nothing unusual I can recall. There are three others that have knowledge of the Saint… my superior, General Grenville Dodge, and my immediate subordinates, Bowman and Andrews who are above suspicion."

"Sometimes the least suspicious are the most suspicious."

"Bowman helps me at every turn and comes from an impeccable background. He performs errands, second guesses messages from spies and breaks down the latest intelligence, formulating successful hypotheses. He has worked hard to get where he is, and he's very dedicated. Andrews is young, intelligent and gets the job done. Impossible to think about any one of them betraying me. If they were to hand me over, they would have done it years ago. I trust all of them with my life."

"May I point out it was almost your life."

Lucas gritted his teeth, impatient with his southern sojourn when the answers lay in Washington.

She tilted back her head. "There are two others who trust the Saint implicitly."

"Who are they?"

She spread her hands, palms up. "Why General Grant and President Lincoln."

"Extraordinary. I rarely have their ears."

Pressing her lips to his ear, she whispered, "Now tell me how clever the Saint is."

"He is very clever if he has Lincoln's and Grant's trust. I am glad he is on our side."

With avid interest, he saw a spark in her eyes and an amusing twitch of her mouth. She was a dazzling vision and like a schoolboy with his first infatuation, she could cut him into little pieces if she had the whim.

"Have you ever had any nightmares, Lucas?"

She was teasing him, and he slid his hand from her cheek to her nape, resting there. "Interesting you ask."

"What are they?"

"Girls. Always give me nightmares. They always wanted to kiss me…it was a terrible torture growing up, especially as the girls grew up…they frightened me more. Why one time…"

Rachel threw a pillow at him and fell back on the sofa in peals of laughter. Lucas grinned and folded his arms behind his head, enjoying himself enormously. He opened his mouth to reply, but his gaze was drawn to where her shawl dropped, revealing the threadbare cotton nightgown she wore. Perfect, pink nipples protruded. He tried not to look at how the diaphanous garment stuck to her like a second skin, tried not to look at her slender waist leading down to curvy hips and…he imagined, the dark curls of the deep vee between her legs.

His pulse leaped, and he shifted to hide his physical reaction. He gazed out the window at the moon, a silver dollar high in the sky, illuminating a band of clouds that swelled and elongated.

He cursed. How she held the power to stir him. She was what every man dreamed of, a vision of incomparable beauty. What could one more kiss hurt? He had no intention of taking the kiss that far. Perhaps if he kissed her again, he'd eradicate the need he had for her.

Fool. And he could bag the sun and throw the fiery ball across the universe.

When her scent entwined him, his nostrils flared. Her nearness and the sultry look in her eyes unleashed something primal in him, drugged his mind. A pulse beat at the base of her throat. He imagined his tongue exploring that area down to the soft tips of her breasts and beyond.

The thrill of something timeless brushed against them as he circled his arms about her and pressed his lips against hers. The kiss started slow and thoughtful. Her lips softened willingly, her arms trembled as she circled them around his neck. Her warmth and the fierce thudding of her heart sent his own heart racing. Her soft full breasts flattened against his chest nearly undid him.

The latent attraction erupted with such force, and Lucas took full control. He reached down and pulled her tight against him, thrusting his tongue deeper to wield her passion. He breathed her, tasted her, tasted the sweet tea in her mouth and savored her. His kisses, gentle at first, became more forceful. His hunger suddenly released, he thrust his tongue again and again…like a branding iron, searing her, having her.

He cupped the back of her head and she melted against him. He caressed her bottom, and her hands splayed against his chest. He outlined the tips of her breasts with his fingers and her nipples grew taut and she gasped into his mouth.

On her gasp, he drew away from her, his chest heaving.

Cold air smacked against his hot skin, clouted him awake. Breathing hard, they stared at each other. Her lips were swollen from his kisses, and her hand burned against his chest. He wanted to kiss her again, yet reality seeped in. He'd go back to Washington, resume his career, and then what?

He lowered his arms from her, regretted the confusion reflected in her face. "I will go—"

"Yes, you should," she whispered, although her tone and demeanor said different. They had a war between them and a great many other things.

"Wait," she said.

To Lucas, Rachel seemed innocent to the sort of passion he experienced with her. Her behavior seemed incongruous with her strange affair with the Saint, a man who he'd not yet seen.

"I don't want to be by myself." Her voice sounded small, helpless, and childlike. "Could you just hold me?"

Lucas stared at her. Her lush golden eyes shone with tears. She'd been alone for years. She'd witnessed her father's brutal death.

He shouldn't, but how could he not allow this one small concession?

The air was still and the flame barely flickered. The books on the table around the candle cast shadows that radiated out as hands on a pendulum clock. The wick blackened, and the wax slowly turned to liquid, running down the side and onto the brass plate.

She didn't move, and she swallowed before wetting her lips. He wouldn't call his musings dishonorable, more along the order of wicked, with absolutely delicious sensual imaginings. Not altogether wise, considering kissing her senseless had lust exploding through his veins and roaring through his ears.

He pulled her close and wrapped her in his arms.

She laid her head on his shoulder and suddenly all seemed right with the world. She yawned, and soon he felt the soft puffs of her breath against his neck. Did he hear her mutter something ridiculous about him kissing like a prince?

Oh, the night would reign long.

After all, he wasn't a saint.

Chapter 10

Humming a familiar tune, Rachel crossed the yard to the barn. In the beauty of the day, her cheeks warmed from the thought of Lucas' kiss. She had other kisses to compare. Captain Johnson's kiss was like a foul reptile tongue or Ernest Columbine, whose kiss was like whitewash painted on a fence. Nothing she'd care to repeat or to remember.

However, Lucas's kiss was what a young girl dreamed of—like a princess would receive from her prince. Was the kiss something she'd regret? He had fired a latent primitive force inside her…warm, melting twinges low in her belly…making her yearn for something more.

Yet, her longings were a fool's dream. A choking bitterness rose within, for the very thing she wanted the most, she could not have.

She wanted Lucas. How she dared to dream. Yet the vagaries of life were as wide as they were severe, leaving her with no choices. Like new continents, they would remain undiscovered and unexplored, oceans apart and a sea of doubt between them.

Caution. She had to be cautious when dealing with the future.

So entrenched in the war, she could not allow love concerns to muddle her mind. Love would complicate matters, and give rise to many questions that she was not prepared to answer. No. It would be far too dangerous to get involved with Colonel Rourke.

Yet, when she lay in his arms last night, it was impossible not to imagine a perfect life—a husband, a family, a home. Her life when her parents were alive seemed so far away now, a memory of a distant past. And then Colonel Rourke came into her life. She sighed. Something similar to regret touched her.

She gave herself a mental shake. Do *not* think of the past, nor ponder what could have been, what could be at this moment or in the future. It is a futile effort.

Lucas had made his position clear. He wanted promotion and recognition. Pride spoke for him. Proud men possessed a habit of looking down on things and people. Of course, if one is looking down, then he couldn't see the important people to the side of him.

She had made her decision and it was the right one. Of that, she remained certain. No room for doubt or futile guilt or the "what ifs". After the war was over, and slavery abolished, and all the dreadful horrors and privations gone—she would forget the interlude had ever taken place. But could she?

The wind blew, kicking up whorls of dust, and she coughed as she turned the corner of the barn. A lanky soldier and two horses rested in front of the door. Her heart stalled. Bands of fear tightened around her chest.

The soldier stepped in front of her. He pushed a chaw of tobacco into his bristled cheek. "You can't go in the barn."

Whatever was going on, it was bad. "Step aside, Soldier. It's my property." As the soldier protested, Rachel dodged him and stalked into the barn. He was on her heels. She picked up a plank, swiveled, and then smacked him across the head. Down he went. She brushed the dust off her hands.

Her eyes adjusted to the dim interior, worn barrels, a pitchfork, beat-up water buckets, bags of feed grain slumped against the poles, dusty frames of wooden stalls, the heavy bosom of the loft above, gray pigeons clinging to the rafters. From her first slow breath, her nose twitched with moldering hay and manure.

Everything was quiet as it should be except for the horses snorting and wheeling in their stalls. A muffled cry came from the back. Rachel picked up a pitchfork, and edged along the stalls, the crackle of dry straw beneath her feet. She looked over a gate. With lash in hand, Captain Johnson stood over a half-naked Sally, a servant who came once a week to do Rachel's wash.

"I'll show you respect, you black bitch," he said and raised his whip.

Sally kicked at Johnson, a look of terror on her face. She crawled into a ball as the lash descended over her ebony skin. Johnson's eyes shone with his excitement, his mouth curled in a malevolent sneer as he brought his whip down again.

"Stop!" Rachel shouted, gripped the handle of her pitchfork and pointed the tines at him. "Get out and off my property. If I ever find you on this property again I'll kill you." She nodded at Sally. "Sally, go into the house and fetch Simon."

Dazed, Sally stumbled to her feet, holding her torn dress in front of her. "But Miss Rachel, Simon went into town."

To let Johnson know she was alone was the last thing Rachel wanted Sally to say.

The stink of cheap whiskey and the smell of sex lingered in the air. *Poor Sally.* The servant girl teetered around Captain Johnson and fled.

"You think a pitchfork's going to stop me from taking you, Rachel." He leered at her, his excitement combined with anticipation, evident.

Knees shaking, Rachel kept the fork steady, parrying him every time he tried to cut around her.

His upper lip curled. "I've had enough of your haughty refusals. How I'll delight in a nice Virginia peach and compromise you in the delightful process."

"You wouldn't dare." Her chin quivered, and she swallowed. The liquor had made him bold and he was twice the size of her.

He took a step closer. She backed up, holding the tines to his ferretlike face. He rushed at her and she thrust, scoring deep furrows in his cheek. He slapped the fork away and her weapon clanged against a stall door. Johnson put his hand up to his face. Scarlett against white smeared his palm.

"You bitch." In two steps, he flung her to the floor. The back of her head smacked on stone and she shook her head to clear the dizziness. The dry taste of chaff stirred up and onto her lips.

He straddled her, leered into her face. Rachel did not bother screaming. Her fingers curved into a tight fist and she struck him. The blow glanced off his cheekbone.

He grabbed her wrist before she could land another blow. She cried out as he squeezed her delicate bones together, then he pulled back a hand and struck her again. Stars flashed before her eyes. The barn became a black-edged blur; her head throbbed as if a million shards of glass pricked her skull. Tears came to her eyes.

"The worst kind of punishment comes to Northern sympathizers. I'm going to ram my cock in you until you beg me to stop."

His weight pinned her, his fetid breath hot on her face…his hands were everywhere on her body. Rachel bucked beneath him, sobbing. She kicked and screamed, yet his coarse whiskey tongue licked her skin, his skeletal hands clawed her breasts. Pigeons flapped from their roosts. Her fingers knotted in his hair. She jerked with all her strength. "Let me go," she screamed.

He tore at her skirts. "That's right, beg me, Miss High and Mighty. When I'm done, I'm going to whip you. I'll not mar the parts that can be visible. I'll relish your scars beneath every time I take you to our marital bed."

"No!" Fresh panic jolted her through her veins. Her hair loosened from its chignon, and tumbled, damp and tangled about her face, suffocating her. He raised his hand to send another blow.

Suddenly Johnson lifted up, his weight released and he flew across the barn, his head snapping against a vertical beam.

Rachel glanced up. *Lucas.*

Lucas' eyes narrowed dangerously, a tic pulsed in his jaw.

"Colonel Rourke, we meet again," Johnson said, never taking his eyes off Lucas. "My dear Rachel, my assumptions about your activities were correct. You must be involved with the Saint to have aided Colonel Rourke's escape. Clever girl. I never thought you were as stupid as you pretended. You're a traitor."

Rachel pushed down her skirts, struggled to stand. A figure dashed behind Lucas. She shouted, "Behind you!" at the very time a soldier jammed his pistol against the back of Lucas' head. The other soldier had come conscious again. She should have hit him harder.

"Let Colonel Rourke go," Rachel pleaded. "I'll do anything you want. I'll marry you."

Johnson moved behind her, plucked a knife from his boot and held it at her throat. "I don't need a harlot of the north as a wife."

"You can have the plantation," Rachel said. "I'll sign it over. It's all you ever wanted…you killed my father for it."

"So, you know about that. I enjoyed hanging your father. He deserved it. And once you're hung as a spy, you won't have to sign papers of legal ownership. The property will be mine."

"Let her go. You've got me," Lucas said.

"I tip my hat to you, Colonel Rourke, a man with fine abilities, a dangerous enemy and a daring spy. For your reward, you can watch me sample her charms." His knife pressed against her throat. Trickles of warm blood ran down her neck.

Slow and deliberate like a spider spinning its web was Johnson's humiliation of her, his performance calibrated to provoke Lucas. His eyes darkened with barely controlled rage.

Johnson snorted. "The belle of Richmond has a predilection for the enemy. Before I get done with you, my sweet," Johnson goaded, "you'll tell me everything you know."

Rachel signaled Lucas with her eyes, the guard distracted by the tableau. She kicked her leg back, at just the right angle, her heel smashing into Johnson's kneecap with the same thrust she'd used to kick a water bucket. She felt the crack through her boot. Johnson went down. She pivoted sideways to avoid his knifepoint.

A shot went off. The other soldier dropped to the floor, blood pumped from his chest. Johnson grabbed her ankle, tripped her and she sprawled, skidding her palms against the stone.

Lucas dropped on Johnson, his hands encircling the Confederate captain's neck, suffocating him, until he was pawing for air.

His coming death did not move her. He had murdered her father.

The sound of horses drummed up the drive. Rachel scrambled to a window. Sally melted into a cornfield. "Soldiers are coming. They must have heard the shot."

"Damn. No time to take care of this cur." He hissed, dispatching Johnson with a quick jab to the head. He tossed the rebel captain's unconscious body into a pile of dung.

They raced to the house, a hairsbreadth before the riders galloped into the yard. Rachel opened the trap door of her desk and threw her notes and maps into the fireplace.

"Why did you do that?

"I don't want to get caught with the evidence." She tapped her head. "I have it all up here. I did tell you I have a photographic memory."

There was shouting outside. She tore back the drape. Captain Johnson rose from the dark mouth of the barn, pointed to the house, an evil grimace shown on his face. The soldiers had surrounded the house and cut off all means of escape. Rachel watched in horror as they tossed torches onto the roof of her home.

Lucas yanked her from the window. "They plan to burn us alive. I want to keep you out of this. I'll give myself up, perhaps they'll go easy on you."

Rachel raced up the stairs, and said, "You heard Johnson. You know what fate I'll receive at his hands. As it stands, your and my corpse will be displayed as a monument to infamy." In the rear of her armoire, she snatched a Confederate uniform. "We travel together or not at all. Now get this on and be quick about it."

"I'd rather dance with the devil than put that thing on."

"You may get your wish sooner than you think. We are as near to hell in this house as we'd be on a scaffold."

A steady barrage of shooting splintered wood and shattered windows. Lucas jerked her to the floor. "They want to make sure we don't leave the house," he said, switching out of his clothes and dropping his watch into his pocket.

Rachel tugged on her travel clothes, fought to even her breathing as billowing plumes of smoke filled the house. She seized a bag that she kept for such an emergency and called out to him. "We can escape through the cellar." A shower of plaster sprayed over their heads from the gunfire. Too close.

They clattered down the stairs, the house burning, and snapping like a fiery wind through a canebrake. Flames licked the walls and swept across the ceiling. Ropes of fire chewed through the drapes and spread across the floor in rippling sheets.

Outside, the Rebels hooted and shouted, "A beautiful fire."

Memories assailed. Her father...the barn. Rachel froze. Her quicksand feet would not move. Blinded by thick smoke and sweltering heat, she coughed uncontrollably and collapsed. The fire would swallow her up. She would die here, and no one would care. Had Lucas left her behind?

"Where are you, Rachel?"

He was there, beside her. He swept her up in his arms, pushed her face into his shoulder. Broken glass crunched beneath his feet and he stumbled. She looked up. The glowing embers leaped and twirled in a fiery dance. The hot swirling air and noxious smoke clouded her vision, singed her hair and scorched her eyes. How could Lucas see where they were going?

He kicked open the kitchen door and the fire beat a wall of intense heat that threatened to burn their lungs and cook them from the inside. He dropped them to the floor and pushed her. She crawled across the room, bruising her knees, pains skewering her skin as sparks burrowed into her clothing. At the cellar door, he wrapped a rag on a doorknob, hauled it open, and once through, rammed his shoulder against it, sealing them. "I hope you have a good plan because I don't feel like having a cellar for my coffin."

Wheezing breaths ripped at her throat as Rachel drew sweet drafts of fresh air into her lungs. The cellar remained the last haven before the house sank into it. She gave her bag to Lucas, lit a lantern and led him to a root cellar. Jars of cherries, peaches, jams, and pickles clinked on the shelves when she stumbled over a crate of potatoes. From a basket, she grabbed a bunch of apples, handed them off to Lucas to place in her bag, and then gave him the lantern.

The hollow wails of the fire caused her to shiver, and then she breathed a sigh of relief, reaching the east wall lined with shelves and baskets. At a side molding, she pressed a button and the wall sprang open, scraping across the dirt floor, and revealing a tunnel.

"Brilliant. I never would have guessed."

She closed the door. "I had the tunnel built after my father died to help slaves as well as prisoners from Libby Prison escape."

They hurried through a long and narrow passageway, the moist earth cool beneath their feet. She swiped at her nose, the stink of mildew lingered with smoke, and fluttery cobwebs stuck to her head. Soon shafts of daylight spilled into the dark interior.

"I need you to lift the stone above us," she said.

Lucas complied and heaved himself up. He extended an arm, pulled her out, and then examined the structure. "A crude replica of an abandoned well. No one would ever guess it's intended purpose."

"And concealed in the woods across the field from my home over there," she pointed where a smoke cloud mushroomed above the trees. "I must go back—"

"Are you crazy? I'm not letting you go back into that inferno. I'm sorry about your home. But nothing can be done."

A bitter agony welled inside her, the loss of the Bible her father had given her. She sobbed. She cared for no other possession.

He slid his arms around her as her home crackled and exploded, folding into the cellar. Couldn't stop to worry about the things she couldn't change. She pushed away, picked up her bag and led him through the woods.

Chapter 11

In an open meadow filled with blooming purple aster and goldenrod, two horses grazed, flicking their tails in the late afternoon light. Rachel's clothes were torn and dirty from Johnson and the fire. Lucas wiped the soot from her face with his thumbs, and then helped her remove a pile of brush, lifting a tarp and hauling out two saddles.

"Amazing, you think of everything," Lucas said, saddling the horses. After tightening the cinches, he cupped his hand to give her a leg up.

She straddled her chestnut-colored mare and took the reins. "You realize this will not be any stroll in the countryside."

Lucas mounted and squinted at the sun. He sweated with the heat and lifted the detested wool of his gray collar away from his neck. "It will be dark soon, so we'll go around Richmond and move north."

She tied her bag behind her. "No, we will head south. It will be the least likely place they'll look for us."

"Are you joking? They'll believe we've perished in the fire. Johnson couldn't have done us a better favor."

"He is no fool." She raised her head in that infuriating stubborn fashion when she took a notion she was right. "We'll ride south, circling north."

Lucas was about to argue with her, but when he looked into those eyes of hers, he remembered the ordeal she had just been through, and mentally clicked off everything that had happened to her. She had been brutalized by a sadistic monster. Her magnificent home had been burned to the ground and had almost entombed her within its walls. There was no safety net afforded to her now that her Northern sympathies had been revealed.

Over and over, this mere slip of a girl had stood up to countless hurdles and survived. She overwhelmed him with her spirit and inventiveness. He shook his head, amazed at her ability to mourn a significant loss, yet have the poise and determination to put it in the back of her mind and move forward.

Lucas *knew* what she'd left in that fiery inferno. He recognized what had finally broken down her unfaltering confidence and made her cry. She didn't really care about the home or its contents. Without her telling him what she wanted, *he knew*, and it surprised him, knowing how attuned to her feelings he'd become. His chest tightened. She'd risk her life for attaining the Bible her father had given her. Lucas vowed he'd make it up to her.

They had to get moving or risk discovery. Again, he saw a tear fall from her eye that she swatted away, turning her head so he wouldn't see her. His gut clenched.

There was no logic in her proposal to move south. He'd allow her to make the decision...but it would be the last time.

"South," he conceded. "What about Simon?"

"He will have seen the smoke and knows what to do. We have rehearsed our arrangements for the inevitable. I forgot to ask you one question, Colonel Rourke."

"Ask away."

"Can you ride?"

He stared at her, and then a sly, little smile returned to that lovely face of hers. She prodded her horse ahead of him in challenge. Lucas spurred his mount and, at breakneck speed, slipped over pasture fences like a fox hunter on a chase. She kept up, neck and neck, and he marveled at her ability to keep up with a southern boy born in the saddle.

After a while, they slowed their mounts to give them rest. For Lucas, their pace remained alarmingly slow. There was little time to waste. To get the critical information on the Copperhead activities to responsible authorities before their diabolical plot was hatched lay paramount. The Copperheads could change the outcome of the war.

In her bag, Rachel possessed forged passes to get them out of Richmond. Her forethought and planning, he held in esteem. They traveled thirty miles through a rain-drenched night, along broken roads, dodging prowling troops. They moved through Virginia towns, avoiding patrols with the skill of a chess players. They passed through harvested cornfields and plundered barns and orchards. They slipped by wagons full of dust-covered wounded and Union prisoners on their way to Libby.

The ragtag Southern forces marched in barefoot or in broken brogans, others with blood in their boots, gaunt, tired, and with very little food except for hard corn to break their teeth and less to fill their stomachs.

"This war must end soon," he said. He pressed his horse in the tasseled corn, the dry leaves scraping against their clothes. The sun's last crest lowered behind a hill to gild the field. Rachel slumped in her saddle. They had rested little. He was accustomed to hard rides from his days as a scout and still longer days in the cavalry. The journey stretched on. She never complained. The prospect of a good warm bed and night's sleep was inviting, but Lucas dared not offer any respite due to constant danger.

He turned to the left, up a slope, leading to a road. Breezes shushed through the grass and an eagle cried overhead. The hairs on the back of his neck rose. Warning bells rang. He glanced around. Something was not right.

Ever wary, he stood up in his stirrups alert for any foreign sound. As a scout, the night had perfected his senses. His survival depended upon acuteness of eyesight, hearing, smell, touch, and taste as well as his power to reason. Then there was another sense. A sense that told him something was wrong before it happened, a nervous tingling that scraped beneath his scalp and tensed his muscles.

Suddenly, the pounding of a large assembly of horsemen boomed to their rear.

"Hide in the woods," Lucas snapped. She dug her heels into her horse's flanks and bolted headlong into the woods. Lucas stayed on the road, waiting for the Rebs to gallop up to him, and then rode straight at them. The startled patrol pulled up short.

"This way men," Lucas shouted. "Spies have gone down the road! I think it is the Saint!" The magic name was enough to make the Confederate patrol spur their mounts forward.

Lucas waited until they'd disappeared around the bend, and then plunged his horse into the woods, through barrel-like boughs, tearing at massive vines, coming up short of Rachel. "We can't afford to head south. The entire Confederacy is locked up around Petersburg."

"We can't afford not to. It's not the intended direction our pursuers will think of," she said with outrageous impertinence when he stared her down.

Was it possible the creator made someone as stubborn as him?

"As it is now, I daresay there are no pursuers. On the other hand, I don't care for the eventuality that I may be recognized. North is the direction we will ride."

He could see the wheels turning in her head, burning up gears and spitting out the practicality of his decision. But first, the machinery had to penetrate through that block of pig-headedness. He cleared his throat to hurry her to come to her senses.

She leaned back in her saddle, reached back and grabbed two apples, tossing one to him. "By continuing south, there is the strong chance we can cross the lines to General Grant's forces on the other side of Petersburg."

Good God. If she lifted her chin any higher, she'd paint the sky, and if he wasn't so irked by her excellent logic, he might have laughed out loud. But he was not in the mood to hint at the possibility of her greater wisdom. "I'll earn a bullet wearing this uniform for my troubles." He kicked his mount into a canter, heading south. He didn't have to look back. He knew Rachel followed.

Scarcely had the night arrived, the last glint of sun to fade like a still glowing coal in a fire, and on he pushed for hours in the darkness. Lucas glanced back to check on Rachel and found her nodding off in her saddle. He took her reins and pushed on some more, and then took heart and led the horses a safe distance off the road.

He lifted her off her horse, steadied her until she was able to stand. "We'll rest for the duration of the night." Over the mustiness of moss, he spread a blanket under a tree. She sighed as she lay on the ground. Autumn had made a graceless and premature debut, and she curled into a ball, shivering.

Lucas raked his fingers through his hair. The woman had gone on and on for two days without rest and never complained once. Men were conditioned to hardship and the elements. Rachel, despite her uncommon upbringing in the wilderness, was not. He'd been a blockhead, arguing with her at every turn when she was thinking of his well-being. He sat down and pulled her up into his arms, tugging his greatcoat around her, and cocooning her with his warmth.

He lay back against the tree and glanced up to where a bright moon illuminated a sky, where the stars were so clean and bright they appeared an omen of success. She burrowed deeper in his coat. He groaned.

"Lucas?" She popped her head out of his greatcoat.

"Yes."

"Thank you for warming me."

"Get some sleep," he said, and she fell silent again. Lucas saw a star flash brightly, and briefly across the sky, before burning out over the horizon.

"Did you see it?"

"Uhm-m." He rested his chin on her head, breathing in roses and horses.

"Chief Standing Bear said a shooting star was an influence of past conditions affecting the present and the future, similar to waves hitting the bow of a canoe. Such a prophetic sign indicated a portent of change, such as a storm, or poor harvest, or a healthy child to be born."

Lucas chuckled. "Ah, the mechanisms of omens...if you say 'money' three times before the star burns out, you will be yanked from poverty. Or like an adolescent, placing a rag over his face and wishing away his pimples."

"I like Standing Bear's philosophy better."

Her long ago friendship with the Indians made her unique, unlike the majority of people who made it a point to hate the unfamiliar. Rachel embraced them and gathered values and wisdom from their way of life. Her underlying sensitivity touched his heart.

"What are your opinions on Lincoln?" she said.

Lucas smiled. "The man has many credits which are inherent in his character. I respect his ironclad will in preserving the Union. It's been a long, aggrieved war, yet he has never become bitter. His unyielding faith in victory, I believe, will yield triumph in the end. He is honest, sincere and his ambitions are directed to a higher purpose."

Rachel turned, offhandedly amused. "Your adulation of President Lincoln sounds unwavering."

"I've met the man a few times, but I believe he has great nobility of character that lends itself to his selflessness and kindly spirit."

"He received less than forty percent of the popular vote. He is tall, awkward and some say, apelike." She waited for some goading, some crossing of swords.

He raised his brows. "Your perspective on our President seems to fall short of the mark."

"Not at all," she said, silently pleased at his defensive stance of the President. "I am curious of your thoughts about meetings with the man. He has affected you."

"Most definitely, and who knows, maybe someday, I'll arrange for you to have the opportunity of meeting him."

"Perhaps," she said smugly and snuggled warmer into his greatcoat. Seeing the falling star made her think about her family and, suddenly, she wanted to know about Lucas' family. "Now, Colonel Rourke," she teased, "I know little about you. Tell me about your family and yourself. It is only fair." She could almost feel the heat radiating from his chest as he took a shine to the topic.

"Even though I came from a very well-respected Virginia family, privilege came with demands. There remained an expectation of hard work, both of physical and mental nature. We labored as hard as anyone else on the land we owned in the Shenandoah. Education was paramount as well. The atmosphere in our home was proper yet energized with discussions where we boys were required to lead debates on any chosen topic. I grew quick to pounce on any failure of fact or logic. And I can say, discussion ended afterward with many fights behind the barn."

Rachel considered Lucas. From one of Virginia's foremost families, he would seem the unlikely champion of the Union especially with two brothers high up in the Southern military. In the seat of wealth, he'd grown as the second son of a plantation owner.

"Despite the philosophy of slaveholders, my father and brothers decided long before the war to free the slaves. Rachel, you and your father helping to free slaves belonging to other plantations is honorable and has struck a chord—history will remain the judge of war."

To think Lucas was an abolitionist. Never would she have guessed, and his admonition raised him a notch in her esteem.

"With this conflict, I couldn't straddle the fence. I chose the Union regardless of going up against my family."

His arms tensed, and her heart ached for him. "I'm sure it was a difficult decision for you," she offered. The division of North and South cut deeply, dividing families and not surprisingly the Rourkes faced the same difficulty.

"I've known the tragedy of Manassas, suffered battle wounds at Antietam. Worked for General McClellan under the approved formation of a new company of scouts to find out what the Confederates were doing. The familiar Virginia countryside being my backyard and the easy drawl of my accent lent credence to my creditability of being there. Through a developed slave network and dedicated Northern sympathizers, I was able to secure information for the North and promoted upward."

Accustomed to horses and hunting, the usual nuances of a country boy, he'd worked his way up the hard way, earning his significant post. In contrast, men of southern gentility presented a less worldly figure, cunning bred out of them by the impotence of leisure and wealth. Lucas cut a fine figure, far removed from southern aristocracy.

He remained silent for a while. He'd tell her what was bothering him in his own good time.

"I dream of reuniting with my family, of the warm summer days and cold nights of the Shenandoah. My home. But that is all changed." He paused in reflection.

"Still, I like to remember the good times we shared growing up. There are four of us. My older brother, John, who as you know is a general, and I expect what I'm about to tell you will remain confidential?"

"Of course."

"I helped my brother escape. I had him locked up with Quakers in Pennsylvania. I didn't want him to get killed or carry on the war where others would die, nor did I want him to die in a prisoner of war camp. He was very clever and escaped."

Treason. She widened her eyes with the revelation. That he trusted her with his secret touched her heart.

"My youngest brother, Zach, didn't agree with either side and went west. I haven't seen him or my brother, Ryan, a CSA Calvary colonel, since before the war. Ryan and I didn't end well. We had a terrible fist fight...would have killed each other if my father hadn't intervened.

"Ryan hates me and said he hoped never to meet me in battle, promised I'd end up with a bad fate." He shook his head. "My brother, Ryan's, last venomous words to me were that he'd hang me if he ever caught me."

She lightly touched his arm. "It's sad how the people you were once so close with can become just another stranger you don't know."

Lucas stared off into the blackness of the night. "There's no lower curse than a family hand that strikes you when you are down. When Ryan makes his mind up, that is the direction he takes. He is the most muleheaded and unforgiving—"

"Yet it's impossible to take hate away from people. I've seen firsthand what hate can do. We are all hurting and will be hurting for a long time."

Didn't they all carry their scars? To Lucas, the love of his family far out-distanced wealth and privilege and promotion; and his separation was met by a death due to that departure. "Grief may not be as heavy as guilt, but it takes more away from you."

"Sometimes, I'm plagued to know what Ryan's reaction would be if he discovered me here. Would he help me? Turn me in? More likely, he'd kill me."

Rachel sighed. Who could predict the motivations of men in the theatre of war? "I can't believe a brother with so close a familial bond would kill his brother."

"I don't want to meet Ryan to disprove your theory."

"I imagine you must have been the soul of respect when you were a young boy," she said as an offhanded attempt to tease him out of his morbid mood, and she could practically feel him smile behind her.

"Why one time, my brothers and I decided to entertain the family with the play, *The Miller and His Men*. From behind the curtain, I created the effects, employing an added amount of magnesium, gunpowder and dried puff balls for awe and grandeur. The firepower was that of a cannon, bringing the production to a triumphant conclusion...and the servants fleeing for their lives. The explosion was enough to give my father pause, and the fact that his ears rang for weeks afterward."

Both of them broke out laughing, experiencing a sense of peace and satisfaction, and thoroughly taking pleasure in each other's company. Even with the danger they were in, a short reprieve from their troubles seemed well-earned. She had gone through so much in the past few days, the ride exhausting her. Now she had a second wind and wanted to keep Lucas happy.

"You're absolutely incorrigible."

"My mother had far worse feelings with the smoke, sulfur smell and fallout of white ash as I nearly set the house ablaze and destroyed the wallpaper in the parlor. My brothers and I had the hair burned off our heads and were bald for a month."

They both laughed again, an undeniable magnetism building between them. How odd to think they'd have this conversation at a ball, a recital, or in a parlor. The war had made extenuating circumstances, removing them far from the typical nuances of engagement. Lucas locked his arms around her, and she gloried in their shared moment.

"I can only imagine," Rachel said. "There were penances?"

"I remain a quick study of the woodshed," Lucas chuckled and added pointedly, "Miss Pierce, if I had been your father, there would have been many trips to the woodshed for you. That brings me to another topic. I must admit…there is another side to me. I have obsessions."

"Obsessions?" Rachel turned her head, awestruck by his confession. She was so curious, she scarcely noticed his hand lifting to her shoulder.

"I like to kiss girls."

Rachel glanced up, and her heart lurched. She cleared her throat, pretending to not be affected, but his nearness was overwhelming. Part of her wanted him to kiss her, and the other...she couldn't remember why not...for the life of her. He buried his hands into her hair at the nape of her neck, and she smelled him—earthy and the fragrant scent of pine needles. His lips touched hers, slow and thoughtful, surprisingly gentle. He drew back, and her lips were still warm and moist from his kiss.

"It's a peculiar obsession of mine." Lucas said, but it sounded a million miles away and made no sense to her at all. She peered up at him. His eyes bathed her in admiration. Her pulse leaped. He didn't give her a chance to question him before his lips pressed against hers, pulling her closer into his embrace, and her world was filled with him.

Rachel heard the click of guns first and tore away from Lucas. Three Confederate soldiers pointed their guns at them. Lucas stood, shoving Rachel behind him.

A lieutenant with wildly uneven teeth and a smile with increasing severity eyed the two of them. "What are you doing meandering in the woods alone with a woman. Soldier? Why aren't you with your unit?"

Lucas stepped forward until he stood inches from the lieutenant's face. "What's the use of a husband when his wife, pregnant with his child, needs help getting to her home?" Lucas snapped, pointing to the captain's insignia on his uniform. "And besides, what business is it of yours?"

Under Lucas' cold stare, the lieutenant mumbled something, stepped back and apologized. Lucas stood his ground until they lowered their guns and shuffled east, disappearing farther into the woods. Lucas was still the one in command.

He flexed his arm muscles, and then saddled the horses. "Rest time is over. In the future, we must be more vigilant."

She could see he was angry with himself for being caught unaware, and if it hadn't been for his quick thinking, they'd both be dead. Long years as the Saint had taught her to be prudent, but with Lucas, her head was not where it should be.

The horse's flanks twitched when Lucas boosted her into the saddle. He mounted and turned his horse around. When he continued his silence, her pride became bruised. Was he blaming her?

They sloshed through a shallow creek, the morning mist rising like a blanket to the sun. The cold nipped at Rachel now that she was away from his body heat. A painful lump grew in her throat. Gone was the cheerful and teasing Lucas. And gone, too, were the warm kisses shared beneath the tree despite being in the midst of a war zone.

The rotting smell of decomposing leaves lifted from the forest floor and the crunch of twigs beneath the horses' hooves filled the silence. Piecing thorns from overlying branches scraped her skin. A relationship with the colonel was unrealistic. Regardless of her troubled spirits, she would never forget their time together and stored it in the corner of her mind.

"I believe you may demand more of yourself than is necessary, if you understand what I mean, Colonel Rourke."

"No, I don't understand what you mean."

Why did he refuse to see that he held himself accountable for the whole world?

"War brings change," Lucas bit out. "War changes people. It gathers its grains and fires them into contemplation about themselves, about life. There's no turning back, only the sad forward motion wreaking disaster for the losers and salvation for the victors."

Chapter 12

A week of plunging through cramped woodlands, hacking at misshapen thickets had taken its toll. The last straw was when Rachel's horse had taken a stone in its shoe, crippling the poor beast and inhibiting further travel. Against Rachel's protestations, they found their way to a railroad depot, and bought tickets. To all visible travelers, they appeared nothing more than a married couple.

"You are the most muleheaded, stubborn, illogical man—"

She stopped and smiled at a passing gentleman on the train platform. She leaned in closer to Lucas, keeping her voice low, and hissed, "You were the one who was worried about someone recognizing you and, at this moment, we are exposed to the eyes and ears of the Confederacy."

He took her hand and placed it in the crook of his arm, strolling across the platform. "To my line of reasoning, we haven't been trailed. Blending in with the regular population is a simple and expedient approach to get to Grant's lines."

Like an attentive husband, mollifying his fretful wife, he patted her hand and led her to the line boarding the train. Her temperature rose two degrees. "We should have taken the cautionary route on back roads with little exposure. Next time, I decide the direction we take."

They took their seats in the back of the car. A Confederate colonel stared at her. Rachel held her breath. A long brittle silence ensued. Lucas winked at her and looked out the window.

"Good day," the colonel nodded amicably. He took off his coat, settled himself in the seat facing them.

Lucas assumed a polite expression and introduced the two of them as Captain and Mrs. Jefferson Davis.

Rachel's jaw dropped.

The colonel's eyes lit. "Any relation to our President Jefferson Davis?"

"Shirt-tail cousins," Lucas nodded. "On my father's side."

The colonel brought out a flask and offered it to Lucas. "Apricot brandy. Will you join me, Captain? That's if your wife concurs," he said, smiling to her.

Rachel gave a disgusted snort. The train moved off with a lurch, and she clutched her bag in her lap. "My husband does not drink spirits." Lucas must keep a clear head.

"A taste will not hurt, sweetheart, and I must be civil and not affront the colonel's hospitality. He is my superior and an order is an order."

The train chugged and whistled and bellowed out steam, increasing its speed until it was moving through towns and around bends at a steady pace. Rachel rested her head against the cool glass, making a study of the passing countryside while Lucas spent his time in cordial discussion of the war and past campaigns with their traveling companion.

"Let's toast to the loveliest of flowers of the Confederacy," said the colonel, raising his flask. Rachel offered him a shy smile and darted a glance at Lucas. He was superb. If she weren't so nervous, she might admit he was better than the Saint.

"To my beautiful and devoted wife, who complies with my every wish."

There lay a pale blue lightening of amusement between his lashes.

Rachel gritted her teeth. "And to my loving husband, who falls on bended knee at my bidding."

"Indeed," said the colonel. "A happy marriage brings such calm in these cruel times. Any children?"

Lucas bent low and confidingly. "My wife is in the family way."

Rachel's face heated to the roots of her hair. It was the second time he referred to a maternity she never had. When she jammed her elbow into his side, his laughter broke off, and he veered his discussions on mundane topics.

She rubbed absently at her arms. What machinations hammered behind his solid expression? How his clever mind analyzed and deliberated various ways to elude a sudden crisis.

"The object of this war is to correct Abraham Lincoln's political misconceptions," said the colonel, his jaw so rigid with principle that it might shatter, losing his teeth all over the floor.

Lucas swatted at a moth. "Let's hear it for General Lee."

"Hear, hear. Unlike General Grant, he knows which end of the pig makes the mess. And do you see how the people will comprehend that Lee's army will be down on them like a pack of wolves?" The colonel chortled with delightful horror.

"Even a fool can see that coming," Lucas opined.

"They will be crushed like a rotten peach." The Colonel boasted and toasted some more. "Beg pardon, ma'am," he addressed Rachel. "We officers' take our natures with us wherever we go." In another thirty minutes, the colonel had drunk himself asleep, with deep hiccupping snores that rattled the windows.

The train slowed to a town. Rachel turned to where Lucas stared out the window. He used his eyes like she did for a comprehensive study of the lines, breastworks, and the caliber of guns. The colonel's snores became so loud, he woke himself up.

"What's that over there?" Lucas asked.

"There's a lot of good Yanks over there." The colonel laughed.

Rachel squinted in the sun. "Doesn't look like much of anything."

The colonel chuckled again. "That's the cemetery."

Rachel swallowed.

The colonel adjusted the sword at his side. "Have you heard that a traitorous Union colonel and his woman were burned to death in a terrible fire in Richmond?"

Rachel gripped Lucas' arm. His muscles flexed beneath her fingers.

"Not at all," said Lucas, his voice smooth and oily.

"Where you been, Boy, under a rock? Been in all the papers. Can you imagine the outrageousness of those infernal Yank spies in the Capitol of the Confederacy?"

"I can imagine. Foxy devils, every one of them. They have a lot of nerve, those wily scoundrels," growled Lucas. "Why, they could be sitting right in front of you and you'd never know it."

Rachel tamped down the urge not to grab the colonel's flask and hit Lucas over the head.

"As far as I'm concerned, those traitorous spies got what was coming to them," said the colonel taking a hearty sip.

The train stopped. The platform filled with people. "I wonder if there will be enough seats to fit all those passengers." She stared at all the soldiers and dug her fingers into Lucas' arm. Someone may recognize him. The train began moving.

She followed Lucas' eyes to the far door of their car. In the next boxcar, Captain Johnson made steady progress down the aisle.

Rachel drifted closer, employing the use of her handkerchief to cover the movement of her lips as she murmured to him, "I told you so."

Lucas cleared his throat. "Those are without a doubt the four most nettling words in the English language, my dear." He tipped his hat lower and rose, careful not to disturb the snoring colonel.

"I forgot to introduce you to an old friend in the rear car, my darling," Lucas said.

With her satchel clutched to her chest, Rachel moved with Lucas out of their car and onto the coupler. The wind blew her hair and she fought a wave of vertigo as the countryside whizzed past. Her stomach heaved. Lucas held her tight as the coupler bowed and swayed.

A plume of smoke chugged from the engine stack and swirled over them. She coughed. One wrong step and they might fall, crushed beneath the train's massive wheels. Rachel glanced through the window. Captain Johnson stopped to talk to the colonel.

"Whatever do we do now?"

"We jump."

She blinked. "Are you crazy? Or are you given to impetuous behavior? Maybe you're frustrated by a woman smarter than you. That's it! You're determined to flaunt your arrogant shortcomings. You, Colonel Rourke..." she jabbed a finger in his chest, "must have had the privy fall on your head, for you are indeed a lunatic."

"Do you have a better idea? I have no hankering for swinging from a gallows tree."

"Do you want a medal posthumously?" She shrieked at him and made the mistake of glancing through the window again. Johnson recognized her and started toward them.

She looked at Lucas, judged the determination on his face. "There is no way I'm going to jump from this train. There must be another way—"

Lucas swooped down and picked her up and tossed her into the air. The sickening feel of free fall pitched in her stomach and hardened in her throat. She screamed, flailed her arms and legs like an albatross not knowing where God intended her to land, or how many bones she would break.

Water heaved around her, splashing mud over her. Thunderstruck...she had landed in the middle of a cow pond. Her feet oozed deep into slimy muck. Her clothes clung to her, soaked and slicked with sludge. After ingesting the water, she'd doubtless expect some parasitic malady. She shoved wet ropes of hair from her eyes, and then dragged her gaze up a slope to where Lucas stood rocking on his heels. The infuriating sound of her deep and quick breathing ran in tandem with the cows mooing on the dike and the hiccupping hilarity of Lucas. Like a cat, he had landed in the tall grasses on his feet, dry and unharmed.

Rachel shook her fist at him. "You are proof of evolution in reverse. They should have drowned you at birth and saved me a pile of trouble. Ever since you came into my life, you have turned it upside down," she spat. Her teeth began chattering, and she pulled a lily pad from the top of her head.

Lucas held his sides and dissolved into laughter again.

"This is what I get for listening to the high and mighty Colonel Rourke." She made no protest when he grabbed her arm and yanked her to shore. Her final indignity occurred when she bent to pick up her bag, slipped on the bank, and fell into the mud again. Lucas wiped his eyes, stood her up and sobered. Rachel started into a full-blown weeping. He threw his greatcoat around her and hugged her.

Cows crowded around, mooing and drinking from the water's edge. "You've had a little jolt is all."

What was worse—his placating her, freezing to death, or her inability to control the flow of tears? "Everything is going badly. One day, you think all's within your grasp, and the next it's swept away. Now that Johnson has seen me, he will have the train stopped at the next depot, sending every available man to search for us."

"You're upset because you've been thrown from a train," Lucas said.

Rachel stepped back. "What on earth would cause you to think I'd be upset about being thrown from a train? I rather enjoy being cold and muddy and standing knee-deep in a cow pond."

Rachel bombarded him with a whole litany of abuses, raining down all her miseries on Lucas' head. She spent the next thirty minutes telling him so, but not complaining that he had picked her up, and brought her to the front yard of a nearby farm. A farmer appeared at his door with a rifle cradled in his arms.

"Our carriage overturned and lays in the bottom of your cow pond," Lucas explained.

The farmer's wife took immediate pity on Rachel's pathetic condition, especially when Lucas added fire to the story by insisting she was in the family way. With his winning manner, Lucas relaxed their doubts and they were rewarded with their clothes dried, a warm meal to fill their belly and a ride into the next town.

Chapter 13

ucas had the farmer drop them off at a crossroad and hinted they were traveling west, opposite of their intended direction. He followed Rachel down a lone country road without interventions or questions from passersby.

He chewed on a piece of timothy grass as they headed to a safe house or church that Rachel knew about. "I take it your Reverend friend's politics differ from those of his Southern neighbors?"

"The Saint has called upon him countless times during this struggle. Father O'Connor's protection is guaranteed."

The scuff of gravel crunched beneath his feet on the sunbaked road where tar looked like poured licorice. "The Saint. Always the bloody Saint. You place him on a pedestal as if he were the holiest of holies. Why have I never seen him? I'm beginning to think he's a figment of your imagination," Lucas said sourly, and then glowered at her when he saw her smile.

Her eyes sparkled as though she played a game. He could have melted into those amber eyes. Instead, he remained guarded, knowing their enemy, Captain Johnson, would have wired the news that they lived, and then ordered patrols to hunt them down. Lucas' first priority was to get her safely North. In that beautiful, rare head of hers, lay all the facts vital to save the Union.

A breeze blew hot air across his damp forehead, whooshed across his sunburned neck, and then ruffled the hardy wildflowers across the forgotten fields. He took off his coat and slung it over his shoulder. "I believe we should revisit our intended direction and head north instead," said Lucas.

In her mud dried dress, Rachel drew up short. "No. Because of you, we'll have the entire Confederacy looking for us. Do I need to remind you that it was your idea to board the train? As a result of the mess you've gotten us in, you're going to follow my orders, Colonel Rourke."

Lucas narrowed his eyes, frustrated with her mulish expression. "I'll bow to your infinite madness this time but, mark my words, you better be right, or else you'll have to live with the consequences."

Full of sunlight and floating like gold dust, he took in the high steeple, pricking the azure blue of a cloudless sky. Whitewashed clapboard adorned the structure, aged and yellow as soap, but solid as rock. He grasped her elbow and marched her up the steps, and then glanced around while Rachel knocked on the sanctuary door.

"Father O'Connor?" said Rachel.

"Yes, my child. What is it?" The cleric adjusted his collar, glowing snowy white in the cool of the darkened interior.

"The Saint has sent me."

The old man's brown eyes widened as he swung wide the

door, allowing them entry. And none too soon in Lucas' estimation. Thirty plus Confederate riders stormed into the front yard.

"They are in pursuit of us," said Lucas.

The ancient priest glanced wildly about. "You could not have come at a worse time. I have ten slaves hiding beneath the rectory and no room to hide you. We are at risk."

From a sacristy table, Lucas jerked off a lace tablecloth and threw it over Rachel's head.

"What on earth—"

"How about a wedding, Father O'Connor?" Lucas ordered. "Perhaps a dicey ploy but maybe enough to fool some Confederates."

"I'll never—" Rachel squeaked as Lucas hauled her on the altar. With his prayer book in hand, the priest had to run to keep up, tripping on his cassock. Lucas shrugged on his coat. Loud banging battered the vestibule door. Soldiers flooded the church.

"What is the meaning of this?" Father O'Connor demanded. "You are interrupting the tender nuptials of this couple as well as invading the sacred structure of this church." With fire and damnation, he railed on and on, and then shaking his fist at them, he said, "My good friend, President Jefferson Davis will hear of this incursion!"

The determined Confederates blinked and stood there waiting for orders from a higher power. A close-lipped, unbending, Orthodox priest would not deter them.

"If I ran my church the way this government runs an army then I daresay Satan would turn my house of worship into an outpost of hell." Seeing no other option, the priest proceeded with the ceremony. Smiling kindly to Lucas and Rachel, he cleared his throat loudly and began.

Ever aware of the audience behind him, Lucas did his absolute best at acting out the part of a happy bridegroom. Up until now, Rachel had stood quietly next to him. To his amazement, she dug her nails into his arm and hissed, "I'm not going through with this."

"With a lynch mob behind us, you will cooperate," Lucas ordered beneath his breath. He gave her one ferocious glance to quell the fireball coming.

"I'm not going to marry the likes of you," she shouted.

"Oh, yes you are." Lucas could not believe his ears. Was this an act or was she crazy? There existed one way to take care of her. He swung her over his shoulder. Like a wild banshee, she kicked her legs and pounded his back.

"I refuse!"

Lucas smacked her backside. Trapped in her veil, Rachel raged like a lioness.

He turned toward the group of soldiers. "My child will have his father's name."

Some of the soldiers nodded, others spat their agreement in viscous streams of tobacco juice.

"You doin' the right thing, Boy," a soldier yelled.

For entertainment purposes, Lucas slapped her on the backside again, enraging the hornet's nest on his shoulder.

"Give her a good whipping now and, then keep her in order." The soldiers hooted.

Lucas turned to the priest again. Father O'Connor's thin countenance and scrawny neck gave him the look of a furious turkey cock, disapproval stamped in the sharp planes of his face. Rachel fought him so much, Lucas dropped her from his shoulder. He yanked her to his side and shoved a revolver against her ribs. He said, "There will be a wedding today or a funeral tomorrow."

There was a wedding.

Lucas nodded to Father O'Connor and the priest's solemn words filled the room. Even the Confederate soldiers were in awe. Lucas' regard moved to Rachel who stood very small and quiet. She was lovely and the forlorn sight of her tugged at his insides. He had an almost irresistible urge to reach across the narrow space between them and kiss her until her anger vanished. He stuck his gun back in his belt then slipped his West Point ring over her trembling finger. The priest, moved to tears, closed his book and pronounced them man and wife.

"Now you may kiss the bride."

Slowly, Lucas lifted the lopsided veil, ever aware of their audience. He looked at Rachel and kissed her long and lingeringly. Loud hoots erupted from the back of the church in joyous revelry. There was not one dry eye. A colonel rode up outside. When apprised of the wedding, he offered his congratulations and heartfelt apologies, and then ordered his men to leave at once.

When the soldiers departed, Father O'Connor spoke. "I assure you the proper registry of your correct names will be documented and hidden here in this church for safekeeping."

Lucas stood stricken. "You mean we are really married?"

"Marriage is a blessed sacrament bound by God," confirmed the priest.

"I don't hold you to this obligation." Rachel stamped her foot and glared at Lucas.

Father O'Connor interrupted. "For safety's sake, you need to leave as soon as possible. I have a friend who owns a slave cabin hidden in the woods, four miles from here. My servant, Joseph, will take you there and provide for your comfort. Of course, it will be temporary. I will send you a message as soon as possible. You two can work this out on your own and out of prying eyes."

The priest steepled his fingers, pointing them heavenward. "One more word of counsel. Happiness is often found somewhere you don't expect. As the events have developed today, I have become certain that what has been placed in motion is truly blessed and shall endure a long and permanent witness to the will of God. I will keep you both in my prayers."

Lucas blew out a breath. Looking at the brewing hornet's nest in Rachel, he'd need more than prayers.

Chapter 14

To escape to the backwoods cabin had been a simple matter. Father O'Connor's man had been thorough, leaving a veritable feast, and surprising Rachel for times were hard. Inside the basket, Rachel had plucked out a smoked ham, oat bread, apple pie, cheese, and a jar of peaches. Apparently, invoking the Saint's name had come with prominence.

"I think I could eat solidly for a week," she said, licking apple pie from her fingers, and keeping the conversation light, knowing they had important issues to discuss.

The single-room cabin was cozy and surrounded by abandoned beehives. A taint of sweet honey tinged the air and the scratch of squirrels crawled through dead leaves beneath. To her delight, a copper tub lay upright against the corner, and with Lucas' help, she dragged it down. Water steamed from an iron kettle over the crackle of wood fire, and her limbs tingled with the prospect of soaking in a hot bath. Her arms went slack.

The wedding. Oh, how she had gone along with the ruse to fool the Rebs. To toy with madness was one thing; when the madness toyed back, and the nuptials proved to be authentic, she had nearly lost her mind.

She sank on a rickety bench, clasped her hands together and stared at the large ring Lucas had placed on her finger. Heavy and awkward, she twirled the band admiring the artfully carved lustrous gold with ruby center, reflecting warm and brilliant in the firelight. She clasped her palm to her chest. *They were truly married.*

Her vision blurred. The wedding was nowhere near what a girl dreamed about; flung over Lucas' shoulder was not a conventional courtship, more like the way his primeval ancestor might have done, dragging his bride into a jungle. Neither listening to the ribald conversation of Rebel soldiers, not what a lady would hear, and with certainty would make her mother in heaven swoon.

With somber curiosity, her gaze followed to where his head was bent, studying the fire as if he, too, were weighing their vows. No doubt, he was scrambling to reverse events. Her bruised heart jolted as a pang pierced it through.

There would be nothing she'd like better than to be married to Lucas—if he loved her, and how easy for her to love him back. How she wanted him to reassure her. How many times had she fantasized about kissing him, smelling his hair, the touch of his breath on her face…his hands on her? She wiped her damp palms on her skirts. A longing grew like she'd never felt before. She shook her head.

Do not leave yourself open for that kind of hurt, Rachel.

The marriage existed as a farce, the Saint's greatest role to fool a Confederate audience. The fiasco wasn't Lucas' fault. He'd strove to keep them from getting their necks stretched.

The night, like the cabin closed in. The wind blew, scraping branches against worn outside shingles, and whistling drafts through the cracks in the wall. Rachel pushed off, anxious to escape Lucas' withdrawal, and the suffocating silence between them. There was a slight give of a rotten floorboard beneath her step, causing a mouse to shoot out and exit a hole in the corner.

She strung a rope across the middle of the room and draped a threadbare sheet across the line, satisfied her privacy was guaranteed. Lucas stirred, emptied the kettles of hot water into the tub and taking a bite of apple, chewed, and then wiped the juices on his pants before returning to his wobbly stool.

She stood on tiptoes and glanced over the line. "No peeking," she insisted in an unsteady voice and hooked a dented lantern on a rusty hook.

He arched his brow in that all-knowing attitude that set her teeth on edge. "I'm a gentleman."

The way he said it made Rachel's bared toes curl against the cold wood planks. She glanced over the line again, satisfied he busied himself, whittling. The draw of a steaming bath overcame her misgivings about disrobing in the same room. She shrugged. Hadn't she undressed in the hearse when she rescued him? That was different.

Rachel reached behind her and unbuttoned her dress, sliding the fabric from her shoulders where it settled on the floor in a soft swish.

"Need I remind you, this was your decision? You're the one who insisted on Father O'Connor's safe house. You'll have to live with the consequences."

She ripped at the laces of her corset, Lucas' words as scouring as the scrape of his knife against the wood. "You can't outwit fate by standing on the sidelines placing little side bets about the outcome. Either you jump in, take the risks, or don't play at all," she told him.

Lucas grunted.

If Rachel had learned anything from her undercover work, it was that those who seized the offensive typically held the high ground. "May I point out, my decision was made on the heels of your fool judgement of insisting on the train." Rachel dropped her corset, took a breath, and paused before peeling off her chemise and exposing her breasts to the chilly air.

"Well..." If a voice could convey a shrug, Lucas' did so. "After the events of the last few days, you know, and I know, that we've already taken the first steps down a joint path."

Rachel stood behind the sheet, naked and shivering, her arms wrapped around herself as she took in Lucas' words. She barely noticed her nakedness, as it was her insides that seemed so entirely exposed and vulnerable.

Woodchips hit the floor. "In terms of making decisions, we've already made ours—you yours, me mine."

She kicked her mud-caked dress that the farmer's wife had attempted to clean across the floor, stepped into the tub, and lowering herself, sighed as the water rose to her shoulders.

"Still, between individuals like us, there is a need for a proper yes or no, a simple, clear answer to a simple, clear question," he said.

She picked up a bar of soap that smelled like honey and rosemary and began to vigorously scrub. "To my estimation, our marriage is not legitimate," Rachel said, allowing the hot water and honeyed soap to soothe the chill and the aches from her stiff muscles.

Lucas' rude snort echoed off the splintery walls, amplifying his contempt.

"You don't want the marriage any more than I do, Lucas." She regretted the words the moment she spoke. But she had to. She didn't want Lucas commanded by his sense of honor to be obligated to a marriage he did not want. "We'll get an annulment."

In answer, she heard Lucas hurl a block of wood on the fire and imagined red cinders flashing up the chimney. She skimmed her hand across the still water, pricking her fingertips and an unexpected wave of sorrow gripped her.

"You find the idea, distasteful?" he asked.

She lifted a leg above the water to rub the bar of soap all the way down to her toes. The shock and revulsion on Lucas' face when Father O'Connor announced they were wed lay proof enough. A muscle cramped in her calf and while she kneaded the pain, the thief of remorse grabbed hold of her, triggering her to worry about the future. "I find the idea as unrealistic as you do. Oh, the years of regret cast upon us, Lucas. What an appalling waste of energy. You can't build on it and the only good left is for wallowing in." Couldn't he see that to remain in the state of matrimony would bring them unhappiness?

She lifted her arms to pull the pins from her hopelessly disheveled bun and let the curls fall in the bath. His pregnant pause conveyed a shifting reluctance that piqued her curiosity.

"The deed is done, so I'll live by the vows," he growled.

Smarting from his callous remark, and feeling the rejection coming off him in waves, she dunked her head beneath the water, drenching her scalp, and furiously working the suds through her thick waves. To be married to a man who did not want her? Absolutely not.

She rose, sputtering, "Magnanimous of you. Your martyrdom shored up by the blood sacrifice of marriage."

The creak of his rickety bench told her that Lucas had risen and was coming closer. She tensed, but as soon as she heard him pick up another log and cast it in the fire, she relaxed. "I refuse to honor the vows."

"The priest may be right." Lucas whipped the curtain back.

Gasping, Rachel drew her knees under her chin and moored them with her arms and sank deep into the bath, thankful the water was now cloudy with soap. "Leave!" she swore in an unsteady voice.

He moved closer, the barest hint of a booted heel scraping against the floor. So close in fact, she saw his eyes turn cobalt, the rings of his irises darken. Despite the opaque water, could he see the flesh that quivered just below the surface? The idea surged bolts of heat and mortification through her.

"Get out!" Rachel lowered her head, fearful she'd lose her nerve, confronting him.

"Make me."

She sank lower into the water, her rapid breaths generating undulations on the surface.

Powerless, cornered, and naked.

He stepped closer, running long fingers along the rim of the tub. From lengthy days on the road, a dark stubble shadowed his face, giving him a rakish look. Light from the lantern above haloed him, casting him in an aura of gold. Even his thick ebony hair seemed bronzed as he leaned down to grip each side of the tub. His butternut breeches clung to powerful thighs, the corded muscles rippling beneath, in what could be considered indecent. Primitive.

"It occurred to me that there might be something we both didn't expect, *Mrs. Rourke.*"

Damn, he used her married name, testing it for the first time, and she was surprised, he did.

"For one thing, you have courage. In my whole life, I do not believe I have engaged in as many arguments as I have with you these past few weeks."

Even in the steaming water, chilblains raced over her skin. She stiffened her spine and lifted her chin. Careful. Plan tactics. *Strategy before tactics is the slowest route to triumph.* She cleared her throat. "A few heated disagreements are healthy, Colonel Rourke," she said, deliberately using his formal title to keep him at arm's length.

He walked around the tub. "Disagreements? Is that what you call them? Well, I expect, we are destined to have any number of them. A scary thought, isn't it?"

"Colonel Rourke, I doubt such probability will be grounds for either of us to shiver and shake with fright. Nor do I doubt, beyond our professional arrangement, will we be together."

He plunked his hands on both sides of the tub, his mouth lifting faintly at the corner. "Is there anything at all that would cause you to shiver and shake, *Mrs. Rourke?*"

His posture, awareness, and confidence belied undertones of a man who always achieved what he wanted. This was the other side of Lucas. The dangerous side. The side she'd seen when he attacked Captain Johnson. Her heart stopped in her throat. Oh, he was trouble. She clenched and unclenched her hands at the turn of events that put her at his mercy.

"Any number of things," she said.

"Indeed." His husky voice flowed over her like velvet. "What if we continue to work together, professionally, of course— perhaps we may do more than engage in heated disagreements? Might that be one of the things that would be agreeable, *Mrs. Rourke?*"

She met his gaze straight on, saw the rising heat within his eyes and nearly melted. "We are both determined individuals," she whispered, out of breath. "Yet, I'm confident we are rather skilled in maintaining our completely professional connection."

"We may both be proficient at sustaining a degree of professionalism," he said with incredible warmth, "but what if we desire not to do so? What takes place then, Mrs. Rourke?"

Rachel's mouth went dry. Belly-low, a warming came over her, like a moth fluttering around a flame. She could not bring herself to look away nor answer him.

"By all means, continue with your bathing. The soap tends to get slick when wet, doesn't it?"

Her mouth dropped from the innuendo and he laughed while his gaze caressed the ripple of the water with suggestive fascination. Rachel's temperature veered violently from chilled to overheated, and she felt a sheen of dampness blossom above her lip.

Damn him. How she'd like to wipe that smirk off his face. She pinned him with a glare, the same she used to sight a rifle.

"I envy you, Mrs. Rourke, for every time I look at you, or

think about you, my thoughts cause me to abandon all principle and honor."

He did not touch her, but every nerve in her body screamed as if he did. She closed her eyes, the intoxicating scent of him snaking around her leaving her hazy and warm like the water lapping over her. She dampened her lips with the tip of her tongue before she betrayed her good sense.

"Indeed," she said, proud that she kept any apprehension or weakness out of her voice and opened her eyes. With trembling fingers, she touched his jaw. "You're not even shaking."

"There is more to me than you realize." He slid his hands farther along the side of the tub, imprisoned her between his arms and lowered his head, hovering just above hers, his breath warm from the sweet apple he'd eaten.

"You must leave," she said with no conviction whatsoever.

"Are you thinking of the Saint?" His face etched in savagery, he straightened, kicked the stool to the foot of the tub, righted it and sat down. "In the game of espionage, there is a quid pro quo. I will leave when you finish bathing." He spread his long legs out in front of him and tilted back in his chair. "Take the soap and massage the bar over your breasts, giving distinct attention to first one and then the other," he commanded.

She swallowed. Bracing herself, she reached to the bottom, and ferreted the soap. In rebellion, she smoothed it over her neck and jaw, washing, as long as she was careful to keep the swell of her breasts below the murky water. "Is this good enough?" she demanded, her voice betraying her, and falling whiskey low like a lover's caress. A sensual spell wrapped tightly around her, leaving her incapable to resist doing what he demanded and at the same time intrigued with the wickedness of where it would go.

He raised a disapproving brow, and then his eyes widened with the path of the soap, slicking down her neck. "Don't play games with me, Rachel."

"Games?"

He dropped the stool to all fours, took the soap from her. He nudged her arms away, placing one of her hands on the side of the tub. "Do not move." He manipulated the bar over her breasts, offering marked concentration to first one then the other.

"Watch what I'm doing," he demanded. He required her to see what he was doing, swore that she see what he was achieving with her body. He enclosed and pulled the nipple with the soap. His mouth curved indulgently, and a lock of dark ebony hair fell recklessly down his forehead. Lifted and lathered and kneaded. The consequence—something of a dream, fogging the lines between what actually existed and desire.

A sizzle of energy scorched through the water, the air, and she felt she would perish from suffocation. She raised a hand to stop him.

A ragged murmur convulsed in his throat. "No." He placed her hand on the rim.

Her breasts grew heavy, weighted with need and so much more. Oh, how he used this sinful compulsion to gratify his depraved craving.

Her traitorous nipples glistened from the soap, hardening into tight pink points. She gasped, sensation rippling through her, coursing through her limbs, before settling between clenched thighs. Her hips rose. To have him move the soap over her most intimate flesh?

Her mouth dropped open. She caught a moan before it escaped, lowered her hips.

Their gazes collided, the fires in his eyes darkened as his pupils dilated.

The devil saw, recognized the direction of her thoughts. Knew she wanted him to touch her and not stop and that knowledge made her hands ball into fists.

He leaned closer and her heart thudded in her chest. Did he plan to kiss her? His lips twisted, and a moan of protest stuck in her throat, muted by a hard, possessive kiss that seemed to go on forever and became increasingly persistent the longer she resisted, coaxing, persuading, enticing her lips to open. He pushed her on the back of the tub, and his tongue roused, thrust through her like a brand, searing her, having her. Breathing was impossible.

Her hands groped to his chest, firm healthy male flesh tingled beneath her fingertips. To touch him everywhere, to explore every part of him. She wet the cotton of his shirt, brushing her fingers over muscle.

He groaned, making her realize how very feminine she was. A wild sensuality stirred to life and a wealth of hidden feelings leaped from her, blossoming, exploding.

He drew away. Flames licked at the ice in his eyes and an answering heat bloomed deep inside her, deep…to her womb. The gap gave way to chill. She managed to gulp in sweet air, her bosom still heaving.

To her frustration, he dropped the soap, wiped his hands on

his pants, watching her. He took a ragged breath and adjusted his clothing.

"We are two made one by what is sacred. As I took my vows, Rachel, I made a promise that I would always care for you. It is not a careless pledge I took. But I warn you, from here on, there will be no other in your life." Lucas poised above her, demanded she look at him. "The Saint will be no more."

A pit in her stomach opened up. For a long brooding moment, almost a lifetime in the space between them.

"I believe it is safe to say I cannot compete with the Saint," he said bitterly. "Why you dwell on that ridiculous excuse for a man, I'll never understand."

"It's not what you think." How she agonized to tell him everything. To protect him. To protect those working for her. Her heart sank. No…she could not take the risk nor could she contemplate what might have been. The war derived heavy expense, forfeiting any possible happiness.

Nerves rattled up her spine as another thought slammed into her. How might he react if he were to find out she was the Saint? In no way did she desire to embrace that threat. To Lucas, the greatest sin was betrayal. With certainty, he'd draw and quarter her for that betrayal.

He tore the quilt off the bed and threw it at her. "There are no excuses, Rachel. Although your body responds to my touch, it is safe to say your affections lay with the Saint."

"Turn around," she demanded, and when he pivoted, she rose, water spilling onto the floor. She yanked the quilt around her. She allowed him to believe she lay with the Saint, but it didn't take the sting out of being called a fallen woman. He believed the depravity because she led him to believe the worst.

Lucas turned down the lantern, extinguishing them in darkness. "I'll sleep on the floor. You take the bed. When we get to Washington, we'll figure the mess out." He grabbed the other quilt and pillow and fell back on the hard floor.

Mess? Unmistakable regret was his bulwark. Rachel cringed.

She crawled beneath the blankets on the bed, Lucas' back to her. She focused on the shadows dancing on the ceiling from the flickering flames of the fire. A log crashed, sputtering and sparking. In the waning light, Lucas' hair shone with a soft sheen of black satin and she could stretch her fingers out to feel the silkiness. Hot and humiliating tears flowed down her cheeks and onto the pillow.

They were unwillingly joined together by marriage. And like a rock in a stream, the North and South swirled around them, trapping them in a place neither wanted to be. Through a blur of tears, Rachel watched the last remnants of the yellow glow of firelight sputter once; a log slowly fell over into the last mound of embers, glowing briefly, and died, leaving the room with the smell of smoke and bitter chestnuts. What occurred between them washed over her and forever irreparable, left her with feelings of loneliness and isolation more intense than anything she'd ever experienced.

They slept for a time, each cocooned under their own quilt and apart from each other's warmth. She rolled her head to gaze at Lucas and swallowed a lump. For in her heart she had found something. Something she couldn't allow to happen...something forbidden and dangerous...something she must never allow to exist.

In the wee hours of the morning, Father O'Connor arrived with another basket of food and bad news. "You must leave while it is still dark. You have acquired the interest of high-level people in Richmond greatly interested in your return from the dead. Many soldiers scour the countryside looking for a man and woman…spies. My advice is to head south to General Grant's lines. May God be with you."

Chapter 15

He stuffed the food in a travel bag. Ice raged through his veins. The thought of another man touching her? He'd dismember any man, Saint or otherwise. For weeks, he fought a maddening possessiveness and jealousy. He'd never admit it to her. No. He'd not put that weapon in her hands.

For many hours of the night, he remained rock hard, her soft body for the taking inches away. But he didn't want her like that.

Did he love her? He wanted a marriage like his parents where love and sacrifice and total devotion to the other lay paramount. He had strong feelings for Rachel, he most certainly did. Without question, he remained responsible for her, more so now that he had married her. The mystery of her affection for the Saint left little doubt in his mind where her loyalties were.

Rachel yanked the curtain back, closing him out, pretending he didn't exist. He preferred the argumentative Rachel who taunted him, not the cold atmosphere pervading the cabin. He remembered too well her hair fanned out like dark shimmering waves across the pillows, the creaminess of her skin, and her vulnerability. The softness of her full breasts in his hands, how he fanned the flames, and how his tongue urged to take the pinkened tip into his mouth and tease it. She had risen like Botticelli's *Venus*, a goddess rising, water sluicing down her lush curves. The heavy chestnut hair from her head lay in wet ropes, covering her feminine secrets, allowing a hint of dark curls between her—

A dishonorable man would have swept her slick body into his arms and carried her to the bed, sinking into her softness before the moisture on her skin had time to dry. Fully aroused, desire pulsed, his cock hard.

He chaffed like a penned bull, gazed out the window at the clouds gathering overhead until they blurred into one. Good cover for their travel, veiling them in darkness.

Just then, Rachel opened the curtain again. Seeing her, his lungs emptied. "Rachel?"

Gone was the beautiful woman and in her place stood a slave boy. She had bound her breasts beneath an over-fitted jacket, topped her crown with a wig of negro wool and cap and hid the curves of her hips with baggy trousers. She had finished her costume by layering silver nitrate over her face, hand, and arms.

"What do you think, Colonel Rourke?" She twirled for him. "They'll be looking for a man and woman—not a slave and his master."

No evidence remained that marked her femaleness and with that, his constant state of arousal dropped south. He gritted his teeth. The minx stood a genius in disguise. Her ridiculous get-up and chameleon-like change would fool him if he was not aware, and his temper abated with her practicality.

For two nights and two days they made their way unchallenged. From time to time, Rachel inquired of their whereabouts from the local slave population and proved a good source of information especially when she invoked the name of the dratted Saint. Skirting the eastern border of Petersburg, gunfire dueled over distant hills. Lucas had no way of knowing if the shots came from Rebel or Northern pickets. Grant had his noose on tight. It would be heaven sent to fall in with northern pickets. Luckier yet, if they didn't get shot.

"Is there a risk?" Rachel asked, eyeing an open field.

"Of course, there's a risk. There's a war going on." He held no illusions and pushed her within the woodland's boundary.

Her proficiency irked him. She had mastered an art that meant a great deal to her as it did other spies—that of swift, silent movement. Validating her Indian training was her fortitude, survival skills, and unparalleled sense of direction. When there existed a hint of being followed, she had him trace her path on stones to leave no trail. At any whiff of unusual movement, they hid in underbrush to avoid all men. They would emerge at a creek for a drink, and then melt into the forests.

Her talent for obtaining food, he grudgingly allowed, was inspired. Hickory nuts crushed by stones remained time consuming for the little meat they offered. Here and there, she found thickets of chokecherries, but the fruits were so thin around the pits that it offered little except the tart sweetness to appease his hunger. She dug cattail roots and presented them to him as a substitute for bread.

"I'd rather drink vinegar," Lucas mumbled. His stomach had contracted into a hard, little fist.

"At least it will give the illusion of eating something worthwhile," she said, and then slapped his hand when he reached for a cluster of grapes. "Pokeweed. Coma, then death."

They passed through a ragged corn patch; its haunted remains scored by encroaching armies. He glanced up. The heavens roiled heavy with tumbling vapors to the west, muting tracts of blue sky. From its ragged edge, a purple-hued veil of rain approached with the wind.

"It seems like it has rained a lot this season."

"Only twice a year—October to May, and June to September."

Lucas laughed, thankful for her humor. "Well, at least it's easy to predict the weather."

Beyond a stand of birches, the woodlands thickened. They came upon a yellow-haired, Pennsylvania Bucktail. He lay against verdant ferns with a smile on his face. The dead soldier's eyes were open, his hair ruffled in the wind, and his hands curled up to the heavens. A Monarch butterfly landed on his forehead then flitted away.

Rachel knelt and closed his eyes, began to shake and broke out into sobs. Lucas yanked her away to quell the agony emanating from within her soul. Her tears wetted his shirt. No words were enough to protect her from the reality of war and death.

"He died alone," she sniffed.

"Sad fact of war," Lucas said. "There has been no darker or bloodier ground than the gentle fields of Virginia where murder has bred murder and justice distributed on the barrelhead."

"What is said to the boy's mother? What answers are given to his wife or sweetheart?"

Lucas had no answers. He took the soldier's name from his identification papers, covered him the best he could and added some prayers.

A steady and miserable rain began to pour. After several hours of travel, the rain stopped, and skies cleared, giving way to a bright autumn moon. The rains had turned the road into a sea of mud. Lucas righted Rachel whenever she slipped in the soft ooze. He had pilfered a few overcoats from a slumbering farmhouse, and now pulled her collar up and buttoned her coat. A chestnut curl escaped, and he tucked it beneath her wig.

He had a frustrating desire to kiss her soft lips. But the kiss never came. Time and practicality ruled. To begin something he'd not or would not stop might prove dangerous for both of them.

"What do you think of me?" she asked, and Lucas wondered what she wanted.

"I think you have a talent for survival. I think you are more intelligent and more sophisticated than any woman I've ever encountered. What I find out of the question is your career path as a woman." He cleaned away the mud from her nose and cheek and forehead. Despite her disguise, Lucas remembered the raw beauty that lay hidden beneath.

"Well—" she drawled. "I cannot see that my being a woman has anything to do with the course I have chosen."

Lucas twisted coils of vine around her broken bag, heard the throaty inflection in her voice and grew wary. "Right."

"After all," she looked at him, appearing innocent save for

the twinkle in her amber eyes, "I could have been a man." She met his disgusted look with a peal of laughter, so light and lovely to the ear that he found himself smiling in response.

Lucas tugged twigs from her hair, grinning from her mercurial change in mood. He had worried about the effect of the dead soldier. Her lips turned up with a hint of mischievousness, and he knew she was warming up to something.

"There was girl in Richmond who was spiteful every time I came into contact with her. She claimed I was an ugly hag who would dry up into a wizened, bitter old maid, for no sane man would take me for his wife. I held my temper and ignored her."

Lucas narrowed his eyes in the encroaching darkness, and he said, "You ignored her? I imagine it was an impossible feat for you."

"Oh, yes."

"I have the distinct feeling you'd have the last word."

"Not at all." Rachel gave a dainty shrug of her slim shoulders. "There were no words. You see my foot accidentally slipped in front of hers, causing her to trip and fall face first in the mud."

"Of course," Lucas said, picturing the injured girl's rage. "And I'm sure you offered your sincere apologies." He could feel her smile through the darkness.

"My most sincere apologies. I also offered her use of my parasol."

"How benevolent of you." Lucas grinned. "I'm sure that made up for everything."

Rachel laughed. "Not exactly."

"Care to enlighten me?" he said, enjoying her camaraderie despite his growling stomach.

"Can you envision her face when she opened her parasol and a mouse fell out, scrambling over her hair and into her chemise?"

"Poor girl is probably still recovering."

Rachel laughed so hard she had to wipe her eyes.

"Am I to assume the poor girl suffered more?"

"From her screams, she frightened a skunk sleeping in a basket in the back of her carriage."

"Am I to assume, the skunk just happened to be resting in that unique location?"

Rachel dropped her chin to her chest, penitent as a nun. "It is unfortunate."

Lucas broke out into fresh peals of laughter. Their eyes locked as their breathing came in unison. She raised her hand and touched his face ever so lightly. His skin burned where she caressed him, and the sweet intoxicating musk of her body nearly overwhelmed him. Crushing her to him, his lips pressed against hers, and then gently covered her mouth. The soft curves of her body molded to him, sending shivers pounding through him. Whether Lucas wanted to admit it or not, he was falling in love with this wonderful, infuriatingly independent woman.

The problem was—it was all wrong. She wanted an annulment.

His obsession with her pounded through his heart, chest, and head. His body was afire. Reason hammered him. He had to stop this now. Dragging air into his constricted lungs, he pushed Rachel away.

"I swore an oath to protect you. You haven't had the normal

upbringing or opportunity to see the outside world. A world governed without war, where a young girl goes to parties and teas and balls. That sham of a wedding doesn't qualify."

She went rigid. He ignored the urge to haul her back into his arms.

"Stop it, Lucas. I don't hold you accountable for anything."

Lucas raked his fingers through his hair and vowed he'd do his damnedest to get her away from the Saint's influence. "To walk the streets of Washington will be none too soon. I'll set you up with a friend of mine. She'll introduce you to Washington society in proper form due a lady. You'll be invited to balls, teas and whatever extravagant party the Capitol offers. You'll be able to meet someone who you can marry once our marriage is annulled. It's the only honorable thing I can do for you. I promise—"

"No promises, Lucas. There were never any strings attached. I knew what I was getting myself into from the beginning and hold no expectation of you. Forgotten. Done. I don't need you, nor have I ever needed you. I have the Saint."

She dismissed him with a lift of her dainty shoulder, and Lucas stared down at her, cold savage contempt running through his veins. His voice dangerously low and hissing with fury, he spat out, "The Saint! Always the Saint. I can't wait until I get my hands on him."

"What does the Saint matter to you except to win the war for the Union, and to gain your promotion and prestige? He has done you no harm. Beware of that dragon of jealousy before it eats you alive," she taunted him.

Her voice broke and tears glimmered in her beautiful eyes. "To cast me aside when we reach Washington? At least the Saint has shown me nothing but loyalty."

He stretched his fingers, struggling to maintain his mask of nonchalance. Snapping the man's neck would come with great pleasure. Lucas swung her around and prodded her forward.

Chapter 16

"We cannot afford to cross the river here," Rachel said.

"We can't afford not to," Lucas stated, his eyes flinty as steel.

Rachel told herself she would not cry, wouldn't let Lucas know how much he'd hurt her. He was weighed down with enough guilt and principle to fill the world.

They had plodded twenty miles through a rain-soaked night, along broken roads and deer trails until they reached a river. She wanted to follow the river farther. He wanted to cross as soon as possible. Lucas slid down the muddy bank, turned and lifted his hand. A superior smile covered his face when he angled his head to a banked canoe.

To reach Union lines and be free of the high-minded Colonel Rourke wouldn't be soon enough. "I can take care of myself," she said, refusing his assistance. She jumped. A dangling root caught her heel. She pitched forward, crashed into Lucas and slammed them into the mud. Her breath whooshed out of her in puffs. Leaf mold peeped up from the ground and prickled her nose. She scrambled off Lucas and rocked on her knees.

He shot up and wiped the unwelcome mud off his clothes. "That stunt might have broken both our necks."

She pinned him with a glare. "I wonder if there is an angel that exists that I can pray to for hopeless causes."

"I hope there is one for stupidity."

She did not dignify the remark, and then eyed the swollen river, flooding well over its banks. The river yawned, swirling in foam, the currents running fast. The risk lay heavy, the crossing screamed for an eternity. She stood frozen.

"We can't cross here. It's impossible...insane." Her knees trembled. There was no way she'd plunge into the maelstrom. She gulped, looked up, anywhere she'd not have to see the murky waters. Even though it was daytime, the moon appeared like a piece of tissue paper in the sky. "See how the hawk flies in front of the moon. The Indians vowed such a sign was a premonition of bad things."

"We'll take the chance. We have no other option and there will be no further argument." He flipped the canoe over and tipped the bow into the water. He flung her bag into the canoe and strode to her. She shook her head back and forth, icy fear forming a cold knot in her stomach.

"What are you afraid of?"

Rachel pointed to the angry river. "Drowning."

He stared at her for a moment until awareness dawned on him. "I can't chase away the ghosts of the past, but I can tell you, we will make it to the other side...it's only a short way."

Rachel gaped at the river, seemingly stretching on for miles when the rational side of her brain said it was only a third.

"I'll be there for you. I promise." He picked her up,

murmuring something about bravery and courage while coaxing her into the canoe. "You believe that admitting to be anything female would scar your soul. It's all right to be weak once in a while.

Rachel closed her eyes. His warm breath caressed her cheek, comforted while he gently lowered her into the bow.

Lucas added his weight and shoved off from the shore. The canoe wobbled wildly beneath her. White-knuckled, she gripped the gunnels. Her heart pounded. The river roared in her ears. With a broken paddle, Lucas fought control of the craft in the dark swirling waters. They glanced off a rock and spun around.

"Go back," she shouted, her voice shrill to her ears. To go back was impossible.

She looked behind. Lucas struggled to get the canoe turned around, fighting with the roiling currents that tossed them about.

"There's a log…" Too late. They slammed into the swirling miasma, trapped. Water sluiced over the canoe, swamping them. Lucas stood, and the canoe rocked violently. He wedged his paddle beneath a log, freeing them, the canoe washing down the river, Rachel huddling in the bow.

"I lost the paddle."

Her life spun out of control, bobbing like errant thistledown on rampaging waters. The canoe skidded off another rock, splashing water on her head. She gasped for air. In wide-eyed horror, disaster loomed in front, an enormous tree fall, damming part of the river.

"Lucas!" Sharp wooden thickets spiked before her eyes. The canoe smashed into the dam and flipped. Water thundered over them with spine-chilling, wicked force. Rachel's head cracked against something hard. Black water choked her, sucking her into a whirlpool. Lights exploded in her brain. She kicked off the bottom, raised her head to get air. The surge rammed her under the buckled canoe. Swallowed into a blackened hole, icy water pinned her in a watery grave. *The river is the master—to eat greedily of her.*

"Rachel!" From far away, Lucas called her name. Her strength ebbed. Her arms fell numb. Her head spun, and her eyelids closed.

Rough hands grabbed her hair, pulled her down. Tiny lights popped in her brain. Strong arms yanked her upward, and then arrived the surreal sensation of floating and being dragged onto solid ground.

Rachel! Rachel!

The name did not register. A hard slap struck her back. Thrown forward, she vomited, coughing and spewing her insides. Rolled onto her back, she shivered and opened her eyes. The world swam. Overhead, long spidery willow branches stretched down.

Lucas. With trembling fingers, she touched his cheek.

"You didn't let me drown. You kept your promise."

Lucas curled up next to her, offering what little body heat his body could give. The sun came out for a few minutes, and Rachel rested, glad to have the warmth. They lay there letting the sun dry away some of the water that soaked their clothes.

"You've lost your bag, but we are safe and sound." He rubbed her hands and feet until the blood warmed her numbed flesh.

"If we might start a fire," she murmured.

He pulled her to her feet. Her knees buckled, and she sagged against him.

"We have to get you north, and you very well know the reason."

So, he was back to that again. Tired, cold and hungry, she detested him for reminding her of her duty.

An inexhaustible demon, he pushed her on and on. He retrieved her hat and wig from the river's edge, wringing them out and tucking her damp hair beneath.

Beneath her lashes, she studied him. What she found surprising remained his contradictory nature. Did his gentle touch spell out that he really cared?

"I feel like a trout, netted and bashed over the head," she said, her head pounding.

"You scared me, Rachel. I'm glad you're alive." He gave her shoulders a squeeze. "Let's get moving. Someone may have heard our shouts."

The screeching of blue jays with a flash of blue fluttered overhead.

"Someone did hear your shouts," said a menacing voice from behind.

Rachel swung around. Home Guard militia surrounded them. How much had the lawless guerillas seen or heard. Her mind scrambled to think of explanations.

They were a motley bunch and looked more than capable of killing them if it took their whim. The leader pushed his horse through the brush, then jerked back on the reins. The horse rolled its eyes white and whinnied fearfully. Rachel reached into her coat pocket for the passes. Water caused the ink to run, making the papers unreadable. She shoved the soggy mass into

Lucas' hands who, in turn, thrust them into the leader's.

Through close-set eyes, he glared at them. Rachel guessed he couldn't read. Being a slave, she dared not speak.

The leader slapped the butt end of his rifle engraved with "Old Betsy" in the wood. "How do I know you ain't Yankees?"

Lucas picked up his cue, emitting his perfect drawl. "We have passes."

"How do I know you ain't spies?"

Lucas stepped forward and clasped the saddle horn of the leader, a marvelous, casual gesture, suggesting he had nothing to fear from them.

"What's your name?" the leader snapped.

"Captain Davis." Lucas spun his yarn, his adopted name rolling off his tongue like quicksilver. His wily deception mollified their captor.

A man mounted on a black Morgan spat a stream of tobacco near Rachel's feet. "I'm darned if that feller ain't turning white," said a man, pointing to Rachel. She looked down, the silver nitrate leaked from her hands, making zebra stripes.

All eyes were on her. "I've expected to come white at some time. My mother's a white woman," Rachel explained.

"Take 'em back to camp for the sergeant to decide," the leader ordered.

Lucas hissed in her ear. "You've got us in a fine mess now."

Rachel knew the minute they entered the Home Guard's camp that the sergeant was in a bad mood. "Hang 'em," he said.

"Now wait a minute here," commanded Lucas.

He never ceased to amaze her, yet his steadfast assurance was to undergo the supreme test of his life.

The sergeant scratched at his lice. "You're either a deserter or those two Yankee spies from Richmond everyone's looking for."

"Prove it," drawled Lucas.

One of the enraged patrol riders threw nooses about their necks, begging to let them swing so as not to delay his dinner.

Rachel eyed the wavering guns and shifting mob.

"Had I my revolvers this would be a different story." Lucas cited the Articles of War, how they lost their passes in the river, and everything else that came to mind. As the minutes passed, tempers cooled. The nooses were removed.

"Your execution is postponed until the captain comes back in the morning," the sergeant said begrudgingly before he scuttled off for his dinner.

Inside a cabin, they were thrust in a makeshift cell. A small consolation was a warm fire. A bar slammed down into place, securing their prison for the night. A lone stool sat in the outer room.

Rachel tore off a scrap of her trousers, made use of the water bucket and washed her face. She yanked off her wig and combed her fingers through her hair. If she was going to hang, at least it would be with her looking in some semblance of order.

"Now what is there to worry about?" said Lucas as if the expectation of hanging was purely alarmist. He opened the gold lid on his watch. "Damn. Our dunk in the river destroyed the piece. It used to keep really good time." He stuffed it back into his pocket.

She expected a more pensive Lucas, not an amiable soul who breathed lazy charm and congeniality. In the spirit of relaxed friendship that had sprung up between them over the past weeks and resigned to her fate, Rachel slid down to the floor, settled beside him, and made a show of examining her fingernails.

"Are you bored?"

"What could possibly make you think I'm bored? I practically drowned. I have twenty Confederate renegades who want to hang me. There's no chance of escape. I'm with the most wanted man in the Confederacy outside of Abraham Lincoln. Why I'm having the time of my life."

"How you cleave to an abiding sense of tragedy." He clucked his tongue. "I thought you thrived on excitement."

"I do when I'm in control. Right now, I'm not in control." She practically wept with his cheerfulness. No doubt, he kept up his lighthearted banter to distract her from the inevitable.

"I bet you'd kick sand in the face of the devil," he said, and then lowered his voice, and took her hands. "You must trust me."

She tried to remove her hands. He held tight and, for one moment, she thought he'd say the words she yearned to hear...*I love you.* He gazed at her as if he were weighing the question in his mind. Rachel waited, but the seconds ticked by, and Lucas made no move to say anything. After a long, tortured silence, she said, "What do you dream of, Lucas?"

He stared at her intently, and then a lopsided grin appeared. "Food. Mashed potatoes, fried chicken, smoked ham, grits and gravy. Lots of gravy."

"You're impossible." The spell was broken. She yanked her hands from his grasp, stood and turned away. She leaned her forehead against a cold, tiny windowpane, closing her eyes against scalding tears. She could brave almost anything, but this? What was she to expect? There were no promises in war.

The night spread slowly in dreadful suspense and awful expectation, and she swiped at a tear. Wasn't she to blame with her duplicity, and her cruel taunts spoken out of sheer perversity? How despicable she was in choosing the right words to infuriate him and provoke him with her mythical lover. But to admit the truth now was like scattering ashes in the wind.

With a lump forming in her throat, Rachel was unable to define her feelings, or explain how she loved Lucas, more than herself, more than her own life.

She pushed away a long-ago notion of a loving and devoted husband and a house full of children. No time for self-pity. In a few short hours, they'd swing from a tree, so it didn't matter anyway. With an effort of will, she opened her eyes to find Lucas standing quietly in front of her.

With the callused pads of his thumbs, he reached out and wiped her tears from her cheeks, then cupped her face in his hands and lifted it, so she had no other alternative but to look at him.

"Lovely Rachel, your eyes mirror your heart."

Rachel sniffed and gave him a watery smile.

"It's okay to be scared," Lucas said.

He'd mistaken her thoughts.

The door scraped open and Lucas dropped his hands. A weary guard thrust a plate of charred roasted rabbit through the bars, and then sat guard on a stool, staring at them.

"This will be the last supper." He laughed at his morbid joke, and then with a jaundiced eye, looked Rachel up and down. "A woman? Doesn't surprise me."

Lucas plucked a piece of meat, gobbled it down, and then grabbed a thigh bone, pointed it at the guard and said, "This is the best I've eaten for a long time. Back in camp they made us soup with the shadow of a pigeon that had been dead for a long time."

The soldier tipped back on his seat and guffawed. "You is funny for a Yank."

"One of Lee's soldiers had both arms shot off, but he was so devoted, he shouldered his way through the battle," said Lucas, making himself agreeable. Soon his wonderful sense of mimicry had the sentry in stitches. The guard shared a piece of wormy bread and Lucas regaled him with hours of anecdotes.

"Why one time…" Lucas began and deliberately lowered his voice.

"What's that?" the guard said, and a dribble of tobacco juice oozed down his beard.

Lucas slapped his leg and bent over laughing as if the joke's ending were too hilarious to repeat. He swiped at his eyes and mumbled something. The guard leaned forward to catch it. Lucas' knee came up through the bars at a right angle, caught the sentry in the pit of the stomach. His fist smashed square into the man's jaw, like the crack of a cane slapped against rock. In a thud, the guard dropped to the floor. Lucas seized the keys off the guard's belt and, in seconds, they were free. He grabbed the rifle and her hand.

"I told you to trust me." He yanked her out the door. The figures of men outlined against the leaping fire, lay rolled in their blankets.

"The prisoners are escaping."

Men stumbled to their feet. Rifles exploded, flying wide of their marks. Fleeing under the cover of darkness, Rachel and Lucas disappeared into the forest.

"Ever been caught in a firestorm? Stay low, or you'll be slashed to ribbons."

Musket balls cut branches from trees and splintered saplings, showered wood chips over them. Rachel pushed off rough cracked ridges of tree bark, unable to discern anything in the cold black night except for the fiery torches behind them.

Lucas fired a shot. A man screamed. A storm of shot burst through the woods from behind. A miasmic smell clung to the air. The ground disappeared beneath her feet. Her arms flailed in the air. Her stomach flew up into her throat. In the obsidian darkness, she grabbed at vines, branches, clawed at roots, and dirt to break her fall. A thorn jabbed in her backside. She slammed into wet leaf mold in the bottom of a ravine, her breath whooshing out.

Lucas wrenched her to her feet and shoved her up the opposite embankment. "You want us to be sitting ducks?"

Zigzagging through the forest like phantoms, they bounded over treefalls and circling trees. Lucas stopped and bit open a cartridge package, sprinkled powder and spat the bullet into the muzzle. Slamming the ramrod down, he slotted the rifle on his shoulder, took aim and fired. With no more ammunition, he dropped the rifle.

"What do we do now, throw rocks?" she said, out of breath, as they approached a roadway. Rachel tripped, snaring her foot in a woodchuck hole and stuck in a tangle of roots. Shouts came from behind. The Home Guard militia charged hot on their trail…a matter of seconds.

"Go," she yelled at Lucas and sagged against the ground like a cornered rabbit.

"I'd never leave you, Rachel."

Holding torches high, a wall of ragged men surrounded them, bearing rifles and drawing revolvers out of leather holsters. The cold steel of a Colt barrel touched the back of her head. Rachel heard the hefty click.

As promised, the captain of the Home Guard had returned. Lucas' glib tongue was unable to turn the tide. The militia stayed too full of rage and whiskey for fast talk.

Rachel stumbled to rise. A guard yanked her up by her long hair. His two front teeth were gone, and he lisped, "Pretty thing, ain't she, Captain?"

Rachel kicked him in the shins.

"You spyin' witch." He raised his fist. "I'll—"

Lucas sprang at the brute. The Confederate twisted away.

"I'll nail your liver to a barn door," the Rebel shouted.

Lucas grabbed him. The man twisted away, but not soon enough. Lucas struck him square across the jaw with skull-cracking force, driving the man into the mud.

The other men were upon Lucas. Fists flailed. Too many. Lucas was easy prey, pitted against greater numbers. He crouched and pivoted, roaring his rage and eluding brutal blows. He struck back with lightning force and savage punches. Lucas subdued each man that rose and fell upon him. Men sprawled across the ground unable to crush Lucas. He elbowed a man from behind with a vicious crack. The Rebel's nose gushed forth with a shower of blood.

A Rebel surged forward, a knife in his hand. In a bizarre dance, Lucas and the Rebel circled each other, the man thrusting the razor-sharp blade. Rebels cheered and shouted. He swiped at Lucas' head. Lucas reared back, missing the full plunge of the strike. Blood dripped from his temple. He shook his head to clear his eyes.

"You're a dead man. We'll draw straws to see who has your woman first." The Rebel snarled and plunged forward.

Lucas blocked the blow, knocking the Rebel aside, and then Lucas twirled, caught the man's arm and twisted upward. The man screamed. Limp at his side, his arm dangled. His knife fell with a thud to the ground.

More men rolled up from the camp and tackled Lucas. Sheer numbers, he could not stop. A gunshot fired in the air.

"Enough," roared the Rebel captain.

Grappled by men, Lucas was stood up, and his arms tied behind his back. The wound on his head, a slight scratch, furrowed the flesh across his temple. The other men were bruised, bleeding or lay in agony with broken bones.

"Get down to business," the captain said. Ropes soared over a stout tree branch. Pushed up onto prancing horses, nooses were flung around their necks. Rachel glanced at Lucas and her heart broke. A sigh of wind wended through the trees and ruffled his hair. She looked away, saw tiny points of light, lasting stars from the night ready to be chased away with the emerging sun. At least it wasn't going to rain on her hanging day.

"Though we walk through the Valley of Death, we shall fear no evil," chanted the captain, his bloodshot eyes, taking on a yellow hue. "What's your name?"

"Captain Davis," yelled the sergeant, "but he ain't no officer."

"They're being punished because they got caught. You are listening to the Gospel according to Saint… I forget the Saint's name. Thou shall steal, lie, spy all you can, but don't get caught." The captain laughed gleefully, and his men cheered him. Yankees were about to die and that gave them pleasure.

"Let her go, she has nothing to do with this war," said Lucas.

The captain shrugged. "Dear, oh dear. Ain't that sweet. All that brawling for nothing."

Lucas' horse danced nervously beneath him, and he kneed it closer to Rachel. The world around them grew smaller. Songbirds chirped merrily in the woods, the sound incongruous with the reality around them.

"You can be downright stubborn and independent at times for a woman. Too independent. Such independence I like. But limited."

Rachel turned her head to Lucas. Despite their terrible situation, he was trying to make her laugh. She was unable to find the words for they were all balled up in her throat.

"I believe you're the most intelligent and beautiful woman I have ever met. And then there is one more thing I need to tell you," said Lucas.

"Oh, come on now," the captain chided. "Do not delay our hospitality with sweet talk. Hang 'em!"

Rachel's heart pounded. A man with food settled in his beard like a bird nestled in its nest, leered at her. "Too bad, Missy." He moved in between their horses and raised his hands to slap the horses' rumps. Rachel began to shake. Visions of her father haunted her.

A group of riders thundered up the road, mud cakes kicked up from the horses' heels. Rachel's horse panicked. The bristled rope burned against her neck. She clapped her knees into the horse's flanks before it dashed from beneath her.

"Halt. What goes here?" ordered a Confederate Cavalry officer. He drew his horse up and held his gloved hand high.

"We picked up these spies, sir, crossing the river, and so far, they have not explained their presence in the area," said the captain of the militia, spitting a long viscous stream of tobacco.

"You hang them like dogs without a trial? Take those ropes off and untie them," commanded the cavalry captain. "When have we become so barbaric as to hang a woman?"

The militia captain pointed a rheumy finger at Rachel. "The woman was disguised as a slave. That's explanation enough as far as I'm concerned."

Lucas intervened. "She traveled like that for her protection. To protect her from lawless criminals such as these."

The cavalry captain stared the militia captain down. "Do they have passes?"

The militia captain's cheek began to flutter. "Yes, sir. But they were washed in the river and don't look official." Unhappy to be usurped by regular cavalry, he angled his head to Lucas. "That one there, says he's Cap'n Davis, but he is either a deserter or a damned Yankee."

"We have a war to fight, not wasting time overseeing pretend soldiers or overzealous militia. Take the two prisoners back to camp. Our commander will sort this out." The cavalry officer turned his horse.

The ropes were lifted over their heads and their hands untied.

Lucas steered his horse parallel to the militia captain. "Let's let bygones, be bygones."

The militia captain thrust his chest out. Lucas snatched him from his saddle and hit him. The leader twisted away, but not soon enough. Lucas landed another blow, smashing him on the side of his head. Arms flailing like a windmill, the militia captain grasped at his saddle horn. The horse reared, and the militia captain fell into a puddle.

Rachel raised a brow, stunned by the cavalry officer who had turned in time to see the affair, said and did nothing except spur his horse ahead for others to follow.

She breathed a sigh of relief. Their fortune had improved for the moment and she eyed the bordering dense forests, scrambling with possibilities to escape. These were well-trained Rebel cavalry and the odds of outrunning them were nil.

Her chest hitched. All the cavalry commander had to do was wire Richmond for the full details. To trade one execution for another?

The captain broke ranks and sidled his horse to hers. He pulled off his cap, revealing crisp fair hair. He wiped the back of his hand across his wet forehead where the band on his cap had left an uncomfortable looking crease. "What is your name, ma'am?"

She glanced at Lucas and said the first thing that came to her mind. "Mrs... Mrs. Rourke."

Lucas groaned.

The captain looked genuinely surprised. "Colonel Ryan Rourke's wife?"

"Why, yes...yes, I am." She bestowed her sweetest smile,

working her charms on the captain. "I haven't heard from him in such a long time. I've missed him terribly, and simply had to risk all and come to him. Being sick with worry, he'd taken a fever, and me not there to nurse him back to health."

Lucas had a fit of coughing, but she dared not look, concentrating on the cavalry officer instead. Her ploy, to buy them more time, confident Lucas' brother, Ryan was in another part of the state. "Why you're so handsome, Captain—"

"Albury. Captain Andrew Albury at your service, ma'am."

"Is Colonel Rourke at your camp?"

"No, ma'am. He is serving farther south. Our commander has been shot and we are to be assigned a new one in a week."

Rachel pressed a palm to her heart. A few days had been granted to her before they received their new commander. She could plead to him to be escorted to Ryan Rourke's camp and she and Lucas might escape. Events could have not had a better turn. "Now do tell, Captain Albury, do you have a wife?"

Chapter 17

"Are you ready, Mrs. Rourke?" asked Captain Albury.

"A minute please." She whipped the blanket back and swung her feet to the floor, pressing her hand to her head to dispel the dizziness from rising so quickly. She had only meant to lie on the cot for a little while. How long had she slept?

Where was Lucas? He'd been taken away from her once they arrived in the camp.

She glanced around the private tent assigned to her. Claiming to be the wife of the infamous Rebel, Colonel Ryan Rourke, had earned her deferential treatment.

An empty bowl of salty stew lay beside a piece of half-eaten cornbread. She gobbled the remaining bread down, licking the sweet honeyed crumbs from her fingers, and then stepped around a hipbath that had been provided, the men having left buckets of hot water for her to rinse the caked mud from her body. In a small mirror, she checked herself, running her fingers down a calico dress procured by the attentive Captain Albury. The dress was a little tight in the bosom and she yanked it up as best as she could, sighing, having to make do with what she had.

She gave her long hair a last brushing and pinched her cheeks.

She lifted the flap and moved from the tent, noticing the utter astonishment from the captain's face.

"Is there a problem, Captain?" She feigned surprised innocence, her gaze darting around the camp for Lucas.

"Yes, ma'am. I mean, no ma'am. I apologize, ma'am." The captain fought for words. "It's just that—" He rubbed his jaw with his thumb and forefinger, looking worriedly about the camp, his hand falling on the ivory-handled, Colt revolvers on his hips.

"The gentleman attending me during my travels…has he been taken care of?"

"Yes, ma'am."

The captain possessed an economy on words. She glanced over his shoulder. Lucas was tied to a tree. He shook his head at her. Oh, how he had little faith in her abilities.

"Is it necessary to tie a son of the Confederacy to a tree?"

"We really don't know who you are—"

"Has anyone tended his wounds or offered him food and drink?" Her tone was censorial.

"Yes, ma'am."

"He has helped me greatly to reach my husband at great risk to his life. I feel—"

Captain Albury offered his arm. "The new colonel is in camp. We'll let him decide."

The cornbread heaved into her throat. She wanted more time to figure out an escape. "You said you were not to get a new commander until the end of the week."

"That's right ma'am. General Lee decided to mix two cavalry units under one commander."

Damn. "How wonderful." She smiled prettily up to the captivated captain and placed her hand in the crook of his arm. "Lead the way."

Rachel took a deep breath trying to remember what little Lucas had shared about his family and his brother, Ryan, to make her story plausible. This must be her finest role to convince the Rebel commander to release them.

Rows of tents were erected, and the crisp crackle of glowing fires dotted the encampment, affording warmth and a melodious lullaby for the weary, worn-out, bearded Rebels. Some played poker or dominoes, others wrote letters. A bullet-ridden Old Glory waved in the breeze in discord to the metallic pinging of coffee cups and utensils. A low rumble of supply wagons rolled in, spiraling up a wave of dust. She winced. The men were gaunt, barefoot and reduced to eating hardtack.

She liked wearing something feminine again yet fidgeted at the number of stares accompanied by polite nods and friendly waves from the soldiers, making her feel like a queen returned from banishment. Colonel Rourke must be popular with these men. She'd use the status of being his wife to manipulate whoever was in charge.

They passed a hospital tent where a group of nuns worked dressed in black tunics with white wide cornets, giving the appearance of wings. She had heard of the Sisters of Charity, battlefield nurses who had witnessed the worst of the war's atrocities, yet continued with their devoted acts of mercy. They stepped beyond a line of tied up horses, munching on hay, and then drew up to a tent where a flag of Old Glory fluttered and snapped in the wind.

Captain Albury patted her hand. "Wait here while I announce you."

Confident in her posing as Colonel Ryan Rourke's wife, she eavesdropped on the conversation inside.

"We have picked up a Captain Davis and a civilian, sir," said Captain Albury. "They have been unable to explain their presence in the area."

"Do they have passes?" the commander snapped. It was the kind of voice that cut through with hot authority. No, worse, it was the kind of voice that would make the devil jump. She wiped clammy hands down her skirts.

"Yes, sir," Captain Albury said. "But the passes were washed out and don't look at all official which makes me suspicious."

Rachel twisted her fingers. This wasn't going to be easy.

"Let me see them."

"The civilians or the passes?"

"The civilians!"

"I should caution you, sir." The captain lowered his voice. Rachel leaned to hear him. "The woman has the shameful notion she's your wife."

The blood drained from her face. *Colonel Ryan Rourke!* Never in a million years did she expect to come face to face with him. Her luck had run out. Lucas had told her his brother's promise to kill him if he met him in battle. For sure, they'd both be hanging before the sun set.

"This is interesting. Bring her in first," he said.

The tent flap opened. Her wits scrambled. Her eyes fell on Lucas' brother as he sat at his desk with a cigar gritted between his teeth and so menacing, and so like Lucas with his dark hair, strong nose and quintessential smirk. The air in the tent cooled several degrees, and even the shadows deepened as though he held the darkness with him, wearing it about his broad shoulders like a regal mantle tailored for the devil, himself. He tipped his chair back, appraising her from head to toe, in that same carelessly infuriating manner as Lucas had done. His eyes settled on her face.

"Why, you have to be the most beautiful woman I've ever laid my eyes upon. But as to claim to be my—"

"Your wife, darling." It was that touch of Rourke superiority that gave her all the courage she needed. She sped around his desk and clapped her hands on his shoulders. "You don't look at all well. You should have sent for me sooner," Rachel admonished then glanced at the mystified Captain Albury. She cleared her throat. "Could you close the tent flap? The colonel and I should have some privacy."

The colonel dropped his chair to all fours. "Now look here, ma'am—"

"Be quiet," Rachel ordered and waited until the captain moved from the tent. She looked into Lucas' brother's narrowed eyes, liquid pools of cobalt.

Can I trust you?

"If you have a care to cite the real reason for this odd introduction, we can get down to business. I'll remind you that you are on precarious grounds," he warned her.

With certainty, he was a hard man, hardened more by the war. *Would he turn in his own brother?* "If there is any sense of love or bond for any of your family members, you must have it now. We are in dire need of your help."

"We?"

"I ask for your assistance to get us to Union lines."

"To Union lines! End this gibberish and tell me who you are talking about!"

"Lucas," she whispered. That one name stopped him cold.

"Lucas? Where?" he demanded. "I thought he was in Washington."

"He was, but now he's here in your camp. He was captured somehow, brought to Richmond and tortured. I helped him escape. We need your help."

"And who are you?"

"I'm Rachel Rourke, Lucas' wife."

That statement alone made the seasoned cavalry colonel choke. "Lucas married? Why, he's an avowed bachelor. Never!"

She looked heavenward. The man was more surprised to find out Lucas was married than to find him this far into the Confederacy.

He stood and circled her with the unhurried but absolute concentration of a shark drawn to blood. Dark brows lowered in calculating evaluation, his stubborn jaw tilting slightly to one side in an achingly familiar gesture. "I must offer you my belated congratulations. But putting this matter aside, I have a sworn duty to uphold the Confederacy."

"Captain Albury!"

Something broke inside Rachel. How dare he betray his brother? She pounded his back. "You are a cur of a dog, a tar water skunk, the worst kind of impotent mass of stupidity." On and on, she rang blows upon his back, raging with every curse that came to mind.

Ryan turned, grabbed her hands and gave her a shake. "Silence, Woman!"

He flipped open the tent flap. Captain Albury's eyebrows disappeared into his scalp to see Rachel kick his commander.

"Release Captain Davis and bring him to me immediately." He tore down the flap in Albury's face.

"But you can't!" Rachel pleaded.

He straightened to his towering height, a wry expression creating a crease next to his hard mouth. "I can do whatever I please. Now stay quiet, or I'll tie you up."

She stilled with the deadly intent of his voice.

"That's better." He released her and rubbed his shin.

Minutes ticked by while Rachel waited for Lucas to appear. Colonel Rourke dropped into his chair. Over his steepled fingers, he studied her like a rare insect under a magnifying glass. Grief swamped her, threatening to buckle her knees, darting glances at Ryan and to the tent flap. Nausea swirled in her stomach. By honestly appealing their case to Lucas' brother, she had signed their death warrants.

She slapped her palms on his desk, furious and humiliated at being so unpardonably treated. "How could you? You'll hang your own brother? Why, if it were possible for a snake to be a buzzard and hatched from the same mother it would be you. I'm sure there will be a special place in hell for someone—"

One dark brow climbed to his hairline. "Lucas married you?"

"I did," Lucas said, passing from beneath the tent flap and standing before his brother. Both men stared at each other for a long time, each taking his full measure.

"That will be all, Captain Albury. You are dismissed. These are old friends of mine. I'll take care of it from here." The tent flap dropped.

Colonel Rourke pulled out papers then frowned at Lucas. "Your *wife...*" he choked, "has been regaling me with the kindest of words. Before she has me boiled in oil, I find it desirable to have you rescue me."

Nerves tingling, Rachel almost missed the jovial interplay between the two brothers and spoke quickly. "You must not let an unhappy circumstance prejudice your opinion."

Lucas smiled. "It's been a long time, Ryan."

"Too long. But not long enough where brothers can't keep their commonsense and help each other out."

"I didn't know how you'd actually feel," admitted Lucas.

"I know you helped out, John. Admirable."

"John had been captured by Yanks and nursed back to health by a schoolteacher. But there emerged some intrigue with the woman and he ended up in the hands of Irish thugs. They were about to hang him when I discovered his location. I tried to keep him out of the war. I didn't want him in a Northern prison or shot dead in battle. Even found a foolproof place to keep him locked up during the war. Or so I thought." Lucas grinned at the memory. "But you know our brother, John. He escaped. I don't know the rest of it. Did come to find out that the schoolteacher was really a wealthy heiress and he had the gall to kidnap her right out of Washington. Why he risked it, I'll never know, but he did have a personal vendetta against her."

"He did," Ryan informed him. "But now things are straightened out. They're happily married and she's at our home in Virginia, expecting their first child."

Lucas shook his head disbelievingly. "Strange things have happened in this war."

"I'd like to think that someday, we'll all be back home and consider this time a bad dream." Ryan paused and looked at Rachel. "I have to say you've caught yourself the loveliest of flowers."

Rachel blushed, remembering all the horrible things she'd said to him.

"She's a handful," Lucas admitted, and she wanted to give him a good kick.

Colonel Ryan Rourke picked up a pen, dipped the nib in ink and began writing. When he finished, he handed the papers to Lucas. "These passes will see you through the next five miles south where you can run into Union lines. There are two fresh horses in the back of my tent."

Ryan unrolled a map and pointed. "There's a parting of troops at Brook's Crossing. You should be able to get through easy enough. I'll keep my boys circling farther west so you won't have any skirmishes with them. I will warn you that you could get shot." He angled his head to the Confederate pants Lucas wore.

"I'll take care," Lucas promised. "I owe you an extraordinary debt." He extended his hand but, instead, his brother threw his arms around his shoulders and embraced him. Rachel grew warm from her head down to her toes. Despite the war, brothers remained brothers.

Colonel Ryan Rourke turned to Rachel and kissed her on the cheek. "Welcome to the family." Rachel had been so worried and was so emotional that she could barely say a simple goodbye and thank you.

Chapter 18

"I told you, Lucas, I'm not a gambler. I'd rather not risk my life on a 'maybe' when the odds have been so stacked against us. I say we take the bridge."

In the shadow of the trees, Lucas squinted over Brook's Crossing. Serene. Quiet. A sparkling river meandered through the forests. Up against the bridge, a fallen tree leaned drunkenly against the embankment. He rubbed his hand on the back of his neck in disbelief of her obstinacy. It bordered on lunacy. They argued again as to which way to go.

"As an officer..." Lucas pulled rank, observing her gritting her teeth, "I find it best to plan military affairs on whatever is impossible and imminent. But as you can see," he waved his hand over the vacant woods on the other side, "there might be something to be concerned about."

"You are trying to be clever with me. I'll have you know that I'm being quite charitable." She smiled, placating him as if he were without any brains whatsoever. "But I'll not countenance any further arrogance on your part for there is no justification or grievance to excuse your sarcasm."

Light danced across fern fronds and glittered off the morning dew. He smiled inwardly. He had complete admiration of her. The way she stood up to his brother when she thought Ryan was going to hang him. He shook his head. Never had he met such a woman and wondered what Ryan thought about the hellcat. "The location of Confederate troop weaknesses my brother divulged has held true. My brother committed treason to protect us by giving us the safest route and sending his cavalry elsewhere. Time is of the essence. Troop movements can change at any moment. I don't have the luxury to argue with you. We should risk going a mile farther through the woods to cross."

"Either you do as I suggest, or you can go on your own, get caught or catch a bullet through the heart. And I won't shed a tear."

A slight breeze rustled through leaves and he allowed an instant of pretended offense to steal into his expression. He mounted and spurred his horse to the east away from the bridge. Rachel grabbed his reins and stopped him.

"Where do you think you're going?" she snapped, swinging her icy gaze up to him.

His breath whistled out. With her cheeks rosy from the sun, her hair curling in thick waves about her shoulders, and that bare dip between her heaving breasts—was there any defense? He smelled wild flowers and saw a soft spongy bed of moss that led his mind to other things. "It's Sunday, isn't it. That part of my brain has it upon reflection. I think I'll take a stroll." In one fluid motion Lucas snatched the reins from her grasp.

"Wrong."

How he loved hearing the rebelliousness in her voice. Lucas took his pocket watch out to check the time. "I do have enough

wits to realize I am heading to General Grant's lines. After you."
She mounted her horse. He waved a hand and let her pass with a
slap on her horse's rump.

Rachel turned, her eyes shooting daggers. "You know
what's wrong with you? You can't admit when you're wrong.
You get everything bound up in that pea brain of yours, rolling
and twisting any peculiar thought which pops up, until it has so
flattened and confused you into a resplendent state of
bewilderment."

That startled a chuckle from Lucas, along with the ticking tap
of a woodpecker. "My head's a whirl, Rachel. Indeed, how you
maneuver me into the addled state of a moron."

"It's a miracle you can pull on your boots. That accomplish-
ment alone must have taken years. Ponder that glorious success
in your life for the time being and follow me." She turned her
horse a hundred and eighty degrees, spurring past him. "I'll get
you there safely."

Lucas wheeled his mount, wending around rough-barked
trees to catch up beside her. "I'm truly blessed to be in the
august company of a military genius. Why Caesar himself would
be awed. The Romans falling on their knees. I cannot think of
how to thank my maker for His divine providence."

"And I'm blessed with guidance bleated from a man with the
aptitude of a goat."

"We'll go your way, this time, for assuredly I am humbled by
the blazing glory of your intelligence." He watched her stiff
carriage, thoroughly enjoying goading her. He had decided
beforehand to take the bridge but the devil in him kept it from
her. "When I contemplate sharing your illustrious company, it's

no wonder why all my common sense flees with the wind, laying in its wake, complete idiocy."

Rachel lifted her chin a notch higher. "As usual, Colonel Rourke, I am the antidote to that sad reality."

With effort, Lucas resisted the temptation to snatch her from her horse and kiss away that smugness. They had gone through a lot together. Rachel was a stubbornly brave, willful woman who worked for him. He was responsible for her. He remained duty bound for reasons she could not understand. They'd be safe in Union hands soon. Perhaps they'd never see each other again. He could not make a commitment, the way she deserved. *Honor.* His mind repeated the word, but his gaze fell on her lips.

He glanced up to the brilliant blue sky, pondering the possibilities of a life together. He found himself smiling.

After crossing the bridge, Lucas grew wary. Too quiet. No birds singing. No squirrels running up the trees. The hairs on the back of his neck stood up. They were being watched. As his brother had described to him, they had traveled close to Grant's fortifications, but how close? He looked down at his butternut trousers, gripped his reins, and then scanned the area in front of him. No challenge came from the woods beyond.

Lucas' head snapped up. A bullet whizzed past his ear. He tackled Rachel off her horse. They crashed to the ground. He rolled with her off the road and behind a hefty boulder. More bullets ripped through the leaves overhead, spraying debris. Friend or foe?

"Need I jog your memory, this was your idea," he reminded her. A shell hit the earth thirty yards ahead of them before it burst. "I have no doubt those are Yankee cannons greeting us."

Lucas raised his head above the rock. "Yes, sir, those are our boys in blue. What a pretty sight."

"A wonderful welcoming," Rachel demurred.

Lucas reached over and ripped off a piece of her petticoat.

"What do you think you're doing?"

He tied it to a stick and waved it overhead. "Surrendering." He counted to three and the gunfire ceased. The Yanks dragged a cannon out of the woods, pointed it right at them.

"Don't shoot!" Lucas thrust his hands in the air. When he deemed it safe, he called to Rachel but instantly regretted it. Men mesmerized into grotesque statues, frozen with open, gaped mouths, and blatant stares at Rachel. Their casual whispers spoke their unconcealed admiration and lust. Lucas narrowed his gaze on them.

Rachel tripped on a rock. Lucas thrust his arms out to catch her. A shot fired from up in the trees. Lucas grabbed his chest and crumbled to the ground. Rachel screamed and scrambled over him, protecting him with her body. An idiot sharpshooter must have thought he was reaching for his gun.

"You fools! You do not know who you've shot!"

"Lucas! Lucas! Oh, please tell me you're not dead." Union soldiers gathered around him. Rachel grabbed one of their guns and pointed it at the soldiers.

"Stay away from him. Every last one of you. We're Yanks!" Then she threw the gun away and cradled his head in her lap. He couldn't breathe. He couldn't speak. Rachel's hot tears fell on his face. Rachel's tears. Her warm fingers, stroked his head. In the next instant, she pulled back, grabbed his bandanna, and reached to press it to his wound. Then she stopped.

Lucas glanced down at his chest. The bullet burned like hell. He flexed his fingers over his wound, then frowned. No stickiness? He sat up. No blood. He looked at Rachel, her expression now as quizzical as his must be. He reached into his pocket and pulled out his father's pocket watch and examined the bullet embedded in the gold.

A profound look of relief crossed Rachel's face. Tears welled in her eyes.

He held out the watch, turned it to see all sides. "Damn. I wanted to give this to my son. Thought I could have it dried out after the soaking in the river."

Rachel's eyes widened, her expression switched from relief to astonishment to murderous intent in the flash of a second. "You…have a son?" she snapped.

"Someday I will, if I get out of this mess." He grinned.

And if the look in Rachel's eyes were daggers, he would be dead.

Chapter 19

"Thanks to you, Rachel, we are now in the unenviable position of being prisoners of the Union Army. Everything we have gone through is for naught. The information you have stored in your head is more critical than ever."

"Don't you think I realize that?" She whirled on him and started pacing the makeshift jail set up from a commandeered farmhouse. A fire burned in the fireplace, a bed in the corner, a stool and end tables added to their meager arrangement. Bars were hammered over the windows of what had been someone's parlor. Outside, a wood pile rose next to a cutting stump surrounded by wood chips. Beyond that was a privy and hundreds of tents with blue-coated Yanks milling about.

"You certainly didn't during our interview with Colonel Crawford, did you?" Lucas drawled with distinct mockery. With regret, he recalled how they'd been dragged, tried and judged before the irascible Yankee colonel.

"And what are you implying?"

Lucas folded his arms in front of him and leaned against a whitewashed wall next to a framed replica of *Dante's Inferno*.

Right now, he was so hopping mad, he felt like one of the enraged souls caught in the circles of hell. "Don't you think it was a little over the top, telling him you had intimate connections with General Grant and were a personal friend of President Lincoln, demanding to write a letter to them? Colonel Crawford sure bought that tale."

"A lot you know."

How she had the impudence to glare at him as if she carried a secret, her boots thumping across the creaking floorboards. He laughed at her inflated importance. "At least I do know what will get us an interview with General Grant."

That stopped Rachel. She faced him, her hands bunched on her hips. "What is that?"

He sighed. "I told him the truth. I was Colonel Lucas Rourke, head of Civilian Spying."

She rolled her eyes heavenward. "I'm sure that impressed him. Your filthy Rebel uniform coupled with the Reb passes found in your pocket will certainly win us an audience with General Grant. Why, he might even extend an invitation for tea. If he doesn't hang you first."

"If you cared to notice, after an hour of your inane prattle, Colonel Crawford and his subordinates pitched us a chilly enough reception to freeze the Arctic. Your presumed wisdom fails to accept a simple fact. They now regard us as Rebel spies." He examined the burn mark over his heart where his pocket watch had miraculously stopped the bullet. He'd been lucky. "And what did you write in the message you assigned Colonel Crawford to deliver to General Grant?"

"None of your business."

"None of my business!" He kicked a brass chamber pot across the room where it banged against the wall. Never would he condescend to beg her.

"I must tip my hat to you, Rachel. I couldn't believe you had the audacity to threaten Colonel Crawford and his men, browbeating them with your trumped up political connections. Then suggesting to the colonel that a false step might cause anyone in your way to have probable cause for demotion, reprimands and court-martial! Your acting's rich. Your real calling should be on the stage." Lucas threw himself on the bed and folded his hands behind his head then hooted with hilarity. "You have a lot to learn about the military."

"If that's how you feel about it, Colonel Rourke, then keep your opinions to yourself. You may be surprised to see what magic I work."

A wind blew against the house, whistling down the cracks of the chimney and shaking ill-fitting windows. Lucas didn't think her chin could get any higher, working herself up in such a lather that she couldn't stop.

"Not only are you balled up in your arrogance, you're vain as well, which ranks next to stupidity. I should have fled the minute you landed on my doorstep for never have I met someone who attracts drama like flies to a hog's corpse."

"Still most remarkable I think..." He paused stroking his chin with his thumb and forefinger in careless reflection. "...what really convinced Colonel Crawford was when you demanded, no, I mean commanded him to give us clean clothes, a bath and food. I thought the colonel would chew up his mustache.

"Of course, you had to add whiskey to the list."

"You can't mend a broken egg. I have to have whiskey to toast a woman who commands and knows how to scheme so well that I will meet my maker in record time. What did you write in that note to General Grant?"

"You don't give up, do you Lucas?" The toe of her boot began to annoyingly tap on the wood floor. "That bit of news is so tantalizing you can't bear for me to keep it from you. Very well, I'll tell you the truth. I invoked the name of the Saint."

Lucas' temper flared. "The Saint. The omnipresent vanishing coward. If I could once identify the Saint and lay my hands on him—"

"The Saint may be closer than you think."

He narrowed his eyes on her. "What do you mean by that?"

Something bothered him about her too cavalier attitude with the Saint. Was it his wounded pride or something else? In the back of his mind, something didn't add up. It nagged him like a flea on a coon dog's tail.

Rachel shrugged her shoulders and stepped toward him, her hips swaying and her breasts swelling above the bodice of her dress. There should be a law against that, especially since his cock rose to half-mast, enough to create a lack of available space in his trousers.

"He is a cunning scoundrel, don't you agree?"

Lucas said nothing and stared at the ceiling, counting the cobwebs, her evasiveness and preponderate adoration like bile jammed in his throat. With sarcasm he could no longer contain, he placed his hand over his heart. "Upon my honor, your misplaced worship grieves me. It truly grieves me."

"Not for one second, Colonel Rourke, do I detect any remorse. Need I remind you that you were the one who was tricked by the Copperheads and kidnapped? Need I point out, I was the one who saved you from your certain fate, helped you get through the forests and Southern lines. Instead, the thanks I get almost got me drowned, hanged, shot at, and now imprisoned."

Lucas sat bolt upright. "And need I remind *you*, I saved you from defilement, carried you through a burning house, talked us out of a hanging, and I did get shot! What do I get for gratitude?"

They were arguing so loudly, they barely heard a knock and the door scrape open. Two Union soldiers brought a tray of food, a freshly pressed uniform for Lucas and a clean dress for Rachel.

The younger Union soldier placed a tray on the table near her. He was taken by surprise and stared at her slack-jawed. "And pray, who might you be, miss?"

Lucas glowered at him. "You're dismissed," he ordered.

The soldier set down the tray. "Ma'am, after you eat, I'll escort you to a tent where you can bathe in private." He scurried past Lucas to place the clothing on a stool, and then ran out the jail door almost forgetting to lock it.

After the soldier left, Rachel turned to him. "You needn't be so rude."

"He should know enough to keep his eyeballs in his sockets."

Rachel folded her arms in front of her. She glanced at the food, then to Lucas, and shook her head. "Care to admit who is the most effective now?" When he didn't answer, she made clucking sounds with her tongue. "My. My. Fried chicken, mashed potatoes and gravy. Lots of gravy," she emphasized.

Lucas jumped from the bed, grabbed a plate, and sat down again.

She sauntered over to him and handed him a bottle of whiskey. "I believe this is yours," she said triumphantly. "Have you lost your tongue, Colonel Rourke, or has your conceit unhinged your mind?"

Lucas shoveled food into his mouth. "It's on account of my esteemed position."

"Ha! You can't even admit I have abilities and influence."

"I don't care how it got here. I'm hungry," he said between mouthfuls, manners bolting out the window. "I see they have guards posted on us outside, so you were not that convincing." She wanted a response, perhaps affirmation of what she'd accomplished. No way was he going to give her one inch.

"You are the most frustrating man I've ever met."

"It's a gift, Rachel," he said, grinning from ear to ear.

"More of a curse."

Lucas found that notion hugely entertaining and heaping more food on his plate, he pointed a chicken leg at her. "You best forget it. We are safely behind Union lines and you are under my command. You will not embark on another mission. No more dances with danger."

That raised the hackles on her neck. He guessed what was already spinning in her mind. "Need I remind you that your father was caught?"

"Your problem is that you possess an overriding sense of responsibility that disallows you to grant control to another human being. Unfortunately for you, it almost became your demise."

He wanted to shake her. "Despite your strong opinions on my capabilities, from here on, I will take matters into my hands and you will do as I say."

Rachel dropped her plate, stood, her skirts snapping with every step she took until she was within inches of him. "Your rabid possession of me must stop. Believing that someone belongs to you is equal to southerners who believe their slaves are their possessions and belong to them."

He jerked his head back. He didn't consider possessing her in that way. Maybe he had, yet his mind went astir, reaping the full benefits of the boon displayed. Slim white ankles showed beneath her skirts.

Rachel put her hand up against his chest. "We still haven't finished. You're in terrible danger unless you forgot. Someone set you up and that someone is still loose. You must tread lightly from here on, avoid mistakes and always be prepared."

The guards came and escorted her to a bathing tent. Lucas took advantage of the shaving materials, soap and a hip bath provided. Feeling clean again, he dressed. With this much service, Crawford must have doubts about them being Rebel spies.

He scrubbed a hand over his face, a besieged mass of frustration. *Rachel*. Her wit knew no bounds and painfully challenged him at every turn. And then too, she had an inner strength and cleverness unmatched in any woman he'd ever known. She had faced the enemy countless times, to the point of sacrificing herself for him and nameless others. Despite the risks he'd thrown her way, and the fact that he'd mercilessly pushed her forward, her unfailing bravery rang through.

She returned. Silent and keeping a safe distance from him, she poked up the fire, pushing around the red coals and setting free a few burning embers. Cinders twisted up in the hot air, and then slowly spiraled down, settling on the hearth. With a brush in hand, she worked on untangling her heavy hair until it flowed like a waterfall of rich chestnut silk. Lucas almost feared to move unless she flew away. He watched, mesmerized. "You are a witch, a beautiful tormenting witch."

"A witch." With a gay laugh, she returned to their easy camaraderie. "Weren't you taught it rude to stare so openly?" Her amber eyes glowed with playfulness.

"I was but admiring you. How can I help it when I'm gifted with a windfall? Does a sane man throw it away?"

"You accused me before of inane prattle, yet you babble now."

He liked the blush that stole across her cheeks.

All his senses were involved with her, her loveliness of spirit stirred his soul, creating a need so deep...

Outside their prison, the guards spent the evening playing cards. Lucas heard troops in drilling and the mournful sound of a bugle, spilling *Taps... Day is Done...* The War. The reality slammed into him. The war had them in its ugly clutches. Even now, he remembered how close they had come to death's door.

He grabbed her hand, and she stared at him, a question in her magnificent eyes.

"This isn't how I planned it, Rachel...but I believe we should begin again."

"Nonsense. Whatever you say, it doesn't matter."

Her mood was different.

"We've come a long way, haven't we? I believe Colonel Crawford believes our story. He is careful and checking our account. It will be a matter of time…"

She was shutting him out.

"I don't care about Crawford." He grabbed her wrist. "That is not what we need to discuss."

Memories flooded him. He recalled her outrage when he threw her from the train, and her courage and resilience when she had to face crossing a swollen river. The fact that she cried, not for her home that burned to the ground, but for the humble Bible her father had given her. He contemplated her daring when she had rescued him from the hands of Copperheads and admired her swift aptitude, enabling her to handle crisis after crisis. Even when it meant wearing ridiculous disguises.

"We are man and wife. By some strange fate, our destiny is sealed. There must be total honesty between us. Your past, your feelings cannot be secret."

She stiffened, tugged her wrist free. "You are making this difficult for me, aren't you?"

"As much as possible."

A reluctant smile touched her lips, and she sighed with sadness. She moved away, her back to him. "It won't work," she spoke over her shoulder.

Lucas' temper soared, He checked it. "We can get over that."

"I have my work, and you have yours."

"What other ways have you devised to keep yourself detached from this marriage?" He couldn't believe she was refusing him.

"You're not good husband material."

"Not good husband material!" The entire conversation was laughable. Here he was submitting to her, and she wanted no more than to serve her singular obsession that she had clung to during the war. Did she feel nothing for him? That she could let him go for some silly mission? For the first time, he realized that if he didn't want to marry her, he would have made up excuses at the wedding. Then another thought snaked through his brain. His insides burned like fiery acid.

"The Saint. Admit it, Rachel."

She turned, tears forming in her eyes. "I won't be married to you. In your mind, you feel obligated to do the honorable thing. I don't want a marriage built on that."

This time, he shouted. "That is the most insane, idiotic, senseless—" He stopped and decided on another tack to convince her. "I'm a man of very few words at times, but I have a definite objective." He drew close to her. "Just for tonight…could we put aside the war and behave like a normal wedded couple?"

Rachel's fingers turned white where they clutched the chair. The guard had told her General Grant was away from the camp and due back at any time. So little time remained.

She felt Lucas' longing, his eyes upon her as he stalked her across the room. No—consumed her across the space of a room. She knew what he requested. How could she tell him that no matter how she might resist, there was never a time when she didn't want him? Her voice came fragile, and she had to clear her throat before continuing. "I doubt there's a woman alive you couldn't have if you put your mind to it."

"You exaggerate my abilities."

His smile reached her with devastating effect. Oh, his melting smile.

To bandy spiteful remarks proved easier to safeguard her feelings. She had control then. Yet, acerbic witticisms failed to come to her lips. She backed into the wall, dragging the chair between them.

He was dangerously appealing. Damp, dark tendrils curled over his forehead. She was incapable of tearing her eyes away.

Lucas tossed the chair aside. Still he did not close the gap between them. Beneath his scrutiny, a brief shiver ran through her and her palms began to sweat. This was to be their wedding night. Her heart pounded. Part of her brain screamed...*do not commit.*

"Rachel."

The air between them sizzled in a wordless clash of far-reaching desires and fears, carrying them beyond friendship, beyond human bond and any other passion. That missing part of her life, that isolated part of her that desperately needed and begged for her soul to become one. *Husband and wife.* Even if it was for only this night.

"I thought we might..." She couldn't finish, not with his fathomless cobalt blue eyes fastened on her while his deep, husky voice caressed her, pulling her further under his spell.

"Exactly."

He wanted her to bridge the distance between them.

"Come here." The naked longing in his eyes burned into her.

"Lucas, perhaps—"

"Rachel, you talk too much—"

He wanted her.

She took a step, then another.

Lucas jerked her into his arms and his mouth swooped down to capture hers. Her heart hammered in her ears, while she gave herself freely to the hunger of his kiss. His arms moved around her, and he groaned when she clasped her arms about his neck. She inhaled a mixture of soap and manly scent—Lucas' scent.

He pushed her back until she bumped against the wall. His mouth skimmed her jaw, down her throat, his teeth grazing her ear and his fresh-shaven jaw smooth against her skin.

Before I go…

A part of her told her that she should stop, that she should think this through, but the other voice in her head drowned her out. She wanted him more than she could breathe.

Rachel gasped when he gathered her into his arms and carried her to the bed.

With no opposition from her, Lucas reached behind and unfastened a row of buttons, pushing her dress away. She shivered as the calico gown glided down her body and pooled at her feet. Naked now, Rachel covered herself. He moved her hands to her sides, her nipples grazing the soft cotton of his shirt.

"You never need to cover yourself. Not with me."

Trapped in a whirl of heady arousal, she watched, intrigued as he shirked out of his shirt, reveling in the lean muscularity of his chest, arms and shoulders. Lower down on his abdomen his navel was circled with dark hair, muscles flexed and relaxed with the flow of his movements.

She longed to run her hands across his skin, to glide her

fingers over every muscle and sinew of him. Pulsing heat spread between her legs.

"The guards?"

"To hell with the guards." He growled and strode to the door and kicked a chair beneath the handle.

Rachel moistened her lips with the tip of her tongue. He watched her with hunger in his eyes. A slight sheen lit his body, sleek and strong, without the excess bulk conspicuous of the commanding officers. He finished shedding his navy breeches, and her eyes widened, her gaze riveted to his manhood… impressed and even a little frightened.

He picked her up, laid her on the bed, scanning his eyes over her nakedness.

"You are truly lovely," he drawled, and a strange delicious tension scorched below as he devoured her with his eyes, touching her everywhere. He lay next to her, the heat of his body running down the entire length of her, and…keenly evident, his manhood pressed against her thigh, and the barely controlled power wound in his body. Rachel closed her eyes not quite understanding how things were meant to be. How would they fit? She had seen stallions in the pasture…but this was something else.

He drew Rachel up beside him and stopped. She opened her eyes.

Lucas took her hand and placed it on his chest, the strong pulse of his heart drumming beneath her palm.

"We are two to be made one by what is sacred. As I took my vows, Rachel, I made a promise that I'd always care for you. It is not a careless pledge I took." From the rich timbre of his voice, her heart beat to match his pulse. "I warn you from here on to the end, there will be no other in your life…nor will there be any secrets between us."

Rachel was mindless to his warning, so lost was she when he used his thumb to circle her nipple. She raised her fingertips to trace his jaw and trailed them down his neck, entranced by the sensual feel of his firm skin and the silky texture of his hair. She memorized everything about him, sensing his vulnerability and reached up to stroke his cheek.

Unable to resist, she kissed his throat and then his shoulder.

Lucas shuddered. "How many times have I conjured this in my mind?" He pulled her body until her breasts pressed firmly against his chest, and her thighs tangled with his own. His hand wandered down her waist, drawing intricate patterns, moving downward to stroke her thighs. She trembled beneath his caresses.

Her curiosity of him was just as searching. Her finger followed across his belly where his muscles rippled, hard and lean. She dreamed of this, touching him, absorbing the beauty of his body with her fingertips, lightly tracing the dark furring of hair running down his chest, and down to where his maleness lay. She circled around it, never touching him there and heard his intake of breath every time her exploring fingertips drew close. She reveled in the power she had over him and raised her eyes to his. They were a darker shade for blue now, darkened with passion, hard and penetrating.

"You are playing with fire," he growled against the curve of her shoulder, but his words were lost as he took her mouth, and then seared a trail down her throat and shoulder. A warm hand closed over her breast, caressing in circles then capturing a nipple and squeezing it between his fingers before trailing to her next breast.

He crushed her to him, his hands exploring the hollows of her back and down over her hips. Automatically she curled into the curve of his body. Her breasts tingled against the muscles of his chest. His hands and lips were everywhere, the gentle message sending currents of desire through her. His mouth moved to her breast, his tongue caressed her sensitive, swollen nipple.

"Do you like that?"

"Yes." She arched toward him.

His hand seared a path down her abdomen and onto her thigh. He stroked there, and she groaned, pushing her hips into his hand. His palm sought the warmth of her woman's mound, circling her wet cleft. She jerked.

"I love the way you respond." He did it again. She writhed.

Urging her thighs further apart, he slid his fingers deep into her. Again and again, came the probing of his fingers, the pleasure coming pure and explosive. She breathed in deep soul-drenching drafts.

He kissed her, parting her lips, and setting her nerves ablaze with a slow search for her tongue. Rachel's hands crept around his neck, her breath labored, her body turning light and hot. When he dragged his mouth from hers, she kept her arms around him, her head spinning.

"You are ready for me," he said against her mouth. "So moist and hot and silky."

"Yes, yes." Rachel gasped in sweet agony, not wanting him to stop.

He rolled on top of her, separating her thighs with deliberate pressure of his own. He continued to stroke her with his fingers, and Rachel thought she'd spiral off the ends of the earth.

"Look at me."

She opened her eyes, saw the unleashed power of his manhood.

Suddenly, guilt rocked through her for she had not been honest with Lucas…about her role as the Saint. *There must be no more secrets between us…*reverberated through her mind.

"Lucas…I must tell you—"

"The Saint will be no more," he commanded.

He thrust himself into her body, filling her completely. A sharp, unexpected pain slashed through her. Rachel cried out…shoved against his shoulders.

"Rachel!" His face was taut with emotion.

The pain vanished, and she didn't want him to stop the lush, exquisite feelings flowing uncontrolled. She moved beneath him then, adjusting her body to his, welcoming him into hers, melting against him, and the world filled with him. To have more of him. She gasped with pleasure. She wriggled. He fit well. Very well.

He grabbed her shoulders to still her movement beneath him. "Why didn't you tell me you were a—"

"It doesn't matter."

"It does matter!"

"Lucas." She took his face in her hands. "I can't explain… why are you angry with me?"

"I'm not angry with you." He almost shouted, and because she squirmed beneath him, he moved against her. She wrapped her arms around his neck, offering him her parted lips, matching the erotic rhythm as he moved inside her, tenderly drawing upward and thrusting deeper and deeper. Rachel responded with each demanding stroke of his body. Passion radiated from the core of her being until he freed her in a bursting of sensations, flooding her with hot pleasure. She wrapped her legs around him as Lucas made one final thrust, his body jerking convulsively again and again as his warmth spilled into her.

Rachel felt Lucas move onto his side, carrying her with him. Her breath came in long surrendering moans and her eyes unsteadily opened and focused on the patterns of light dancing on the wall and ceiling from the flickering flames of the fire. A log crashed in the fireplace, sputtering and sparking.

She reached up, outlining his chest with her fingertips then raised her head and nipped at his nipples. He groaned and grabbed a fistful of her hair, holding her in place. He stared at her with startling intensity, his blue eyes darkening and penetrating, his wide, muscular shoulders filling the entire scope of her vision.

A look passed between them more eloquent than words. "I need you, Rachel." He lowered his head with a slow demanding kiss. "I want you."

He kissed her thoroughly again and she felt his manhood hardening more, if it were possible, toying against her triangle of springy curls. She whimpered and moved her hips in response.

"Are you able to do that again?"

"If I can't get your notion of saving the world out of that lovely head of yours, then I'll have to resort to other measures."

He nudged his knees between her thighs and hovering above

her, his gaze bored into hers. "I love you. You are mine forever, Rachel."

Her breath caught. He had said three powerful words and there was no going back from them. Shattering tenderness swept through her. Heart pounding, she lifted her hips, welcoming each driving thrust, her woman's body reacting to the indescribable, splintering feeling that built with pulsing leaps deep in her womb.

With aching affection, she held his face with her hands. "I am yours, Lucas I love you with all my heart."

His hands were everywhere, his manhood, engorged and molding her to him with steady thrusts. Her impatience grew to explosive proportions, his expert touch hurling her over the brim to higher and higher levels of ecstasy.

"Lucas!" Rachel shattered into a million glowing stars. She arched against him receiving the last of his liquid warmth and filling her with sweet agony.

They lay entwined as lovers, drifting off to sleep, and then making love again…and again. The musk and scent of his body filled her nostrils and she floated in languid contentment. It was all a dream, a beautiful, wonderful fairytale…and that's all it could ever be.

Chapter 20

*L*ucas had slept so soundly that he'd not heard the guard come in the night to notify Rachel that her note with the signature *"S"* had received General Grant's attention. Rachel gazed out the window as she dressed, the North Star appearing as a brilliant point of light against the velvet night. The waxing moon, soft and smooth as a silvery disc, slanted light over Lucas' sleeping form.

Later, she'd pen a letter to Lucas, but it did little to assuage the thickness in her throat. He'd be furious. He'd hate her.

Lucas had told her she was his, and she'd cherish that thought until her last days. He gave her many things. He was the first man who really understood her. The first man to whom she bared her soul. He understood her mulish independent streak. Intelligent and noble, he plied her with challenges yielding nothing but his consideration of her. Despite the reckless risks she took, he had saved her many times. But falling in love with Lucas was something she had never imagined.

No. She should never have become involved with him. The attachment complicated her life too much.

Yet she'd never give up one moment of the time she spent with him. She was young with Lucas, almost carefree. She had fallen in love. She had learned what it meant to give herself completely, body and soul, to another. Each moment she cherished, and set fire to memory, so they'd be forever imprinted on her mind, as warm and real as they had been when they were first made.

But if anyone would chance to see her face now, they'd never guess the misery beneath, or her shattered heart for without a doubt, Rachel knew Lucas would never admit that he needed her help. She knew the danger he was in. The only way to help him was to meet with General Grant, go to Washington unhindered and figure out who was behind the Copperhead plot.

She moved silently to the bed. Lucas slept, a contented smile on his lips and so appealing in repose. They had made love several times, the last with such ferocity, it humbled her. Rachel smoothed back his hair shimmering in the moonlight, and kissed him one last time.

God help me. She tasted the saltiness of her own tears. In his sleep, Lucas mumbled something about loving her. As the cold thinning light heralded the approach of dawn, Rachel's heart broke in two.

"You're a woman!" General Grant boomed like two cannons.

She had been informed that the Commander of the Union Army was calm and staid, but the idea of the Saint being a female had not occurred to him. Rachel smiled. She expected nothing less. "None of your officers must know I'm the Saint. No one. It is imperative more than ever that no one knows."

Several of his attending generals, officers and clerks had been called upon and now crowded around a large table inside a large home that had been confiscated. Rachel divulged all the pertinent information stored in her head. She pored over maps, wrote down names, drew descriptions of places and Southern movements of lines. The torrent of information amazed those sitting around her as they nodded nods heads in approval and wide-eyed amazement. General Grant frowned at times as he bit thoughtfully on his cigar. She did not reveal Colonel Ryan Rourke's encampment. He had helped them escape, and she owed him.

The questioning rose like a wild tsunami. Rachel tried to keep up with the torturous changes in rapid-fire conversation. She had always passed on information through her network, never coming in personal contact with Union officials. How odd to be discussing matters of war with generals. She shrugged. It was really no different than sitting in a parlor discussing the weather.

With her knuckles, she kneaded a growing ache in her lower back, and then remembered the gesture to be unladylike. "As you see—" She stifled a yawn and she worked to keep her weary mind focused. Her lovemaking with Lucas all night long had taken its toll.

In no mood to agree, General Grant sighed irritably and motioned to one of his aides. "Get Miss Pierce a chair and pour us some coffee." Rubbing his wrists, he added, "I hate the advent of winter. The cold and dampness makes my joints ache."

After hours of uninterrupted deliberation, she completed everything she knew.

"Oh, and one more thing—" She looked to General Grant for permission to continue.

"We don't stand on ceremony here."

"Colonel Lucas Rourke is in camp." Rachel explained how he'd been kidnapped from Washington, brutally tortured yet never divulged any information. "He came to my rescue several times during our escape. He is a true hero and should receive recognition and promotion."

She stared at every man present to make sure there would be no misconstruing of Lucas' disappearance. If assumptions caught fire with alleged desertion, he could face demotion, court-martial or hanging if they believed he worked as a spy for the Confederacy.

"A hero?" Grant paused, lit his cigar. The fragrance of rich tobacco wafted over them.

"He saved me several times. Without him, I'd not be standing here telling you of this plot."

She impressed everyone.

A general standing next to General Grant interrupted. "Excuse me, did you say Colonel Rourke?"

"Yes. Is there something pressing?" Rachel asked, ready to defend if necessary.

"I'm General Webster. He nodded to her. "My daughter, Susan, will be delighted with the news. You see, they are very much in love and to be wed."

"Wed?" A coldness hit at her core. Everyone's faces blurred. She placed her palms on the table to steady herself.

You've lost him. A hysterical voice roared in her head, but another voice, a pitiful, more heartbreaking one, said, *you never had him.*

"My daughter's been inconsolable since Colonel Rourke's disappearance," said General Webster.

"Well...may I offer my happiest felicitations to both of them." Chest aching, Rachel turned to General Grant, and pasted on a brilliant smile. "I'll need a pass from you and transportation arrangements made to Washington immediately. Time is critical." To put as much distance between her and Lucas as possible.

"Done. Anything else you require, Miss Pierce, see my quartermaster. And thank you, young lady, for all you have accomplished."

"General Grant." She looked to him. "I need to ask a favor."

He nodded in understanding. "Gentlemen, this meeting is adjourned."

She waited for the men to file out and took a deep breath. "Colonel Rourke, at times, is a trying man and tends to get in the way—" She felt like a juggler given one ball too many. "You must keep him in this camp for at least seventy-two hours after I depart. He has a tendency to overthink a situation and it is imperative more than ever that no one knows I am the Saint or my whereabouts. I can further the Union's cause operating with anonymity."

"Including Colonel Rourke?"

"Especially Lucas—I mean, Colonel Rourke." Grant's eyes widened. He had not been picked as Commander of the Union forces because he was stupid.

"I imagine there will be some discussion on Colonel Rourke's part, but I have my work cut out for me. You must trust me on this," she said in a vain attempt to smooth over her mistake. Grant remained too much of a gentleman to comment.

"What you're attempting to do with the Copperheads is dangerous."

"I'll make do," she said in a strained voice. "If I may borrow your secretary's desk, I wish to pen Colonel Rourke a note."

Beyond the horizon, the sun plummeted, and so did her heart. She was leaving for Washington within the hour and she might never see Lucas again. Sitting at the desk, she picked up the nib pen and stared at the day's last scarlet rays, tamping back her tears. So much for faithful platitudes. If he couldn't remain loyal to a woman he was betrothed to, then what did that mean for her?

Maybe all this time, she'd been deceiving herself. She'd fallen in love with Lucas. He was attracted to her, and she held no illusions that he might love her with his endearing words, claiming she belonged to him, but he had a fiancée!

Did his declaration to her mean nothing? Deep down, she must have known there was no hope of a future with him. Her mind raced. How could he return to the arms of another woman? Was he forced to marry Susan? Did he love her?

Whether he desired Rachel, it did not matter. Against a world turned upside down with war and hate, she had fallen in love. So complete was her love that she would rather sacrifice her own life than his, and she'd do it willingly, without hope of his love in return.

No way did she desire any of his explanations. To hear the truth would hurt too much. *Be practical.* Their idyll here had ended. He'd return to the woman he'd planned to marry, and she, Rachel, would be forgotten. She dipped her pen in the inkwell.

Dear Lucas,

There are some roads that can never be revisited. Our marriage was a temporary pact made in undue haste and for our safety. Soon you will see our relationship as an alchemy of opposites. I release you from our vows and further obligations. We'd only bring misery and torment to each other. As I have work to do, I ask you not to interfere.

Sincerely,

Rachel Pierce

Chapter 21

*L*ucas pounded the door and shouted at the guards for the thousandth time. "Where is she? Why are you keeping me locked up?"

For two whole days Lucas cooled his heels to the point of exploding. No answers or explanation to her disappearance. He had paced his prison until he could count every crack in the wood, every cobweb on the ceiling. Something was wrong, very wrong. Then he saw it. An envelope addressed to him. Must have been placed there by the guards when he fell asleep. He ripped it open.

"Releasing me from obligation! Who in the hell does she think she is?" Lucas hammered the door with his fists, and if it wasn't made of stiff oak would have crashed through it. "I demand to see General Grant."

It was a blooming of madness. He'd foolishly drunk from the nectar of the forbidden fruit intoxicated with the idea that love, only love would be permanent. How he'd emerged the sentimental fool.

She wanted to annul the marriage. No way was he going to allow her to. The marriage stood. Yes, they were polar opposites, and it was their challenging natures that drew them together.

The irascible Colonel Crawford had visited him with all the deference of a praising pope, yet stayed behind the locked door, apologizing to Lucas that they were to hold him until General Grant was ready to see him.

So, he sat like a caged animal, held prisoner by his own country for upholding his honor and performing his duty, and there was nothing he could do about it. He raged like a madman, the guards shuffling away in case he broke free. He needed to throw his fist into someone's face. Something to take the edge off the tightening in his gut.

Finally, the cell door banged open. Three soldiers had come to call. Lucas smiled and rolled up his sleeves. No longer did he have to wait to relieve his frustration…he'd get out of his prison if it was the last thing he did.

"General Grant wishes to see you, Colonel Rourke," said one soldier. Before the man could salute, Lucas knocked two of them out cold and shoved the other one out of the way.

"It'll be worth the court-martial." He stepped over them. "I'll escort myself to General Grant."

"Look at that," said the guards sitting around a campfire as Lucas stalked out of the jail unescorted.

Lucas ignored the men standing to attention as he passed.

"Colonel Lucas Rourke reporting," he said as he reached Grant and saluted.

Grant raised an eyebrow. "I order you to sit down and take a stiff drink, Colonel."

"I suppose you know where she has gone," Lucas snapped.

General Grant raised a brow. He remained mute on the

subject and that left Lucas to think of only one reason for her disappearance.

Lucas bolted from his seat. "Don't tell me she took off on some fool mission with the Saint."

"Please sit." Grant offered the invitation with steely politeness. He clamped the cigar between his teeth and stared at Lucas. "You do not know the Saint's identity?"

"No," said Lucas.

Grant's eyes lit with surprise. "I will offer you this. Miss Pierce has the country's best interests at heart and that is my first and foremost obligation." In their five-year acquaintance, Grant had never talked to him like this, in a friendly paternal banter. After a minute, the general drew his cigar out of his mouth. "I detect a romantic interest on your part, Colonel Rourke, that you should not allow to cloud your thinking. It is a hard and fast rule of mine to never let one's passions govern his emotions."

Lucas shot out of his chair. "Romantic notions be damned! She's my *wife*. I want her immediately!"

Soldiers flooded the room to surround Lucas.

Grant waved them away. "This takes on a very different meaning then." He lit his cigar with a lucifer until the end grew like a bright red coal, studying Lucas at his leisure. "I take it you are concerned for *Mrs. Rourke's* security?"

"Yes." Lucas gritted out, tamping down his anger. He'd get nowhere being a hothead. Rachel's dismissal had him festering inside like a sealed volcano.

"Since you are her husband, I will make one small concession, but I must have your sworn oath you will not interfere with her work."

"You have it, General Grant."

"Very well. In twenty-four hours, I will tell you her whereabouts. Not one second sooner. Miss Pierce or rather, Mrs. Rourke, is one of our finest agents, and I will not compromise her or my word to her. I remind you of your oath not to interfere, or you will be court-martialed. Am I clear on this, Colonel Rourke?"

"Twenty-four hours!" Lucas ground out.

"I'm trying to win a war, not run a Sunday school," Grant said with a wry tone of impatience. "I would like to speak to you before you go," he added.

"Speak now," said Lucas, "I'm leaving now."

"Lock him up," ordered Grant. Several soldiers seized Lucas. "I should have you court-martialed, Colonel Rourke, for countermanding my orders, but I'd be losing the best man the Union has to offer. I'm sorry, Soldier. I have done all I can do. It is one of the cruel fates of the war, which is cruelty itself, and there is no refining it."

In exactly twenty-four hours, Lucas was released by General Webster with whom he had a vague familiarity. Lucas learned two things from his interview with the man. He learned how the general related to Rachel the tale of his daughter who had tried to hoodwink him into marriage, and knew, without a doubt, the firestorm now brewing in his wife. Secondly, he'd tricked the general into divulging Rachel's destination.

Chapter 22

She had a good clean start. Lucas landed in Washington in eight hours later, a feat that took a normal man twenty.

"Colonel Rourke, how else do you explain being in the south and abandoning your position?" asked General Grenville Dodge. With a jaundiced eye, he tilted back in his chair and gazed at Lucas with unflinching directness. Lucas sweated beneath the heat of Dodge's glare and, with it, the uncomfortable feeling of being suspect.

"I won't be browbeaten into a false admission or trapped by an accidental answer, sir." Two subordinates flanked each side of him in the narrow office. Lucas suffered the welcome of a plague rat.

"You will tell me, and you will tell me now," thundered General Dodge.

"I was kidnapped under a ruse set up by Confederates, sir."

Lucas had the uncanny wisdom not to give further explanation. General Dodge was an old hand at playing games and, with certainty, this was his superior's wish. The interrogation was for the benefit of his two companions. Lucas kept his mouth shut.

"I'll have you know, you are under house arrest until I get to the bottom of this."

"Colonel Rourke has been nothing but loyal to the Union," protested Lieutenant Bowman. "I cannot think of a better officer and one who has risked his life many times and—"

"Colonel Rourke is a seasoned officer. He has made an unforgivable foray in the south that is undeniably questionable," ranted Dodge. "I cannot lead this high office with a hotbed of sensitive information while allowing one irresponsible son of a bitch under my command to jeopardize the Union."

Lucas straightened. "I would expect nothing less, sir."

Lieutenant Anthony Bowman would not be deterred and his bold defense surprised Lucas. "I can vouch for Colonel Rourke—"

Dodge's face mottled with rage. "By God if I hear another word, I'll have Colonel Rourke court-martialed. As far as I'm concerned, he's not fit to serve in the United States Army let alone the Office of Civilian Spying. Lieutenants Andrew and Bowman, you are dismissed."

Bowman glanced in Lucas' direction and shrugged his shoulders. Lucas waited, listening to the door close after the two departing officers.

"At ease, Colonel Rourke. I wanted to speak to you alone and appreciate your silence."

"It was understood, sir."

Dodge, a lean, thoughtful man who never cracked a smile, discerned many things. Palm up, he gestured to Lucas to have a seat. "I needed a demonstration to throw those two off the scent. I've known you a good many years and never doubted your loyalties. But we've got a rotten apple in our midst, and I'm beside myself to ferret him out. I have dispatches from General Grant supporting your story and complimenting your heroic endeavors. He mentions the danger you are in. I agree. That's why I've decided to post guards on you day and night under the guise of house arrest."

"But General, sir, I will not be able to move—"

"Nonsense. I am confident you will be able to move about the city on your own recognizance. Now, tell me what you know about this Copperhead disaster that is about to be let loose. We need to round up these fiends as soon as possible."

Lucas spent the next hour sharing all the information he knew. He wished Rachel were here with her photographic memory. *Where was she?* When Lucas finished, he studied his immaculately dressed fifty and then some superior officer. Dodge's long face broke into longitudinal stripes by creases, haggard by pressures from the war, and blue eyes, sincere now, almost lost under a tangle of gray brows.

His calming voice cut through the silence. "As soon as I received the missive from General Grant, I wired our agents in New York, Baltimore, Chicago and notified those in Washington." Dodge drummed his fingers on the desk. "Do you have any idea who could be our Judas?"

"My instincts tell me there is a connection between my kidnapping and what's about to be hatched. Make no mistake, General. I will find the enemy. There is no other option."

"In what ways can you suggest we find this rat?"

"I'm going to offer myself as bait. Have your men loosely guard me."

"Your life is in danger. It would be a huge loss if you—"

"I'll take that risk. I will not fail."

"Am I to assume you have an idea of who it may be?"

"I have my suspicions. Andrews and Rogers."

Dodge whistled through his teeth. "My thoughts exactly. No one else?"

Lucas shook his head. "Maybe Bowman, but I doubt it. He's basically a greenhorn."

"Sometimes the least suspicious are the most suspicious."

Rachel had told him the same thing.

"How are things in the south?"

Lucas rolled his head to get the crick out of his neck. "The South's on its knees, but still has plenty of fight."

"I received word about the disastrous results of this crater business in Petersburg. Hundreds of our good men were slaughtered. Any information I can get to end this damned war…" His voice drifted off for a moment, his pride in his position evident yet frustrated by uncertain events. "Hell, I'm in the intelligence business, but I'm not a damned fortune teller."

Lucas did not answer.

"Quite remarkably," Dodge continued, "I've received a message from President Lincoln regaling you, verified by the Saint."

"The Saint." Lucas narrowed his eyes. Had Rachel met up with the Saint? That meant Rachel and the Saint were in Washington together. His blood boiled.

"It seems you have earned the impressive trust of the Saint during your travels." A frown furrowed across Dodge's forehead. "Tell me, what does he look like?"

"I can't say. I've never seen him."

"Well, according to President Lincoln, the Saint holds you in high regard. Now tell me, how is it you get vouched for by a spy you've never met?" General Dodge then added, "I can't complain. The Saint's loyalty and information have been indispensable. We couldn't have been as effective without it. Yet I still think it odd no one has ever seen him. I sometimes imagine he is a slave, yet other times, I entertain the possibility our Saint—" Dodge gave a sardonic laugh. "Might be a woman."

Lucas' heart stalled. *Might be a woman?*

"Damn."

"Pardon me," said General Dodge.

"Nothing, sir. Nothing at all." His blood ran cold. His gut clenched. *Damn you, Rachel. Damn you to hell a thousand times.*

She'd made a fool of him…and he'd never seen it coming. Grant knew. He remembered the astonishment on Grant's face when he had asked, *"You don't know the Saint's identity?"* Even President Lincoln knew.

Lucas had been with her for weeks, yet he'd never guessed. He gripped the arms of his chair, his knuckles whitening. Her disguises, her ability to move in all kinds of social circles, her resilience in getting out of the worst of trials. The South would never suspect. He never suspected. Her undying faith, loyalty, and complete trust in the Saint…it was all because…she was the Saint!

"Is something wrong?" General Dodge prompted.

Nothing except his damned stupidity. "No sir, nothing at all." She had baited him countless times, his jealousy inflamed by a mythical lover.

The Saint may be closer than you think.

Lucas gritted his teeth and stood. The Saint…under his nose and he'd been a blind fool. It galled him…how cunning she was, and him so stupid. Oh, how he itched to get his hands on her.

"If you don't mind, General, I'd like to go to my quarters and rest."

"Somehow, Colonel Rourke, I have the distinct feeling that rest is the last thing on your mind."

Chapter 23

"What we gonna do now, Miss Rachel?" whispered Simon. "There's a whole passel of those Copperheads you been lookin' for downstairs and they's here on foul business. I can smell it as bad as privies ripe after a winter thaw."

Rachel and Simon hugged the walls of the upstairs balcony mindful to stay in the shadows. For a whole week, they had been under steady employment at the 310 Elm Street house in Washington, the same address she had seen on the maps in Rutherford's office in Richmond. Paid two gold coins for a contrived absence, the former maid had taken ill. In her place, Rachel had swept floors and cleaned until she was blue in the face.

The home was a huge rambling sooty brick structure, indefinable on an insignificant street with no traffic and too plain to gather any notice. A perfect place for those with nefarious purposes to meet.

There had been no activity other than the presence of an invalid and his doctor's occasional visit. Their surveillance was about to be given up when a mysterious Mr. Walsh appeared.

Then without warning, a whole horde of men appeared in the entrance hall.

She peered over the balcony and stepped back. John Jenkins, a neighboring slaveholder from next to her Richmond home greeted his companions. He'd remember her. The scar across his right eye gave him an eternal squint. She was the one who gave him that scar years ago. She had hit him with her father's sword when he had beaten his loyal salve to death for a minor infraction.

Rachel grabbed Simon's hand and yanked him in a storeroom. "We'll hide in here."

Except for the muted light frayed and thinned out from behind the chimney brick, they were engulfed in darkness.

Days ago, Rachel had surprised her servants at her home in Washington upon her abrupt arrival. They had been set into a flurry of activity to get the house in order, a modest home her father had procured for his visits to Washington. Before the war, her father had placed most of their remaining assets in northern banks and investments. Astounded, Rachel had learned his speculations had accumulated a considerable sum.

"What's the worst that could happen today?" Simon stuck out his bottom lip in that same petulant way Rachel adored. She had missed Simon's peculiar complaints.

"The worst," she conceded, "is that we get caught and shot for our endeavors." That would be hard to swallow since they'd not be able to find the real leader.

"But if you, the Saint, can't do anything to stop that den of snakes, Miss Rachel, how's the whole United States government gonna do it?"

Rachel smiled. Simon's undying faith touched her heart. "It means we have to work harder and think better to beat them at their own game."

The men filed into the library beneath them. Rachel and Simon placed their ears close to the back of the chimney flue, a perfect conduit for sound to travel. A half-hour passed with greetings and mundane cordiality and she allowed her mind to wander, thinking of Lucas.

Ever since she'd left Lucas at General Grant's encampment, she had been desperately trying to keep busy to purge all thoughts of him. As time ticked by, thoughts of Lucas emerged with nothing fruitful for her efforts to forget him. She rubbed her temples. The image of him with his fiancée taunted her.

Their marriage was a cruel quirk of fate and should never have taken place. She experienced a real loss at the prospect of seeking an annulment. In her heart, talking to Lucas wouldn't matter. He'd wear the responsibility tag on his lapel, and they'd just end up arguing all over again. They weren't compatible. Too different in ideals and philosophies. She'd be miserable existing under his tenets of belief and what he demanded, and he'd be miserable in hers. There was no getting around that. A hot tear rolled down her cheek and she brushed it away, forcing herself not to yearn for what she could never have.

Having to come face to face with Lucas again would provide more agony. Better to not see him at all instead of being reminded that he existed.

"And it will be a victory," Mr. Walsh laughed, taking repeated pains to inform his companions. "We are fit, prepared and well organized to embark on the largest conspiracies to thwart the tide of the war. It's proof of the Confederacy's resolve to crush the Yankee bastards." The men, no more than a lair of cackling and vengeful demons, cheered at the prospect.

"But when will it happen?" another asked, his voice as irascible as a rusty file scraping across metal.

"Soon. Very soon," Mr. Walsh confided.

"But we need to know—"

Rachel squeezed Simon's hand. Their patience and diligence had paid off.

"The hell you do. When the time comes you will be notified. One of our significant others is coming to town and keeps all his notes locked up in his library safe. He will give me direction on when to commence. I'll meet him this week at a ball I'm attending."

Rachel inhaled. For the Copperhead leader to remain anonymous he must be a well-known public figure. She pressed her ear closer to the gap in the flue.

"Perdition and hell fire will summon our Confederate brethren. A diversion is to be created. We're planning to wreck bridges, ferryboats and rail properties inside and around Washington. All strikes will be conducted simultaneously. Our main goal is to surprise and attack quickly. Our objective—to kill President Lincoln and Secretary of War Stanton."

An assassination attempt on Lincoln? On Stanton? Her jaw fell open at the boldness of what they were planning.

"And Colonel Lucas Rourke." Walsh pronounced the name with sulphureous contempt. "We didn't do it right the first time. We will make sure the second."

Rachel's muscles tightened. *Lucas.*

"Colonel Lucas Rourke? I thought our boys had him in Richmond," another man contested.

"They did, but somehow he escaped with the help of the dratted Saint."

"The Saint you say! If we ever catch that scoundrel, we'll hang him from the highest tree then feed his guts to the hogs."

Rachel fingered her neck.

"That's another issue," the leader snarled. "Unfortunate as it may seem, Colonel Rourke is back in Washington and too close for comfort. His untimely death shall be more important than ever."

Lucas was in terrible danger. What had Lucas come to close to finding out? Maybe he had been kidnapped and taken to Richmond for more than just information. A faint sensation grew out of different degrees of uncertainty, her spine tingled and hummed a mystery, untying knots. A thought froze in her brain. No. He was getting too close to someone.

A moan in the far end of the storeroom startled her. She crept through the darkness with Simon beside her, reached her hands out, felt ropes bound around someone. "I'm trusting you to not make a sound," she warned. His head nodded up and down. She untied his gag.

"How long have you been here?" How much had he heard? Simon and she had been working in the house for days aware of all the comings and goings.

"I was thrown in here two hours ago. You and the boy had gone for supplies," he said in a thick Irish accent. To Rachel, he sounded young.

That was true. She took her knife out of her pocket and cut

his ropes free. He grabbed her hand in a hearty shake. "Jimmy O'Hara's the name. I work for Colonel Rourke and must warn him. We must leave here with that lucky bit of information and the fact that they will wish to dispose of me."

He'd heard the Copperhead's conversation, too. Rachel agreed. Leave now. No time to question him further. But how would all of them get down the stairs and out the front door without being noticed?

When the library door rasped open, she tensed. Mr. Walsh bellowed up the stairs. "Where is that damned maid?"

"You can't go down there, Miss Rachel. Someone may recognize you and they'll know of you helpin' Colonel Rourke escape."

Rachel moved to the door. "You and Jimmy escape while I distract them. Simon, you must get this information to the top of the chain, the one person I know who will listen as soon as possible. And warn Lucas!"

Simon grabbed her arm. "How is you gonna escape?"

"I'll get to the kitchen and go out the back door. Now hurry."

Rachel jerked her arm from Simon's grasp and tiptoed out of the storeroom and to the top of the landing. "I'm here, sir. I must have dozed off while sitting with Mr. Edwards. He's ailing awful bad with his fever and all. I wish you wouldn't holler so. You'll wake the poor man."

"Get the men a cordial." Walsh's gimlet gaze fixed on her with all the charity of a hawk spotting its prey.

"Yes, sir," Rachel moved down the stairs. Two guards stood next to the front door, their interest in her insulting. She slowed her progress to give Jimmy and Simon time to escape. Her palms sweated as she gripped the railing, hoping the rest of the Copperheads remained in the library. She passed Mr. Walsh whom she'd met earlier in the afternoon when the doctor came. She felt his eyes on her. She skirted around him to the kitchen. He grabbed her arm.

"You're not the regular maid."

"No, sir. She's sick and gave me her job while she recovers."

"You've heard nothing," he demanded.

Knees shaking, Rachel pasted on a blank look then looked where he pinched her arm. "Am I in trouble for falling asleep? Please don't fire me. I have seven brothers and sisters to feed."

He pushed her. "Get the cordial and be quick about it."

She hurried to the kitchen and stopped cold, a gasp locked in the back of her throat. Two guards barred the back door. No way could she escape. She took her time arranging glasses to surround a decanter. She bobbed a curtsy to the two guards, picked up the serving tray and headed to the library.

The door was ajar. She glanced to the guards at the front door lost in conversation and took a deep breath. She backed in and placed the tray on a side table. Blank papers next to the tray aroused her interest. Like a magician, keeping her stagehand moving to keep the audience busy, she let her other hand do the trick. The papers were in her skirt pocket, neat and tidy before anyone noticed. She finished filling the glasses from the decanter.

"Walsh, I thought you said no one was about," demanded one of the men.

Rachel felt twenty pairs of eyes on her backside.

Mr. Walsh's tone was resigned but chilly. "Weren't you paying attention? I told you I hired a maid to care for Edwards."

Rachel kept her head bowed and moved to leave.

"Hold there, don't I know you?"

Rachel counted the steps to the library door. Never would she forget the deadly quiet of the room. She could hear the muffled clatter of horses and wagons with the jangling of harnesses passing down the street. A woman spoke sharply to a child, producing a solid wail. In the room, the clock ticked loudly. Rachel was by herself with a despicable group of men who would slit her throat on the spot.

Jenkins, a troll-like man with a pointed gray beard swaggered up to her. With tiny, button eyes, he stared. The scar across his right eye brightened to a deep red.

"I do know her. Why this is—"

Rachel moved fast. She hit him over the head with the decanter, and then hurled the tray into the crowd. Cordial splashed. Glasses splintered. Shouts of fury and surprise, and the cry for vengeance curdled her blood. Rachel ran. Headed off by two stunned guards, Rachel sped up the stairs. At the top, she heaved her mop bucket on the guards, hitting one square on the forehead. She heard the crack of his skull as he fell on his companion. Together they crashed and tumbled down the stairs, blocking the rest of her pursuers.

"Get her," screamed Walsh. "She's a spy!"

Rachel knew the rambling house like the back of her hand and forced herself into an all-out run. Suddenly, a hand shot out, grabbed her, and yanked her into Edward's room. Rachel smothered a shriek. "Jimmy O'Hara."

Jimmy locked the door, and then threw up the window, the sash violently vibrating. "Jump."

She looked out. Too far. The idea of jumping evaporated with the likelihood of breaking her neck. She shook her head.

"We have to, it's the only way."

Boots pounded down the hall. They searched every room.

"Go, Jimmy, and get help."

"No way, mum. You're the Saint. I ain't leaving you."

He'd heard Simon's comment in the storeroom.

Edwards moaned in delirium. The mattress the man slept on was a massive, bulky boxlike affair set up on cross-ribbed slats and possessed an air space equal to the deepness of the supporting box.

Rachel whipped out her knife and slashed open the side of the mattress. "Hurry, Jimmy," she urged then squirmed inside. "Either get in or jump out the window."

She scored an opening in the bottom of the ticking to breathe. Jimmy joined her.

Rachel pressed her nose and mouth to the tiny slit, sucking in the dusty air. The warm darkness throbbed with her racing heart.

Men approached...cursed. "Edward's door is locked."

Wood splintered as the door was broken down. Numerous men, their boots stomping across the floor, entered the room. Above her, Edwards tossed and turned in pain. Items torn from the closet thumped on the floor.

A feather tickled her nose. She smothered the temptation to itch it. She pressed her face against the slit between the boards, trying to fill her lungs and blow away the errant feather.

Someone pushed on the mattress. The bed bowed, and then

they moved beneath. She could smell the man's cologne. "No one under the bed. Nothing here, Captain Johnson. She's gone and so is the prisoner we had tied up in the storeroom."

Rachel froze. Captain Johnson. He was bold enough to be in Washington?

"The window's open, you idiots. They've escaped. Pick up her trail on the streets and don't come back to this address. We cannot risk discovery."

Men flew from the room. Captain Johnson paced. "When I get my hands on Rachel Pierce, she'll wish she was dead a thousand times."

Her blood turned to ice. The cold snap of his boots beat a livid rhythm down the stairs. The front door slammed. Rachel let out a breath. Other than Edward's snoring, no sounds emanated from the house. She and Jimmy squirmed from the slit in the mattress. Jimmy peered into the hallway and motioned for her to follow. He opened a window over a first-floor porch roof and helped her out. Jimmy jumped to the ground.

Rachel scooted down on her bottom, and then flipped on her belly, her legs dangling off the roof. She closed her eyes, swaying like a dead leaf in the winter wind, terrified to let go. "Catch me, Jimmy. I don't want to break an ankle."

Strong hands reached for her calves then moved up her legs. Rachel gasped, outraged that a young boy would take such liberties, vowing to give him a brutal set down once she was on the ground. Rachel lost her grip. She fell in a whoosh, caught in iron-tight arms.

"Thank you, Jimmy. You can put me down now."

But he did not put her down.

She opened her eyes.

"Lucas!"

"Exactly."

How happy she was to see him. The subdued tone of his voice stopped her, his grim face, a carved mask. She could see it in the flaring of his nostrils, in the high color of his cheekbones, and the glare of rage that glittered from his eyes. He wasn't smiling.

He set her on her feet and hauled her down the street.

"Jimmy, do something," Rachel quailed. Who could be worse at the moment...Lucas or Captain Johnson?

"Jimmy O'Hara will do nothing for you." He shot a glance at Jimmy who ran to keep up. "He's in my employ."

"Lucas, I must tell you, this place is riddled with Copperheads."

"Quiet, Rachel. You're in Washington, my town, and your insane activities end now."

"Indeed, Colonel Rourke. Then who is going to protect you?"

"I can take care of myself."

Rachel snorted. "That's why you ended up in the Capital of the Confederacy."

"I'll be watching my back more closely."

"Lucas, you need to know—"

"Not one more word. I command you to cease all your impetuous dealings and leave it to the big boys who can handle it."

Rachel dragged her heels. "You forget, I'm working for General Grant who is higher in authority...and I'm not enlisted in the army. You cannot command me."

Lucas scowled and yanked her forward. "I don't give a damn about what Grant wants. I'm your husband, and I command you—"

"You two are married?" Jimmy asked.

"No, he is not my husband. That was an unfortunate circumstance, and you are not to repeat any of this, Jimmy." She looked to Lucas. "I'll not hold you to the vows. No one need know anything about it. It's forgotten. See—" she snapped her fingers in the air. "Just like that."

Lucas gave Jimmy a warning that said, *get lost* as loud as if he'd roared the words, and then dragged her in a storefront alcove. He plastered her against the brick. "You forget we consummated the vows several times over as I recall with many fine remembrances."

"How dare you. What if Jimmy were to hear? He's an innocent."

Lucas laughed. "Jimmy does not have one innocent bone in his body."

Jimmy had helped her escape. She needed to defend Jimmy's honor. She tried to push Lucas away. He wouldn't budge.

Think, Rachel. She could not. Not when Lucas was near. Not when her senses whirled. A slow smile spread across his lips. It bore a strange note, hinting at a memory that somehow disturbed her more. Oh, she'd know the heat of his body, his warm lips upon hers, and his arms embracing her. There had been the touch of his hand on her breast, and a gentle caress along her thighs, and…the haunting sense of pleasure that now surged through her body. His manhood was hard against her thigh. She closed her eyes. *Would she yield to him right here?*

She swallowed and closed her eyes, longing for his touch. His fingers stroked from her chin to her jaw, testing the downy skin there. Oddly, she salivated, and was forced to swallow as a wash of foreign awareness poured over her like warm honey.

What spell did Lucas weave about her that she should desire again that divine happiness that left her blood pounding in her brain, leaping from her heart, and making her knees tremble?

"There is no escaping me." His silken voice deepened to a husky velvet. A threat of inevitable seduction. A promise of possession.

She opened her eyes. All the feelings of loneliness and isolation heaved like a cruel, crushing wave. She wanted so much to finger the firm line of his jaw, to take his ruggedly handsome face into her hands. In the narrow space of time, a hot ache grew in her throat as she studied his cobalt-blue eyes, fury mixed with arrogance, and burning tenderness.

No! They were wrong for each other. She could not let this attraction…no lust, go any further. It was unfair to both of them. There remained the fact of his fiancée. Above all, Lucas had to be protected. A large conspiracy existed. She must have time to put the pieces together without her mind cluttered.

Distracted by a shout, the clank of harnesses and pounding of hooves, she looked up. A runaway team of horses ground down on them. Rachel shoved Lucas away.

"Simon!"

She lifted her skirts and ran toward the wagon. A youthful hand pulled her up and in. Simon's usual sense of industry did not fail her. Jimmy sprinted and hurdled in the wagon and lay panting at her side.

She glanced back. Another wagon traversed the intersection blocking Lucas' pursuit. The last thing she saw was a chilling rage crossing his face. But it was the words he mouthed that chilled her to the bone.

I know you're the Saint.

Chapter 24

"War is fighting battles, not prayer sessions and hymn singing," said Lieutenant Bowman as they passed a group of women standing on wooden crates, righteously weary, yet singing and chanting their praises from divine avocation.

Lucas did not listen to his good friend. He'd left the Willard Hotel where out of frustration and a need for diversion he had dined with Lieutenants Bowman and Andrews. There was no particular destination as they walked past grazing cattle, leaving behind a slaughterhouse situated at the base of the unfinished Washington Monument where offal rotted three feet deep and clouds of buzzing flies swarmed. Along Pennsylvania Avenue, the air was better, yet dampness hung, and he pulled his greatcoat around him. From street stands, hawkers trumpeted cake and ginger pop.

"Where is she?" he muttered aloud.

"Pardon me?" said Bowman.

Lucas scrubbed a hand over his face, and then through his hair, tugging in frustration. "Nothing." He had not slept for two days. He was tired, and he was in no mood for conversation. He had checked every hotel, every place he knew, everywhere. Still he did not find her.

Jimmy O'Hara. A vein pulsed in his jaw. It would be a very sorry day for the young Irishman who dared to tip his hat to Lucas as he rode off with Rachel. To think Jimmy was on the United States payroll and worked for Lucas.

Jimmy was a young hooligan who had grown up an orphan on the streets of New York, and then moved to Washington. Jimmy's street-wise experience in the Irish underworld made him a treasured resource during the war years and to Lucas. Now, Jimmy had thrown in his lot with Rachel. Not that that didn't surprise him. Every male, young or old, she had glued to her.

Jimmy was Lucas' new strategy. The boy would lead Lucas to Rachel. Yet to catch Jimmy was like snaring fog in your palm.

"Are you going to marry her?" asked Bowman.

"What?" Lucas jerked his head around. Bowman smiled at him, and Lucas caught the jest.

"By the look on your face, it appears like you've been love-struck, harder than a double mule-kick," said Andrews, to his left. He was a good-natured man. Was he the traitor?

"No. It's a religious conflict," Lucas lied and glanced behind them. A hint of a shadow crossed the street. Jimmy O' Hara trailed them. Lucas bided his time. Trapping season was about to begin.

"No," Lucas fenced. "I'm a Catholic, and she worships the devil."

Bowman laughed and clapped Lucas on the back. He bent to Lucas' ear, low and secret as they turned down Maryland Avenue. "I must admit, I'm love-struck, too." Bowman clutched his heart. "She is the most beautiful woman I've laid eyes on, and none equal to her. I've met her at the last two balls and fought the groundswell to have a dance with her. She has a way about her. A wit and conversationalist like I've never before witnessed. Newly arrived this week and already the toast of Washington." He sighed heavily.

"Don't swoon on me." Lucas' voice was curt and unforgiving, out of turn with the jovial mood of his two companions. "No woman alive is that sensational."

"Except she's very mysterious. I wanted to call upon her, but no one knows where she lives. What's most remarkable are her eyes. Like amber that shimmers in the sun."

Amber eyes? Newly arrived? Lucas stopped. "Rachel."

Bowman was thunderstruck. "You know her?"

Lucas scowled. Here he was scouring Washington for her, and she was waltzing at balls?

Bowman turned west, an inky labyrinth of chaos in a seedy stretch of town. The sky quickly drained of all color, streetlights pricked the dark canvas of the firmament, and, above, the first stars appeared a line of smoky obsidian that clung to the horizon. The neighborhood was rife with the stench of the nearby canal, doubling as a sewer. His first impulse had been to avoid that area, but his present temper did not object, so he thwarted his initial inclination. Most of the soldiers called it "going down the line" where more than five hundred brothels offered horizontal entertainment to refresh the troops.

She had to be staying somewhere. Hundreds of possibilities flooded his mind. He had received a hand-delivered note via Jimmy three days ago, warning him of the intended assassination plots which he sent up the chain of command and sent out spies on the street to keep an eye on any suspicious activity. They also detailed his own danger. The little fool. Didn't she realize the danger she was placing herself in with Copperheads knowing he had escaped from Richmond with her? These were dangerous men she toyed with, not the standard issue infantryman she could easily deceive. Lucas' worst fears haunted him. What if he failed to get to her in time?

A muscle ticked in his jaw. Someone needed to tame that wild streak in her. If he caught her, and he knew he would, he'd teach her the lesson of a lifetime, keeping her naked and locked up for the next decade.

Damn. He wanted her again. Scoundrel that he was, he desired her splayed across things, bent over other things, on her back, over him, under him, beside him, claiming every inch of her.

"Any more balls this week?" Lucas grimaced in disgust. No doubt like a hound after a hare, she'd be attending and gathering information.

"The Adams are hosting the ball of the season. Oh no, you don't," protested Bowman. "I saw her first. She's mine."

Lucas gritted his teeth.

"I've been thinking about General Dodge's speculations. I believe the Saint is a woman, don't you?" Bowman said.

Lucas mouth went dry. "I doubt it." Lucas wanted to throw everyone off track. There would be bloodlust aplenty if anyone found out the Saint's real identity.

Had General Dodge had this conversation with Bowman? Maybe he hadn't. Lucas shoved his hands in his pockets, fisted them, then relaxed.

"And this business about the Rebel Captain Johnson is a witch hunt. He's long gone. Probably down the Mississippi and out of New Orleans," said Bowman.

A slight chill went up his spine. He didn't comment. No one, not even Dodge, had shared that bit of sensitive information about Johnson in Washington. If Lucas had figured out who the Saint was, then it would be a matter of time before the Copperheads figured it out. Lucas appearing at the Elm Street address and finding Rachel had been a lucky guess. But Rachel's presence there would set alarm bells ringing for the Copperheads.

The click of a revolver pressed to the back of his head jerked him to immediate awareness. Behind them several thugs swarmed.

"Let's take a little detour down the alley, Colonel with your friends."

Shoved forward, Lucas stumbled. With certainty, a well-chosen spot for an ambush. No witnesses, dark, and an easy escape for the villains once they completed their dirty work.

Lucas itched for a fight.

The first thug came at him, eyes wild, launching a right. Lucas ducked, the buzz swept over his head. The thug's momentum carried him in a curve, his kidney exposed for the taking. Easy enough, a question of force. Lucas hit a short right, a colossal blow, a blow that would have cracked a hitching post. The man pitched backward. Another adversary came at him, Lucas swung, landing a sharp blow into his face, breaking his jaw.

Bowman and Andrews froze next to the wall, their eyes large as deer caught in lantern light. No help there.

Men fell on him. He bellowed out an awful challenge. With lightning quick ease, he swung around, elbowed his assailant in the windpipe, broke another's nose and was doused in a shower of blood. The numbers were too many. He received too many punches and several men subdued him. Both Andrews and Bowman were restrained. Not a good spot to be in right now.

"I like you, Colonel Rourke." A man spoke with a Virginia drawl. "You're my kind of man. But don't confuse kindness with weakness." He smashed his fist into Lucas' gut, and he doubled over. His guards pulled him back up.

This man knew his name.

"I want you to tell me everything you know."

Was he referring to anything Lucas might have discovered concerning the assassination or Copperhead plots by his association with Rachel? "I know nothing." Lucas lied easily.

"No time for games." The Virginian nodded to his men. "You know what to do."

A knife flashed. Lieutenant Andrews slumped to the ground, his throat cut. Lucas roared. He kicked at the men holding him. Andrews didn't deserve to die.

"I'll be forced to dispatch Lieutenant Bowman to the world of spirits as well." The Virginian inclined his head to Bowman.

"Please, Lucas. If you have any humanity, tell them what you know. I want to live," Bowman cried. "Look what they've done to Andrews. Please don't let my death be on your hands."

Lucas snapped his head around to Bowman's blubbering. Once Lucas gave them information, they'd all be dead. With his full weight, he yanked down on his two guards and with savage ferocity, smashed their heads together.

"Now!" Lucas shouted to Bowman. Bowman stayed plastered to the wall, did nothing. Had fear immobilized him? Lucas raised his Colt revolver from beneath his cloak and pulled the trigger. Sparks ripped away from the exploding percussion cap, and the gun beat back in his hand. The Virginian screamed, fell back, clutching his shoulder. A Rebel aimed at Lucas' chest.

As if out of nowhere, Jimmy dropped on him, crashed to the ground and seized the gun. He directed the barrel on the Rebel, his resolve unmistakable.

More shots were fired from up above. Lucas threw his body into Bowman then twisted and rolled to the ground, out of the way. Men grunted and screamed, running in a melee. The smoke billowed and cleared. A score lay dead. Union soldiers trapped the survivors.

"Shall I give you a hand up, Colonel Rourke, or are you going to lay about the entire night?" said Jimmy.

"You certainly took your time." Lucas eyed the boy and a group of Jimmy's close companions who moved like unseen rats about the city.

He nodded his head to his two guards, approaching with smoking guns. They had followed discreetly behind. He would reward their diligence. Jimmy on the other hand…

Lucas gazed at Andrews' body, a look of cherubic peace across his countenance. Lucas bent and closed his eyes. He liked Andrews and regretted the waste of his life.

"Too bad," said Bowman, angling his head toward Andrews. "Do you know who these fiends are? They seemed to know you, Lucas."

Lucas studied Bowman who sounded remarkably calm—that

calmness seemed in sharp contrast to the woman-like wailing and inability to defend himself.

"Go on home, Bowman. I'll have my guards take Andrews' body away and lock up the rest of them for questioning. It's been a long night."

"What of your safety?" protested Bowman. His concern was stilted and contrived. The hysterical Bowman sniveling for his life? Bowman stayed too casual for such antics. His tone showed lack of concern, and that icy indifference bothered Lucas.

"I have my guards with me."

Bowman's glare to the guards grew hard and resentful. "And where did they come from?"

In a low, deadly voice Lucas said, "I ordered them to follow at a safe distance just in case something like this happened. Men, take Andrews' body to the undertaker. Arrest these traitors and question the Virginian thoroughly. I'll join you later to hash out this mess soon enough."

He narrowed his eyes on Bowman. "Go home and get yourself in order. I can take care of this myself."

Jimmy snorted.

Lucas waited for Bowman and the men to leave, and then gripped Jimmy's shoulder. "Despite what everyone believes, I've been long out of my nappies."

As he gave Jimmy a dressing-down, Lucas kept a wary eye on a familiar figure hiding across the street, and, as usual, dressed in disguise as a boy. His mouth twisted in wry derision as a sudden and new revelation occurred to him. The crazy little fool thought she protected him. She stood in the shadows probably gloating over the fact she had taught him a lesson. It took everything in his power not to dash across the street, grab her, and shake some sense into her. But she'd be long gone before he even came close.

"Where's Rachel?" Lucas asked, as casual as possible. He kept up a steady dialogue to keep Jimmy busy, so he wouldn't signal her before Lucas got his hands on her.

Jimmy shrugged, which didn't surprise Lucas.

"Why have you switched allegiances? As I recall, I hired you to work for me."

Jimmy snorted. "Her work is more important at the moment. You got the letter. You know the situation."

Lucas could no more change the belligerent juvenile than he could persuade the dawn not to come. "You realize this end of town is crime-ridden, and you understand she's my wife, and needs my protection more than ever."

Jimmy shrugged off Lucas' hands. "My take on it, Colonel Rourke, is you're a hothead around her, and the important work don't get done when you're about."

Lucas all but lost his temper. No way was he going to put up with an infatuated fourteen-year-old boy. "You are on my payroll and supposed to be working for me."

"I'm not in the military and you cannot command me."

And I don't need a lecture from you where my wife is concerned. I'm very calm around my her."

"Like two badgers going at it." Jimmy crossed his arms, leaned against the wall, watching him like a hawk. He protected Rachel from Lucas. Lucas counted to ten. There were bigger stakes at play. Andrews was dead. His blood turned cold.

It might have been Rachel.

From the corner of his eye, he saw her attention drawn farther down the street. She darted from her hiding spot and took off, no doubt following Bowman.

Dammit. She wasn't going to get away from him this time. Lucas broke into a run.

Chapter 25

The thought of Lucas dead scared Rachel to death. The guards posted on him were not enough. Thank providence she had the foresight to have him tailed by Jimmy O'Hara and his band. When the thugs surrounded Lucas and his two lieutenants, and shots were fired, her heart stopped. The smoke cleared, and she breathed a sigh of relief when she saw Lucas talking to Jimmy. Her stomach pitched.

Lucas might have been killed.

The ever-resourceful Jimmy O'Hara rose as a true hero in her regard. She and the lad had become fast friends, bound by what they heard at the Elm Street house and his adoration of her as the Saint.

She congratulated herself that she had Jimmy protecting Lucas. For other than those two guards, Lucas seemed not to care a whit for his safety.

Rachel pressed her fingers to her temple. Earlier, she had seen Lieutenant Bowman emerge with Lucas from the Willard Hotel. A familiarity nagged her. This week, she had danced with him at balls. He'd sought her out. Oh, the man possessed an underlying cleverness, and her suspicions grew like fire snapping in dry pine.

How odd when Bowman surfaced from the alley, not staying behind to help Lucas. With her kepi cap pulled down to conceal her hair, she followed him. On occasion, she hid behind barrels when he paused to light a cheroot or stopped to ogle ladies of the evening behind gaudily draped windows.

In the shadow of an oddly located Jewish temple, Rachel stood on tiptoes to peer in a window of a three-story brick structure, named *Gwendolyn's Glamourous Delights*. Expensive Brussels carpets, china vases, feather pillows, marble-topped tables and scantily-clad ladies reclined on plush furniture.

Rachel blinked. Harnessed in a corset stood a woman possessing mammoth breasts. Must have taken two days for her to be wired in. If released, her bosom might flow over Washington and smother all inhabitants. The laughing woman caught her eye and pointed to an illustrated sign, *Soldier's Choice,* listing various erotic services. Heat rose from Rachel's toes to the roots of her hair. Were such things possible?

In the distance, the bells of St. Patrick's chimed well past eleven. She rubbed her back where it ached, looked up the street. Damn. Bowman had slipped away.

She balled her fists and forged onward through the churning, sordid world. A rush of piano music filled the street with the clomping of horses and men's ribald laughter, far from wifely dictates and spousal reprimands. Rachel climbed up on a barrel to take another look. Barely discernible in the darkness, she caught sight of Bowman.

Standing Bear's lessons on the fine art of tracking game

proved a useful skill, following a deer for miles before finding an opportunity to let their arrows fly. The Illini had taught her well, but this was riskier.

Thankfully, the information she had gleaned from the Elm Street house had been delivered up the chain of command and the location was now being raided by the Federals. She had assigned Simon to watch in case any of the Copperheads had returned and to tail them. More likely, the Rebels had scattered, maybe even changed their grand scheme once they knew they had been overheard. Yet her instincts warned her that Bowman was involved as a shadowy leader.

Shivering, Rachel pulled her coat around her. Bowman gazed inside a lighted tavern and she melted in a shallow door entrance, counting to ten.

She darted from her hiding spot, passing several clapboard buildings built expediently to house new businesses—saloons, brothels, seamstresses, laundresses and occasional stable and apothecary. Bowman turned another corner. Can't lose him. She quickened her pace.

The night grew cold. Noisy soldiers milled around saloons, and a group of drunkards spilled out of a doorway, catching her off guard.

"What do we have here, but a wee laddie," said a ponderous, drunken sergeant picking her up underneath her arms and holding her high.

"Put me down!" she commanded. He laughed in her face. She gagged from his rotten teeth and fetid breath. Bowman was well ahead.

"Let's have a little fun, boys," he shouted to his fellow

soldiers. "Strip him down and take him up to Lovin' Lucy. She'll make a man out of the boy."

The blood drained from her face. She kicked hard, catching the toe of her boot in the man's Adam's apple. Severely winded, he sputtered and dropped her in the mud. Before she could crawl away, several hands were upon her, tearing off her coat. She kicked and scratched and clawed at her assailants, fighting for her life.

"Attention!" boomed an authoritative voice. The soldiers dropped her. Her breath whooshed out of her. On her hands and knees, Rachel scrambled across the street, tugged on her jacket before any of them realized she was a woman. Unable to see the man who commanded their attention, she thanked the Lord in heaven he'd intervened and used the momentary distraction to break into a dead run.

Entering a well-to-do neighborhood, she slowed her pace to catch her breath. Bowman vanished. She bit her lip, sickened by the prospect of losing her quarry. Luxurious mansions backed up against the pitch-black sky, smoke curling from chimneys.

Then, farther down, Bowman strolled as if he had all the time in the world. He stopped then disappeared again. She approached the place where he had turned, a driveway of sorts with an ivy-clung wall running along one side and a stable along the other, bordered with a wrought iron fence.

She kept to the shadows. Two hundred yards down the lane, Bowman threaded his hand through foliage, slipping through an aperture in the wall. A wood door clapped shut.

Like Bowman, Rachel groped through the vegetation. A key. She inserted it in the lock and swung open the door to a large garden with meandering graveled paths, boxwood hedges, a gazebo and a fountain, all the accoutrements of one endowed with vast wealth.

A stone mansion stood three stories high. Lamps burned in a room on the ground floor. Through French doors, gilt mirrors, rich oil paintings, a pianoforte and other lavish furnishings were scattered. Did Lieutenant Bowman live here?

Was he one of the leaders, if not the head of the hydra?

"Is your curiosity satisfied?"

Rachel whirled to find Lucas scarcely a foot behind her, his tall frame leaned against the wall, his arms folded across his chest. Gooseflesh rippled up her back. She darted. Rachel was quick, but Lucas was quicker. His hands closed over her shoulders in a ruthless grip. His face in the shadowed light gave no clue what he was thinking, but his mood was evident.

"What good will running do?" he murmured dangerously. "Where could you possibly go that I would not hunt you down?"

She pushed against him. He'd not budge. "You have no right to hold me here."

"I have every right in the world. I am your husband."

"For some insane reason, you cling to that fiction."

"You are my wife in every sense of the word. Or, will our child be fiction when he or she is born nine months from now?"

She had tamped down the possibility of a child.

"I thought not," he answered for her. "I suppose you thought it was fiction when those drunken louts were about to strip you down."

"It was you who—"

"Yes, it was me who stopped them. Can you imagine their

surprise at finding a woman? I shudder to think what that mob would have done to you."

"Well, I—"

"Of course not. You don't think. You throw caution to the wind. And now you're skulking around in the dark outside Lieutenant Bowman's home."

"His home? On a minor officer's salary?"

"Why are you so interested in him?"

Rachel licked her lips, trying to think of a plausible explanation, but Lucas' nearness scattered her wits. How she longed to see his smile. To feel his warmth. Rachel swallowed. This wasn't the end of her susceptibility to him, a weakness that would be with her forever.

She had hoped they could turn a blind eye toward their mutual attraction for each other, disregard it, or at least brush it off as insignificant. That was the best solution, and that was she'd set her mind to do.

Instead, Lucas had imprisoned her like an animal in a trap, and the force of his grasp conveyed the maddening conviction that nothing she said would make amends. Her heart pounded, furious with her vulnerability to him, especially since she had chosen to be more benevolent.

For an instant, nothing moved in the moonswept night. Not even a leaf stirred. The garden lay heavy, somnolent, and empty. She gazed into Lucas' eyes, eyes as cold and hard as flint in the meager light, and she had no doubt of his intentions.

He was ready to throttle her.

Chapter 26

She had made a fool of him by keeping from him that she was the Saint. Beneath that shimmering, glittering surface he had drowned in her monstrous deception. Her willful intent to obscure the truth, to mislead, to disguise who she really was had emerged into a cold and calculating betrayal.

What was he going to do with her? Lucas stared down into Rachel's defiant face, and he realized what he ought to do, understood what his best option would be, and was furious enough that he almost found that option appealing.

"So, you use threats and intimidation to force me into compliance?"

Lucas stood silent. Her breathing came hard and even. The smell of damp earth, and her scent—roses, clung to the air. He gritted his teeth. Why was everything so black and white to her?

The lamps went out on the first floor. Lucas turned his head, gazed at a brighter path of light. Someone progressed to the second floor, and then the light floated to the third floor and far down a west wing. The light hovered as if suspended then extinguished into darkness. Lieutenant Bowman retired for the night. Lucas turned his gaze back to Rachel, returned her hostility with a cold stare.

"Do you realize Bowman could have something to do with the Copperheads?"

She was predictable and singularly adept at changing the subject. "You're not going in there. I am." He kept a brutal step ahead of her thoughts.

"I'm going with you. Besides, you don't know if you'll find me here waiting for you, do you?"

Lucas glared at her. "Rachel, I will have this out." Lucas snapped and by God he would. He was ready to shake some sense in her, a full measure of determination to bend her to his will.

"Oh, you will have this out. You are bold enough to claim I should be your wife and bold enough to make it understood that I should bow to your every whim. You taunt me at every turn by some false duty you perceive. I do not want you, nor have I ever needed you."

They stood there, each firmly set in conviction, yet unwilling to yield. Anger seethed from each countenance, until their faces seemed twisted like evil demons. Incongruous to the calmness of the night, a mounting rage seized Lucas. He moved closer, pushing her against the ivy-covered wall until he left no room at all. A score or more of epithets were more than ready to spring from his lips, and well he knew that Rachel stood equipped to yield equal of her own. For each of them, there stood a reason too righteous to be surrendered.

"Why is it you are more suited to argument than rational thought?" With no time to quarrel, he preferred not to concede to an impasse, and grabbed her arm, dragging her behind him. "It's better to keep you with me to suppress your lunacy." He glanced at the sky. "There's a full moon. I should have known you'd be about."

"Stop this, you're hurting me." Rachel stumbled to her knees.

Lucas hauled her to her feet. "This is your idea of playing games. Believe me, if the Copperheads ever get a hold of you... your treatment will be much worse."

There waited a rat to be ferreted out. He trusted Rachel's instincts. But he'd never admit it to her. He, too, had his suspicions of Bowman and needed to lay them to rest. "Make sure you do everything I say and don't make a sound."

His temper escalated to the breaking point, his memory fresh with Andrews" pointless death. In two seconds, he forced open the French doors that led into a library.

"I see your talent for opening doors comes in handy," she said in hushed tones.

"I had plenty of practice in your home in Richmond."

"A lot of good that did."

"My point exactly."

Before Lucas could stop her, Rachel opened the door of the library into the hall and slipped out into the darkness. After minutes, she returned and pressed the doors closed in a light snap.

Lucas came from behind the door and she almost jumped. "What were you thinking parading through the house alone?"

"Surveillance. I don't want to risk an itinerant maid to come upon us. All is quiet. No lanterns lit. The servants have left for the evening or are sleeping. I heard snores on the third floor. Must be Bowman," she whispered.

Lucas stuck his revolver in his belt, went to a mahogany desk, pried open the drawers with a huge sounding crack.

"Can't you do that any quieter?"

He tried to read the papers in the silver moonlight that streamed across the room.

Rachel lit a candle. "Always come prepared," she smiled.

With bent heads, they scanned through papers. There were letters, invoices and bookkeeping ledgers. Nothing remarkable. Lucas shoved everything in the drawers. "Looks like your theory on Bowman is null and void."

Rachel waved him aside." Why would he hide anything in plain sight? Wouldn't it be the most logical place for anyone to look? After all, the Copperheads at Elm Street said he kept his plans in a safe."

Lucas started toward the bookshelves. For the better part of an hour, they soundlessly went through books to see if any were hollowed out and hid any incriminating information. After that failed, Lucas was about to give up. His wavering gaze fell on a painting. He strode across the room.

"Rachel, bring the light over here." He lifted the landscape, revealing a safe hidden in the wall. He paused and frowned, and then placed his fingers on the cold steel, deftly turning the dial, listening for the click of the tumblers. He swung open the safe.

"Another talent, I presume?"

Lucas rifled through the contents. "You've only begun to see me scratch the surface," he boasted. "Bonds, stocks, mortgages, made by Bowman's late father. If there would be anything to incriminate the lieutenant, it would be hidden right here."

A parchment envelope fell to the floor and Rachel opened it.

"A directive to attend the Adams' ball. Why would he keep an insignificant invitation in his safe?"

His jaw tensed with a faraway look on her face. Her calculation summed up his line of thinking. Someone important to the Copperhead scheme would be at the Adams' ball. "In the future, I forbid you to seek out anything more about him."

She stiffened in reaction to his warning. As he replaced everything, Lucas knew the sooner he confronted her about duping him, the better.

She was a ruthless liar.

"So why didn't you tell me you were the Saint?" he hissed, striking at her deceit. She'd pay for making him look the fool and keeping him tapping his toe with Grant.

In the wavering candlelight, she lifted her head to meet his gaze straight on then shrugged. "At first, I didn't know who you were, and I didn't trust you. Besides, I didn't think it was important."

There was boldness in her voice and in the golden eyes that gazed back at him, but despite her attempt at bravado, he felt her shiver of fear, and he formed an idea that might put a permanent end to her antics. It was a beautiful plan, and he felt the excitement of a gambler dealt a hand of aces—the game in his favor. Brilliant. He'd take the risk, using his own devil's box of tricks. He'd maneuver her, throw her off balance.

"You're frightened of me."

She bristled at his words. "I'm not frightened of you."

He took her hand and her fingers trembled. Hot wax from the candle she held seared down his wrist. He placed it on a table. "Liar. You are scared to death, and you should be. Don't faint away on me."

"I've never fainted in my life."

"There's a first time for everything." Lucas dropped her hand and backed her up against the wall. He placed one hand on each side of her head and bent his head until his face was only inches from hers. It was a dominating position and told her he had all the advantage.

"Let me go. What if Bowman discovers us?" she hissed.

"He's way up on the third floor west wing, gone to sleep and not likely to hear a thing. Like you said, the servants, if any are present are asleep. As for you, Rachel, this business is ended. I'm taking you home with me. I'll lock you up if necessary."

A small vein throbbed over a delicate brow. "For heaven's sakes, Lucas. Don't you think I would escape? I've done it countless times before. You can never hold me."

"No, but I can think of other ways to hold you."

She shivered beneath his grasp.

"I don't want you. I never wanted you."

"It's a lie, but you do have your pride. Tell me," he murmured, looking straight into her eyes, her face illuminated by the moonlight coming through the window, "why you continued to deceive me?"

"You were bent on believing I had a mythical lover, so I let you think what you wanted."

His back teeth ground together.

"What of your fiancée?"

"What about her?" Felling less than charitable, Lucas refused to let her know the truth. He'd been made a fool. Two could play the same game.

"Isn't it inconvenient?"

Mirrored in those golden pools he saw her shock give way to hurt. A part of him desired to tell her the truth, and then make love to her. But the other part, undeniably, wanted to put his hands around her throat and strangle her for her deception, and—for her denial of him.

Lucas shrugged. "I'm a reasonable man. I only intend to keep what is mine and for my pleasure. You may fight me being my prisoner." He moved his hand down her neck and beneath her jacket. He yanked up her shirt, pulled off the tight bindings that made her look like a boy. His hand closed over a full breast, rotating the nipple until it became pebble hard. "I encourage you to think of the prospects."

Rachel inhaled.

He plucked at the nipple. "This is the new Lucas. The one you'll not deceive anymore. The one you'll answer to."

"It's over between us."

He laughed, and then trailed a path down her slender waist, reaching down into her trousers. His hand touched her womanly folds, warm, moist. His fingers began a lust-arousing exploration of her soft flesh, the silk of her womanhood open to his demands. Her lips parted in a gasp.

Lucas sought to master her, to demonstrate that she belonged to him, and that any resistance on her part would not be accepted. He planned to probe to her very soul, to put his mark there.

"My dear girl," he replied with mock astonishment. "I wouldn't dream of letting someone go with your talents. It would be such a waste."

"What do you mean?" Her hands clenched to curb her shaking and she pushed at him to get free.

He'd not take pity on her.

Lucas upped the ante. How he wanted to punish her for making a fool of him. His fingers probed her femininity, deeper then withdrew, then probed again. A shudder ran through her.

He saw that her eyes were glazed with pleasure, and he strode to keep her mindless, stroking her, her woman's heat melting over his fingers until he bent her to his will. "I will release you, but that release will depend on conditions."

"Lucas!" she moaned.

She was about to climax. Lucas paused, but his fingers remained cupped inside her, controlling her.

"Do not stop…" she panted. "…what conditions?"

He did not answer. He began to stroke her again. She sank upon his hand, matching the rhythm of his fingers. He wanted her close—near the pinnacle of her orgasm. He wanted her promise, and by damnation, he'd have it at all costs. He brought her to the edge, then stopped.

Rachel sobbed, leaned into him. "Lucas…why?"

"You promise me, Rachel." He began to stroke her again.

"Now, Rachel."

"I-I promise."

"Say it again," he demanded.

"I can't—" She breathed in deep soul-drenching drafts. He knew she could not answer, her cry, a sign of her body's raging call for fulfillment. He aimed to shatter the hard shell she had built so carefully.

Lucas was not immune. It was the most erotic display of his life. Intoxicated by her scent, he pleasured her, attuned to her low sounds, playing a wicked and tantalizing game, making her weak with wanting. His body rock hard now, demanded her obedience, and he increased the tempo of his fingers, slick with her passion, toying, teasing, insistent, demanding, he moved inside her velvet folds unable to assuage his own pent-up frustration.

Lucas flicked his thumb across her hardened feminine peak. She thrashed as if lightning shot through her. Her head fell back, yielding to her searing need he cultivated. He watched her, satisfied as she grew heady with desire, rolling her hips against his hand.

"Lucas, please—" Violent tremors seized her. He felt her body begging for release, but his was not enough. She dug her nails into Lucas' shoulders, trying to capture the elusive peak.

"Don't fight it. You'll never win." His hand performed his magic, harder, faster. "Let it happen."

With each thrust, he felt the pressure inside her intensify, threatening to burst. Rachel climaxed in wave after wave, her heat flooding his hand, her body sagging limply against his, her whimperings, soft and sobbing. She clung to him, awash in a sea of sensuality, her strength drained.

"You're so responsive. I cannot help but think that your concession was pleasant for you."

She stared at him in disbelief. "You've made your point."

Lucas slowly withdrew his hand, flicking her swollen nub one last time, smiling when her body bucked involuntarily. "I warned you, but you did not listen, and as a consequence, you have forced me to take action."

Reality dawned at what he'd done to her. She struggled to button her pants.

"I hate you."

He ran his knuckle down the cream of her cheek, her musk still slick on his fingers.

"I could kill you, Lucas."

"A minor difficulty, but until that happens—" Lucas caught her chin between his thumb and forefinger. He scrutinized her face, admiring her passion-ridden eyes, the pert tilt of her nose and her ripe, lush lips. He kissed her roughly, savagely unable to control the volcano within him. He pressed his hardened groin to her thighs. "I will take you until you are senseless." Her felt her tremor, and his lips recaptured hers again. His tongue traced the soft fullness of her lips, then hungrily explored the deep recesses of her mouth.

Rachel tore her mouth away, but he wouldn't let her go. Burying his face in the crook of her neck, her breath warm and tremulous came quick upon his skin. He wanted to bury his cock into her. It would be so easy to sweep his arm across the desk and take her there.

"Lucas. You must stop this insanity."

A moment passed. When his head came up, his veneer became like ice. Her pleas sobered him, reminded him of the way he'd treated her, yet his seething lust possessed him. She tugged at him for another reason, trying to pierce through his rage, attempting to penetrate the primeval, sensual haze besieging him—to make him aware that they were not alone.

Damn!

Bowman's shout echoed through the house. Rachel, her tear-stung eyes, glacial now, shot daggers at Lucas. He shoved her behind him, keeping to the darkness. The door to the library banged open, light spilled from his lantern, his subordinate bent on catching an intruder.

Bowman leveled his revolver at Lucas and snapped off a fast shot. Lucas twisted. Bowman's aim was not good. The bullet struck the desk, splintering mahogany and ricocheting shards of wood into his belly. The pain stabbed at him.

He checked for Rachel. She had fled. Lucas leaped through the French doors. He didn't want to get caught breaking into Bowman's house. He wanted to keep Bowman under surveillance.

More shots crackled. He retreated to the shadows, escaped through the door in the courtyard and rounded out to the street. He paused, palming his side, warm and sticky from his blood. Far ahead, Rachel clamored on a horse behind someone at full gallop. Jimmy O'Hara. Contempt heated his blood. So much for her promises.

In a mocking tone indisputable to his ear, Lucas stood in the darkness. "I'll see you at the Adams' ball tomorrow night, Rachel. And that's a promise."

Chapter 27

Rachel stood in front of a gilded mirror in the entry hall of the Adams' home. The image of a woman in a red silk gown trimmed with lace and black jet beadwork and a décolletage cut dangerously low stared back at her. When she pinched her cheeks, the words, *femme fatale* came to mind, a tempting woman who had devastating consequences upon those men imprudent enough to yield to her charms.

Her lips turned up from Simon's objections. No way did he want her going out in *that* gown and would have to fetch Grant's army to protect her. Yet she had to put herself face to face with the Copperhead leader. As to guessing his identity, her instincts would be her guide.

She had already created a stir at two other balls she attended, inveigling herself in any way possible to learn more, if anything, about the Copperhead leader. Industrious Southern spies moved like furtive ghouls, elusive shadows in the night, stealthy and impenetrable. Time eclipsed on silent wings with the Rebel uprising drawing near. Her belly knotted. Fortunately, key Northern commanders had been apprised of the Copperhead plot and planned an anaconda approach to round them up…that was unless they changed their plans.

In her bones, she felt this night would reveal all. Etched into her memory was the invitation discovered in Bowman's safe. She swept a slow appraising glance over the crowd. The ball was her last opportunity to find the Copperhead leader, and nothing must get in her way.

She thought of Lucas. Had Bowman wounded him? When shots had been fired, she ran, Lucas vaulting behind her. Simon had checked with a black servant of General Dodge and allayed her fears, discovering Lucas' injuries minor. A part of her desired to go to him and ease his pain. However, there were destructive consequences to that impulse.

She contemplated the darker side of Lucas, the part she had come to dislike. The one who had humiliated her with her own traitorous body. No, it did not serve her well to continue her thoughts. Lucas was lost to her.

At least, he was out of her hair. My, how she liked the sound of that. She smiled imagining the look on his face when confronted by his superiors. A letter to the right man way up in the pecking order had cured her problem, and that man had ordered Lucas to stay away from her.

She didn't need him. Simon could protect her, along with the precocious Jimmy and his vast network.

She waited while an attendant took her cloak and directed her down a festooned hall. She moved to the opening of the ballroom then fashionably paused to obtain the most male attention as possible.

The cavernous room was alive with music and laughter.

Dangling from the vaulted ceiling were huge chandeliers, lit with hundreds of flickering candles, bathing the room in a soft, wonderful glow. Whirling in a realm of colorful silks and satins were ladies of Washington's elite, dancing with a number of Union officers and government officials. Laughter tinkled, wineglasses clinked, and the sweet harmonious chords of a waltz greeted her.

In no time, Rachel became the belle of the ball. From the moment she made her entrance, she had the rapt attention of everyone in the room. Feeling all eyes fastened on her, the occasion developed exactly how she had planned. With a surge of confidence, she lifted her chin and laughed at shared witticisms provided by handsome young officers. Fans snapped shut. Conversations halted. Men stared and flocked to her side, their conduct less than dignified, while worried mamas and young women watched in jealous dismay. Men, young and old, begged for a dance with her. More than willing to oblige, Rachel was led onto the dance floor with one dance after another wondering all the while what Lucas would think of her in a ball gown instead of one of her disguises.

Surprising her, Lieutenant Bowman appeared at her side. She narrowed her eyes, remembering the shots he fired at them.

"Would you do me the honor of this dance, Miss Pierce?"

Ill at ease, Rachel nodded her consent. How did he know her last name? When he noted the puzzlement on her face, he laughed into her ear.

"I try to know everything there is about a lovely woman."

Rachel flinched from the double entendre.

Bowman was memorable. His eyes...where had she seen that color before? He gripped her too close. She moved back.

"You are the most remarkable woman I've ever met. So mysterious and full of secrets."

Beyond a doubt, he was shrewd and cunning, and she dared little to trust Lucas' subordinate despite the fact Lucas said there was nothing to be found in Bowman's library.

"I do not desire to waste time on preliminaries but wish to escort you in the near future to a place, shall I say, very close to my heart."

Her gaze snapped to his. Years of studied diplomacy set ingrained in Bowman's face, making his sentiments difficult to discern, yet the calm in his eyes emerged more frightening than if he shouted at her.

"I would be honored," she feinted, bestowing a sham smile. She glanced over his shoulder to Simon and Jimmy, both with serving trays. A silent communication emitted between them. Bowman was to be watched.

The dance ended, and a portly colonel drew her away to the buffet table. She by-passed the duck soup, French chicken pie, veal, olives, sweet breads, fried artichokes, scalloped tomatoes, and pineapple pudding that the colonel heaped on his plate in healthy amounts, and sipped a cup of fruity punch which tasted sour on her tongue.

A loud stir echoed across the ballroom. Rachel stood on tiptoe to observe the commotion. The blood drained from her face.

Lucas.

He'd ruin everything.

She swallowed her panic, yielding to an unexpected rush of pride at the sight of him, so strong and polished, his bold looks handsomely flaunted in his navy-colored uniform with shiny brass buttons and gold epaulettes gracing his wide shoulders. He oozed power and strength and for the first time, Rachel saw Lucas in his true element, a man who was born to lead. Just by standing there, he commanded everyone's attention—even her.

"Handsome as a devil," said a young girl next to her.

"Why he's no devil, he's as sweet as a lamb." Her two girlish companions tittered. "I will simply swoon if I don't dance with him."

Rachel rolled her eyes at them in disgust. She had no idea what Lucas was doing here or what trouble he'd cause her. To unveil the Copperhead leader meant keeping Lucas from creating a scene.

The band struck up a dance, and a whiskered captain bowed before her. Accepting his hand, she allowed him to parade her onto the floor. Lucas had not looked her way, but she had the uncanny feeling he knew she was there. As her dancing partner whirled her around, she kept a wary eye on Lucas engaged in conversation with several officers.

A pretty blonde emerged, exquisitely gowned, and hair perfectly coifed. She tilted her head to Lucas. He broke rank with his companions, bowed and kissed her hand. As he moved into a dance with her, a ripple of applause split the air.

"General Webster's daughter, Susan," her dancing companion said, following the line of her gaze. "They are engaged, and I've heard it's to be the wedding of the year. Colonel Rourke has just returned from the south and completed a dangerous spy mission. He is a hero they say, bringing all kinds of information on Rebel defenses."

"And to think he did that all by himself," Rachel snapped,

surprising her partner with her sarcasm. "He probably walks on water, turns sticks to serpents, and throws lightning bolts from the heavens." Rachel's blood rushed hot in her veins. To think he took credit for all her hard work.

"I'll wager Colonel Rourke could bind any woman to him with nothing more than a few sweet words," the captain said. "He has a way with women when he chooses. He was a committed bachelor. To tell the truth, I'd never thought to find him waltzing down the wedding aisle, consummating marital bliss."

Rachel thought his conversation inappropriate and was about to tell him so when he continued.

"They say he was gone a lengthy amount of time, even believed dead, so you can imagine his fiancée's joy upon his return. Most said she had been pining away."

Rachel flashed a narrowed glance at the girl in Lucas' arms. The twit could pine away in a pine box for all she cared. Lucas threw back his head and laughed at something amusing his fiancée said, and then returned a devastating smile to the girl. Rachel's breath caught. A bitter stab of jealousy ripped through her. Lucas…enjoying another woman, and not just any woman, his future bride. Rachel's chest ached so much she could scarcely breathe.

Hadn't he'd informed Rachel in Bowman's library that she was to be used for his pleasure? But how could he love the general's daughter when he made so bold a claim on Rachel?

What did she care? After last night, she was over Lucas. She no longer loved him, no longer cared where he was, or what he was doing…or if he had a fiancée.

She must remain detached. She had more important matters to think about instead of getting waylaid by the legendary Colonel Rourke. At least in her work, she found a sense of purpose that helped tamp down the rising despair of loneliness. When she looked at Lucas again, his attention focused fully on Susan, her heart squeezed. *How dare he be so desirable!*

Rachel missed a step. If Lucas came near her again, he'd have a lesson to learn. She had fixed that situation for good.

When Lucas saw the number of covetous gazes following his wife's every movement, he raged with renewed fury. To put a saber through every man who dared to ogle her had merit. Yet he could understand. Seeing her dressed as she was literally took his breath away. Never had he seen her dressed like that, practically didn't recognize her without pants. As she whirled about the ballroom, her hips seemed to undulate beneath the silky fabric, hips that invited a man's caress, and sparked the imagination of every officer in the room.

His blood boiled, taking every ounce of his effort to stay put, orders he'd received from his commander not to go near her. And he knew *exactly* who initiated those orders. Two soldiers stood by a column. General Grenville Dodge glared holes into him, daring him not to interfere. Never did the irascible old general attend social occasions, least of all, a ball.

No doubt, after the harsh treatment and humiliation Lucas had put Rachel through in Bowman's library, the orders were her way to fight back.

Fine, he would stay away. But he could not keep his eyes off her. Her beauty was like staring at the dazzling sun and he didn't care if he went blind, and neither did any other hale and healthy man in the room.

Undeniable facts bubbled and boiled. Why did he come up with the ruse to marry Rachel? Of course, the Rebels dogged their tails. The wedding triumphed as a way to fool the Confederates. Lucas' conscience wouldn't let it end there. One single reality remained.

He wanted her.

He wanted to own her and possess her until she depended on him for the very air she breathed. He was formed and molded by his thoughts between his honor, his need to protect, yet to respect her for who she was. That notion came with cost. His fear couldn't afford it and his pride refused to understand it.

He loved her.

With a war going on, and the madness of the world surrounding them, he'd fallen victim to an outrageous and brazenly beautiful woman who endured his temper, mocked his honor, and refused to yield to his authority. Meeting Rachel was like being in the bottom of a well for a very long time, and then a rope was thrown, and he was pulled up into a glorious heaven. She captivated, charmed and exasperated him as no other woman had ever been able to do. Lucas couldn't imagine a future without her.

She wanted him, too. The knowledge slammed into his heart, nearly bowled him over. If she wasn't so stubborn and involved with being the Saint, she would have known it long ago. He just had to make her realize it.

He danced with Susan Webster, the general's daughter, despite her lies, but for one purpose only. To clear the air. Let her know the rumors and lies she'd spread would not snare him as she hoped it would. "I never proposed to you. So whatever wedding plans you have formed, forget it."

"Well, I never—"

As she blushed to the roots of her hair and gritted her teeth, he pretended to be engrossed in her company while keeping an eye on Rachel.

The whiskered captain pulled Rachel too close for Lucas' comfort, and then risked moving his hand along the side of her breast and down her hip. Lucas ground his teeth. Enough. He abruptly returned Susan to her friends and strode across the ballroom. He was not going to allow some hairy beast to paw his wife, even if it meant a court-martial.

When Lucas tapped the captain on the shoulder he'd intended to slam his fist in his face. But with Dodge breathing down his neck, Lucas suddenly decided to be charitable. He cut in without permission, taking Rachel and leaving the sputtering captain behind.

Rachel gasped and attempted to pull away. Lucas rested his hand firmly in the small of her back, signifying a territorial affectation, tacit and unspoken, yet clearly comprehended by every male in the room who witnessed it.

"You're apparently irresistible this evening," Lucas said, noting her eyes stabbing him like dagger points as he danced with her. "It is an unusual occasion for you to be wearing a dress, no less a ball gown."

"You noticed?" She flashed a sweet smile.

"So has every man here," he snapped. "But that is your intention, to keep them frothing at your heels with all your charms displayed in that damned gown. What are you thinking to go out in public dressed like this?"

"I like men who make fools of themselves. Like you…you don't hesitate one minute to make a fool of yourself. I don't think I've ever been in such inspiring company."

Her cutting remark could have been heeded a mile away. Lucas gave a curt nod to Simon and Jimmy, carrying trays laden with refreshment. With certainty, one signal from Rachel, he'd receive a bowl of punch heaved all over him. "I see you brought your faithful puppies."

"Apparently you have difficulty following orders, Colonel Rourke." She nodded her head toward his commanding officer. "I seem to recall you were to stay away from me…far away."

"A minor interpretation when it comes to being in the company of my wife. Nothing or no one will keep you away from me, and I shouldn't have to be under armed guard to keep away from you."

Rachel glared at him. "That is the sort of abomination you would imply." He looked grim and ready to throttle her, but he didn't frighten her one bit. "The vows are not real, nor are they binding. The marriage was a ploy to fool the enemy." She pushed away from him, but he held her tightly. "Stop it, Lucas."

His strong fingers pressed upon the small of her back as he whirled her around the ballroom.

She tore her gaze away and glanced about the ballroom. "Everyone is staring at us. You dare ignore your superiors and make a public scene?"

"I dare a lot Mrs. Rourke. I dare to hold you in my arms. I dare to kiss you."

He had power over her. *Damn him!* "You must stop this. You have your fiancée."

"Ah," he smiled. "A fiancée could be a problem."

"It is none of my concern." She twisted to get free, but he held her there, pressed to his hardened manhood.

His eyes were half-closed as he watched her. "Are you jealous?"

She flinched as if he had hit her. "Of course not."

Her body yielded to his power as he swung her around the dance floor. He dared her with his cobalt eyes, so penetrating, to remember the kisses the night before and before that...to remember what he'd done to her. To strip her bare, kiss her breasts, hold her hips, to sheathe his hardness. She closed her eyes. Somehow it was more of a dream and the ball, the war, the world blurred into unreality.

"I summon to mind how we shifted among the sheets, Rachel." His voice came husky, against her ear, inciting riots of sensation across her flesh.

"I tasted your lips, the hollow of your neck, your breasts until your nipples grew hard...there is so much pleasure I can teach you. Much more of you I can taste. Would you like that?"

Did she miss a step?

"There is a richness to your skin." He dipped his eyes to her breasts. "Like living silk. I'll never get enough."

Rachel panted. *Pathetic.* She strained toward him, toward mating. A shower of slickness moved down her thighs, soaking her pantalettes. All he had to do was throw up her skirts. *What was he doing to her?*

"Are you ready for me?"

She licked her lips. Dare she kick him? Break his spell? She scanned the ballroom. Everyone was staring at them.

"Lucas!"

He shrugged. "Let them look their fill. The men are jealous, and the women envious that I dance with the most beautiful woman in Washington."

Were they dancing? Too much. Her breath drew tight, her blood burned, turning her insides to molten fire. Her arms ached where one rested on his shoulder and the other held firmly in his palm. By some miracle she remained dancing.

The music stopped. Her breasts heaved as she sucked sweet air into her lungs.

Then she saw...he was affected as much as she. A momentary flash...a glimpse of the real Lucas...the good Lucas yet replaced with a mask of arrogance.

He chuckled. *Did he mock her?* Was he teaching her a lesson like he did in Bowman's library from an imagined offense?

His conceit sobered her. She raised her hand. He caught it, clamping hard on her.

"Our audience."

Rachel blushed from the murmurs. What a fool she'd been.

"You will always remember me."

She scoffed at that notion. How he excelled in using the right words to infuriate her. "Your memory barely scrapes the surface. I think about you as much as my horse. I am so busy with—"

Several officers approached to beg a dance. Lucas stared them down and they all vacated their positions.

"Amazing how you do that," she scoffed.

A satanic smile spread across his face. "Do what?"

"Put murder and mayhem in those eyes of yours. Attila the Hun possessed the same barbaric manners. Go back to your fiancée, Colonel Rourke. I'm on the Saint's business." She whirled away from him with another partner.

Oh, she was playing with fire. But she dare not provoke him to the point where he might throw caution to the wind, throw her over his shoulder, and carry her out of the ballroom. She had to keep a cool mind. End the nonsense of becoming a shameless wanton whenever he was near.

After begging off the dance, she moved down a long hall to the ladies' lounge and paused at an open window to breathe fresh air. Raindrops pattered on branches. She held out her cupped palm, catching several in her hand where they pooled together. Tilting her palm, the water cascaded to the ground.

"How sad that something simple and pure cannot last," she said aloud. The soft thud of slippers caused her to turn around. Susan Webster and her entourage straight from the choir, peered down their noses, and armed with gaily colored fans, employing them with enough dizzying force to blow a house off its foundation.

"Some things are never pure," Susan said, then laughed. Her friends tittered.

The quintessential queen bee, the general's daughter stood in charge and to Rachel's estimation, had not missed a meal. With practiced ease, Susan's smile went taut with a heavy dose of haughty self-importance, disapproval and rudeness. She and her bovine companions embodied all the qualities of a clandestine group of shrews—ill-tempered and full of resentment.

Susan had seen Lucas dancing with her and, no doubt, was nettled that he'd left her standing in the middle of the dance floor. Rachel squared her shoulders and attempted to move through the group, sparing no time for a silly confrontation. They created a barricade of silk and brocade with all the charity of an arrow meeting its target.

"Excuse me, Miss whoever you are."

"Rachel Pierce," she furnished, unable to fathom why Lucas would choose a shallow witch for his bride. He'd have the silly girl for his lunch.

As a veteran of contentious meetings with females in Richmond, Rachel possessed any number of weapons. To have a snake or a mouse handy might prove entertaining.

"Miss Pierce, you are newly arrived to our city? Where do you hail from?"

Susan desired to make it known Rachel was from the south to create an ambience of suspicion. "May I know the reason?" Rachel asked.

"Because I say it's important," said Susan as more of her friends collected around her.

Rachel lifted a brow. "For whom?"

"For the Union," Susan snapped.

"I'm sorry, Miss—"

"Webster."

"Miss Webster, it's none of your business."

"Miss Pierce. You do not know to whom you speak. My father is General Webster. He works for General Grant. We northern ladies are fastidious about our ties to the Union and see outsiders as a threat."

Rachel arched a brow. To think she had the fate of the entire Union on her head and she had to deal with the name-dropping

Miss Webster who secured her status through her father's rank. Wouldn't she be surprised to learn Rachel had met with General Grant, and his generals, including Susan's father.

"I am humbled by your admission, Miss Webster, and most happy with your allegiance to the Union." Her tone carried a whiplash of scorn. "I'm sure someone of your consequence must be busy with sewing socks and polishing boots for our boys in blue."

Like the hair on a spitting cat, Susan's bosom rose. She lifted her arm to give Rachel a full-handed slap.

"Rachel, I forgot to ask if your recent journey to Washington was pleasant," Lucas said, towering behind them. "General Grant sends you his warmest regards."

Susan's hand wavered then dropped.

"Miss Webster." He sounded startled as he folded his arms, yet his dubious look mocked her and indicated he'd seen and heard everything. "I didn't notice you. I hope, Miss Pierce, I'm not interrupting your chat with Miss Webster."

A wave of crimson climbed from the girl's bodice to the tip of her forehead. Had she broken out with hives?

Susan snapped her fan open and waved it. "I didn't see you, Lucas."

"I suppose not." His eyes flicked over her, making clear his contempt.

Shrinking from the confrontation, Susan's support group wavered, and then flew from the hall.

Susan pointed her chin to the ceiling. "Miss Pierce is from the south, and in light of this long-suffering war, her loyalties should be questioned."

Bored with maintaining his indolent pretense, Lucas unfolded his arms and moved to within inches of Susan. "Miss Webster…" He drew on a deadly silence until she squirmed. "There is no question about Miss Pierce's loyalties to the Union. Your lack of warmth and welcoming to a newcomer I find short in feminine qualities. Most certainly, I find envy and pettiness bad mannered and unattractive. Since you are guilty of all negations, I suggest you find other company to keep yourself occupied."

"I-I wouldn't marry you even if you asked me." Red-faced, Susan glared at Lucas.

"Next time, Miss Webster, you should allow the gentleman to do the asking. It might be an occasion to have your dignity restored."

She clamped her mouth shut, pivoted and marched to the ballroom.

Then, as a dark tower of lordly grace, Lucas lazily stalked Rachel…a man who moved with such finesse, she'd not marked his footfalls.

"I thank you for championing me, but I really had the matter in hand." She took a step backward.

"A skunk hidden in your purse? A snake concealed in your pocket? I came to save Miss Webster from you."

Rachel laughed, but as he stepped closer, she danced from his reach. "Lucas, you cannot compromise me here. I need twenty-four hours. I'm so close…" Lucas' lips hovered…so near…she could almost taste him.

"What about your betrothal to Miss Webster?"

Lucas frowned as if the thought pained him. "That was her idea. In my absence, she told all of Washington we were engaged.

Of course, that had to be clarified."

"Wait…you are not to marry Susan?"

His eyes blazed into hers. The candlelight, turned his eyes into dark embers, flashing every bit as hard and hot as tempered iron. Rachel licked her lips.

"Have you not been paying attention?"

He was not marrying the general's daughter.

Her chest burned, and her heart heaved against her rib cage. Finally, her body forced her to drive out a breath she'd kept wedged in her lungs.

The movement drew his gaze to her bosom.

Glancing down, Rachel found that her bodice had drifted lower. Her corset squeezed her breasts high enough that the shameful rosy crescents of her areolas crested above the contrivance, the ample flesh quivering in time to the trembles of her body. To yank her bodice up would give him power over her.

"I've missed you, Rachel." His warm breath caressed her face.

She must not—

He lowered his dark head to the hollow of her throat, dragging his lips across it. She shivered with the heat of his tongue, her hands curling into fists as her traitorous body surged with throbbing heat.

In a sensual haze, she peered over his shoulder, and then thrust him away, pulling up her bodice. General Dodge and two uniformed men streamed in behind Lucas.

"Colonel Rourke, I warned you to leave Miss Pierce alone. Arrest him."

Chapter 28

The library was quietly lit, the spines of many books cast their outlines in deep shadows on the shelves. Rachel closed the doors behind her, silencing the distant strains of the orchestra, and moved to the fireplace. She slumped in one of the several high-back chairs situated about the room, her heart beating a shameful rhythm as she clamored to get a hold of her emotions.

When the soldiers put their hands on Lucas and before he could wrench free, ten more soldiers seized him in their arms, grappling him to his knees, and manacling him. Like a mad bull, he fought against his chains...his beautiful eyes...eyes that moments ago held such sensual warmth...were cold shards of ice that flashed with murderous intent.

How he must hate her.

And she knew for one awful second that if turned loose, his long, sinewy fingers would wrap around her throat. But it was when he lifted his head that impelled her need to flee, to run to the opposite side of the world if necessary. Her blood rushed and her heartbeat thundered in her ears. *Flee.* Oh, God...she needed to flee, run away.

"Enough!" said General Dodge.

By her hand. By her orders. Like a common criminal, they had gagged and dragged Lucas away, escorting him out the rear of the house and away from the eyes of revelers. She couldn't stop them and say he was her husband. No, Lucas would get in her way.

Why hadn't she thought this through? Humiliating him that way, especially after he told her Susan Webster was not to be his bride. The shock of that news must have frozen her brain. She'd reacted solely on emotion, not rational thought.

Her vision blurred, distorting the flames in the fireplace and veiling the motes of dust in the dim orange light. Her fault. *All her fault.* Guilt stung like needles.

After Lucas was taken away, she hoped still to get the information she needed and had danced the entire night away… to no avail. Her back ached, and her face throbbed from smiling. She removed her slippers, letting them fall to the floor and kneaded her sore feet. Yet for all her effort, there was not a hint of any rebel activity. Bowman had departed early. She had missed her opportunity to find the leader of the Copperheads and had nothing else to go on. She'd failed. Lost her chance. Lost Lucas. Forever.

Her chest ached with the irretrievable loss.

She had no notion what she should do, nor did she have the mental strength to decide. In this moment she was only capable of sitting next to the fire and staring at the flames.

How she wished Lucas was there to comfort her. But he wasn't and he would never be there for her again. Tears welled. *Her fault. All her fault.*

She started when the door opened. *Please go away. Let me be.*

She was so tired of the line of cloying males. She closed her eyes, pulled up her knees, and tucked her skirts and hoops beneath her hips, concealing herself from view. As long as no one moved to warm themselves, they'd not see her.

"Let's make this quick. Tomorrow morning at the Ruther's place, five miles north of Washington near Steeple Ridge, we meet to finalize the plans for the night's activities."

Rachel gripped her skirts. The mention of a specific time and place prodded the hairs on her neck to stand at attention. The man's voice possessed a hint of a grating drawl. Familiar. How she longed to peek around her chair.

"Did anyone seem suspicious to you tonight?"

Mr. Walsh's voice, her former employer at Elm Street. She hadn't seen him all night. Dare he be so blatant to make a public appearance? To flee from the room and have him arrested. They would catch her and all would be for naught.

"No. I've kept my guard up. Frankly, I'm tired, and I'm going to turn in, so I can be fresh tomorrow. In the past week, I've been to Chicago, Baltimore, and New York, synchronizing our event. I assume everyone here is set. Have there been any difficulties during my absence?"

"Minor. The attempt to assassinate Colonel Rourke failed. We think the Saint may have been aware and interfered," Walsh said acidly.

Rachel pressed farther into the chair. Her shoes. She leaned over, stretching her fingers and picked them up.

"You idiot! I gave orders to make sure he was dead upon my return, and you call the Saint's presence minor? He could jeopardize our best laid plans."

"Don't worry. Everyone is on alert and ready to meet at Ruther's place."

"I hear Colonel Rourke was arrested this evening. Did you have a hand in that?"

"Don't know what the infraction was, but I'll learn of it tomorrow. He's too close as far as I'm concerned. But with him locked up, that puts him out of our way."

Who was Lucas too close to?

The men bid their farewells and departed. Rachel breathed a sigh of relief then thanked her lucky stars she had been in the library. Fortune had finally smiled on her this night. The only trouble was that she had not glimpsed the Copperhead leader's face. But if she heard that voice again, she'd recognize him.

Chapter 29

Rachel had been escorted from the ball by Jimmy and Simon. She had written messages, sharing intel to other spies working for her in Washington, and to the one man at the top she could rely on about Mr. Walsh and the mystery man. Chicago, Baltimore, New York and no doubt Washington would be hit soon in a coordinated attack. "Make haste to deliver all these letters to the men I assigned. And, Jimmy, be back shortly. Let Simon deliver the bulk of the messages. There is no time to waste."

Men would race out on horseback to comb the Washington streets to counter the plan formed. General Grant and other military personnel would be contacted. She ran her fingers through her hair. No time. She had to change her clothes and travel miles north of Washington and find the Ruther's place on Steeple Ridge, that is, if she could find it in time.

She unlocked her front door. After removing her wrap, she looked at herself in the hall mirror. A jangled mass of anxiety reflected back. Was that really her?

Ever since Lucas came into her life, he'd turned it upside

down. Not so incomprehensible, really. She was in love. She was madly, deeply, completely in love, and too afraid to admit it again to Lucas, especially while he was forced to cool his heels in a military jail because of her orders to not have him interfere.

Didn't love and stupidity go hand in hand?

After she completed what she had to do this night, she'd have Lucas released, maybe even give herself a few days' head start. She thought of the collateral damage as a result of her orders. To describe the rage Lucas would possess as threatening was to call the Sahara dry or the ocean wet.

To come face to face with him? She shook her head and her reflection mocked her. His revengeful nature would bury her.

She picked up the cranberry glass oil lamp, kept lit by the housekeeper. The lamp's crystals clinked against one another as she climbed the long flight of stairs to her bedroom, so looking forward to the tea the maid had no doubt set out. Given the late hour of her return from the ball, she'd given the servants the night off.

She'd wait for Jimmy, and then ride out to Steeple Ridge to learn the last of the Rebel's plotting and beat them at their own game. And that would be the end of it, the end of the Saint. Lucas was right. The Copperheads were dangerous, and it remained only a matter of time before they figured out her real identity.

She was tired, sick of the pretense, exhausted of the war sapping her strength and draining her emotions. There would be nothing better than to take up Lucas' offer, accept their vows and live as man and wife.

But she wasn't fool enough to leave herself open to that kind of hurt. Yes, Lucas had said he wanted her, desired her. But she wanted more. She wanted it all. Any woman could be desired, but—to be cherished…well that's what Rachel wanted more than anything else in the world.

With a rush of wind that beat down on the house, Rachel entered her room. Rain slashed at the windows and pummeled the roof. She yawned, set down her lamp, muted it, and kicked off her slippers. She proceeded with the gradual process of unbuttoning her gown, until the scarlet dress that had created a sensation at the ball fell to the floor in a soft swish. She untied the strings to her whalebone corset and threw it to a chair, cursing the punishing garment. She untied the pink ribbon on her drawers, sliding the silky garment over her hips, and down her legs. She shivered as the wispy chamois glided down her body and pooled at her feet, and that garment too she tossed to the chair.

In nothing but her stockings and garters, she moved to the mirror and massaged her breasts, so mercilessly pinched beneath her corset. She turned from side to side and frowned. Her breasts seemed fuller, heavier.

So many things to think about, her mind was drowning with it. At a time like this, Rachel didn't need thoughts of Lucas to keep emerging, pounding her like wave after wave. A bolt of lightning lit the sky, illuminating the room, followed by a roll of thunder. A weighty feeling plummeted in her stomach, Lucas, cold and alone in jail.

Rachel sighed. On the other hand, she was relieved to have him securely locked up and safe from an assassination attempt. She reached for her nightgown.

"Don't even think of putting it on."

Rachel turned and clutched the gossamer material to her bare breasts. "Lucas?" Her limbs shook. *Stupid.* To think he could be detained.

He hadn't made a sound. But there he was lounging in a chair. Low light and shadows made him look fierce. "Do you believe two guards could keep me imprisoned when I evaded the whole Confederacy?"

Close thunder shook the bricks, rattling the glass of the oil lantern and her, too. "How did you find my home?"

"Easy." His eyes appraised her, pinned her with those cobalt blue orbs, and it took all her power to step backward. "Jimmy may not leave a trail, but Simon leaves a path a mile wide."

His coat was thrown carelessly over a table, his boots stretched out in front of him, and he reclined like a panther confident of devouring its prey. His electric presence radiated as intense as the lightning outside, and from his fingers, dangled her corset and chamois. In his other hand was a brandy bottle he'd no doubt pilfered from downstairs. She was acquainted with his unparalleled strength and quickness, knowing that a dash for the door would not be prudent. Not to mention her nakedness.

"You might like to plot, but I like to surprise." He dropped her undergarments and the brandy to the floor.

Rachel cocked her head and lifted her chin. "What do you want?" she asked, her mind scrambling for options. What worried her more was the lethal edge to his voice, rendering the air to crackle and smolder with his menace.

Naked, trapped, she stood there, having no hint of what to do or what he might do next. Warning bells chimed. One trivial blunder, and she'd not end the Rebel rebellion. All she had worked for would be lost.

She forced a demure smile. "I could at this very moment be planning any number of things."

"You won't get very far this time." He rose so quickly, she cried out. He brushed past her, locked the door and placed the key in his pocket.

With an inaudible gulp, she composed herself. His commanding tone annoyed her, that same infuriating tendency that allowed no one to contradict his opinion.

"Frankly, I'm tired of chasing down the night for you," he said. "Your willful stand on this war has so dominated your thinking that it has become impossible to have a rational conversation."

She bristled, and his lips twisted into a cynical smile. "Sheathe your claws, Rachel. You better start listening to me."

"Really," she said, giving him a negligent shrug. "I didn't listen to you before. Why should I start listening now?"

"In my entire life, I've never seen evidence of anyone I could characterize as stubborn as you." He stood next to her, dominating her with his broad shoulders and her hands itched to undo the buttons on his shirt, to feel his warm crisp hairs graze her fingertips.

A flight of fancy she must stop immediately.

With her nightgown plastered in front of her, Rachel pivoted, knowing he'd have a fair view of her posterior. She had seen how the women in Gwendolyn's Delights were dressed and how they manipulated men.

A favorable answer to her prayer arose as her eyes fixed on the table where blank sheets of paper lay. She had forgotten about the papers she had taken from Elm Street. She sashayed like one of the ladies of the evening, allowing him to view her in nothing but her garters and stockings and rewarded when she heard a ragged oath. Oh, to wield such power.

"Lucas, I took these from the Rebels. They must have some importance." She lifted them for his perusal.

"Why didn't you show me these before?" He plucked a lemon next to a teapot and squeezed it over the papers. "It's an old trick. When messages are written in soda bicarbonate and dried, they are invisible. Adding an acid makes what they've penned appear."

Shoulder to shoulder, they stood while magically letters formed and whole words appeared. She allowed a lock of her hair to fall on his shoulder. She drew it back and his nostrils flared. Good, he'd fall for her charms a little at a time. She had to hurry for Jimmy would be back soon. "Lucas, these are their names, all their contacts."

She pressed a hand to her abdomen. "Except Lieutenant Bowman's name is not listed."

"You will end your obsession with Bowman, and despite your finger-pointing at him, there is no evidence. Impossible. Do not allow your naivety to get the best of you."

She pushed away from him, knowing full well he suspected Bowman. "And you're being conceited. I'm telling you of my concern. You won't find me nodding my head at everything you say, and I'm going to tell you what I think and feel. I have the oddest feeling about him, like I know him from somewhere. "I learned tonight at the ball from Walsh who made a mysterious last minute appearance that the Copperheads will finalize their plans at Steeple Ridge, five miles from here."

He swept his arm across the papers and they flew to the floor. "Not one more word."

"We'll have tea and discuss further," she said, bending over to give him a full view of her breasts while she poured tea. Thank God she had sent off the information before her run-in with Lucas.

"Tea?" He looked her up and down.

"Brandy then?" With the practiced ease of a courtesan, she slowly stooped, and swayed her hips as she snatched the brandy from the floor. She tamped down a smile when she saw the surging heat in his loins. She ran the tip of her tongue across her lips, and turned her back to him, affected by the heat of his gaze and the warm gush in her nether regions. Hands trembling, she yanked a vial from her reticule. For every defense, she now possessed a shaft in her quiver, knowing he was under her control. She popped the top and dumped in the contents, and then offered the brandy tainted with a sleeping draught to Lucas, hoping he'd not seize upon the bitter taste.

Must keep him talking. She turned, poured herself tea, and then swiveled to survey him over the rim of her cup. "I found out at the ball everything is going to occur tomorrow night. You must telegraph New York, Baltimore and Chicago and warn President Lincoln and Secretary Stanton. It's important we move as quickly as possible to round these men up."

"Not we. I will." His smile could freeze the equator. "I'm tired of your recklessness. You are going nowhere. I'm tying you to that bed. I will leave here and make sure the telegraph office sends out warnings."

"I won't back off, not even for a minute." Her resolve was

final, and she cringed when he tossed back the last two drops of his brandy and slammed the bottle on the table.

"I thought not."

She stood her ground, her heart drumming in her ears. He grasped a tendril of her hair and rubbed it between his fingers, as a weaver assessing the quality of rich silk. The color of his cobalt eyes deepened, almost black, too fiendishly clever, and penetrating, eyes that could spark fire and turn her loins to molten liquid. His features were hard, his expression, unrestrained.

He was living, breathing sin.

Standing right in front of her.

When will the sleeping draught begin to *work?* Keep him busy.

Lightning blanketed the sky in blinding brilliance, shifting the deep hollows and chiseled planes of his features into a queer light. The raw intimacy of only a filmy nightgown lay between them. "You could leave, Lucas." Her hopeless compromise faded away.

"Is that what you really want me to do?" His voice was warm and rough. It frightened her more than his vehemence.

"Yes." She smelled the rich brandy on his breath combined with his raw masculine scent.

"You're a lousy liar." He made the accusation. "You are quivering like an aspen. I thought you had more backbone." He challenged her, and then smoothed his knuckles over her cheek. She half-closed her eyes and blushed, remembering the power of his fingers touching her. Her throat constricted, and her senses reeled with conscious perception.

Light coming from the lantern slid along the dark strands of his hair, and his mouth...oh, his fine mouth with lips, smooth, firm, and far too close to hers. Those fine lips brushed against hers, softly, ever so lingeringly, teasing her with intent.

"Tonight, Rachel I'll take care of the rest of the world." He whispered sultrily to the curve of her ear." It's me, you desire." His white teeth grazed her neck. "Badly." He tore away the nightgown, the last barrier between them. "I want you naked."

She nearly melted as Lucas swung her up into his arms and gently positioned her on the bed. Heart pounding, she lay overwhelmed by the full-blooded male and the power coiled within him. Of her own accord, she unbuttoned his shirt then flattened her hands on his chest, pushing, gliding over his silky skin.

"Lucas, we have more important issues," she whispered amazed she possessed any faculties at all. Was he resistant to the dosage? She had dropped in enough to knock out five bulls.

"Dare you try my patience? I am between you and that door." He caught her nape and kissed her with a hunger that insinuated his need. "Never again." His tongue probed her mouth, but the impression succeeded as an overall invasion.

She entwined her arms around his neck and a sob of yearning welled in her throat.

Lucas stopped and pulled her arms from him. He jerked out of his shirt and pants and threw them aside. His body was a profusion of swells and divots of strength and bone. A voice of reason dictated her to move her eyes away, but another more powerful inclination refused to let go of the brain-numbing sight before her. His chest expanded in hard disks, and his ribs scaled down a broad, flat torso, narrowing to obdurate mounds of stomach muscles. She stared at her magnificently nude husband.

"Enjoying yourself?" he smiled and lay on top of her.

His kisses were more demanding, hotter as if he had a whole lifetime to make up for his need of her. She writhed beneath him, terrified of how he made her feel, losing all control. Shameless, she arched her back when he took a soft dusky breast into his warm mouth. He nibbled at it, pulling taut with his teeth, then lavishing his tongue around the swollen peak.

Rachel could scarcely breathe or think, feeling his rapid heartbeat on her breast as he moved his knees between her thighs, her womb clenched on an aching emptiness. Shameless again, she spread her legs and he ground his loins against her softness, rock-hard he thrust into her, and she cried out with erotic pleasure coming from every pore of her body.

Oh, his body. Long and lithe and lethal, it rocked against her in a percussion so ancient, so achingly necessary, it called to the very soul of her. Lucas carried her from one pinnacle of pleasure to another, hypnotizing, and tenderly worshipping her, like a crusader would a relic. His eyes were bright and savage as she soared and shuddered in endless ecstasy. Shameless.

Cries broke out between them. His. Hers. She couldn't be sure. Low. Guttural. Animal. And they were followed by a violent reaction on his part.

She pulled him with her into a glorious place. One made of harsh breaths and moans. Time blended with the storm, as a flash of lightning pierced the night, striking them as its equal impaled through their joined bodies. The gratification just as hot and searing. The pleasure just as striking. And the emotions as obligatory as an agreement one signs with destiny.

"Rachel," he whispered, simply for the pleasure of saying her name. No sooner was the word out of his mouth than his lips found hers again. She moaned, and he deepened his kiss.

He pulled back and shook his head, hanging on to her. The drug she gave him was beginning to have its effect. The look he gave her, she'd never forget. When Judas kissed the savior, selling him for thirty pieces of silver, the look of raw betrayal.

"Why?" He collapsed next to her, and she stroked the damp hair across his forehead. He slept deeply, the drug she'd slipped in his brandy had achieved its predicted result. Rachel flipped her pillow, found a cool place to rest her cheek, and tried to ignore the tears falling down her face.

"Lucas, I love you."

For a moment, she thought he'd heard her. A slight grunt escaped him, and his jaw flexed. He snored…at peace.

Her fate was sealed. No. He'd never forgive her. He'd despise her for what she had done to him. There was only so much a man of his proud bearing could take. She didn't blame him.

Rachel agonized over deceiving him. But he left her with no other option. She had to stop the evil before it commenced. With her network backing her, she had to save President Lincoln and put a halt to the war that brought with it the chains of slavery and reaped so much misery. And as much as there was a crushing foreboding spanning her heart, she must stop the plotters who were going to kill Lucas.

She dressed, her throat choked as she bent to kiss Lucas on his warm lips. He was safe here. Away from any would-be assassins. He'd sleep most of the day and into the night. Just to make sure, Rachel took the key from his pocket and locked the door.

Chapter 30

Rachel and Jimmy had circled the property, frustrated with no conspicuous activity. The farmhouse appeared as any other farmhouse in the Piedmont, white clapboard, shingled roof, porch, hitching rails, barn out back and orchards running up the hillside. Except it remained vacant. She motioned to Jimmy to tie up their horses.

Her sides trickled with perspiration. She shouldn't feel so panicky. She'd been in worse straits. A wind whistled through the trees, snatching at her hair, chilling her bones. "Wait here. I want to move in closer."

"No," Jimmy spoke sharply. "It's too open. We'll move through the trees and keep out of sight. I have a bad feeling. Maybe you shouldn't have been so quick to have Colonel Rourke locked up. We could have used him."

She kept her gaze on the farm below. Jimmy echoed her thoughts. "This is a surveillance. I need to learn what I can."

A harsh bark of laughter rolled over the ridge. They crept across a jagged slope. A group of men, some on foot, a number on horseback, all civilians, stopped on an apex of a bare knoll.

Behind them, the last of the setting sun illuminated the landscape in vermilion and gold, and beyond laid a wooded valley, fenced pastures and shadowed glimpses of a stream. Why they were in the open proved their careless regard and open disdain for the country they'd come to ruin. Their excess of passion would be their undoing if she had anything to do about it.

Wild blackberry briars tore at her hands. She inched through a thicket, her tread light.

"You want to go to hell," the cold muzzle of a revolver shoved against her neck, "I can give you a ticket there." From out of dark shadows, they had been stalked. She turned, sickened, realizing Jimmy had also been taken unaware. The young Irishman shrugged to her.

"I can explain…" she began, trying to shoehorn them out of the situation, "this young man and I were going to pick apples over in yonder orchard when we heard a commotion. If you'll just let us go, we'll be on our way."

In one fluid motion, she pushed the gun away from her and kicked the man in the shin. She rolled to the ground, grabbed dirt and threw it into the other guard's eyes. "Run, Jimmy. Run!"

Hurtling through the brush like a jackrabbit, Jimmy sprang. The guards fired off a couple of shots. Long gone, Jimmy disappeared into the forest like a phantom. She exhaled, saying a prayer. He escaped.

Her guards yanked her up and hauled her to the top of the hill to stand before the enemy. Derision covered their faces and murder glittered from their eyes as they looked her over like a hung deer fresh from the kill. Rachel bore the brunt of all as if a sharp knife stabbed her, cutting all her worthy intentions to ribbons.

"Damn her. She could be as beautiful as Venus, but I'd hang her from the tallest tree," snapped one of the men surrounding her.

She blinked. Captain Johnson! Nerves rattled up her spine. He was her worst fear. Her worst nightmare.

"Miss Pierce." He nodded. "I'm glad to see you. You're pretty precise at turning a card, but I think we've got you on the last shuffle. We watched you at the ball…knew our staged conversation in the library would interest someone with your…talents."

Rachel swallowed. "I'm afraid I don't understand what you mean."

Johnson stood an inch from her face. "Don't insult my intelligence by playing the silly female. We know you're the Saint. Figured it out at Elm Street. That was your misfortune. But to tell you the truth, I was suspicious of you back in Richmond. All defenses and troop movements dispatched to the Union. Every time, it was after you had been present with some trumped up appearance. When I saw Colonel Rourke at your home, it cemented my suspicions."

"Clever you are to make such a deduction, if your allegations were true, but which they are not."

Johnson's eyes narrowed. "Let's not insult either of our intelligences. I congratulate myself for I'm clever enough to have you where I want you."

"I'll betcha she runs like a bitch in heat." A man spat an amber stream of tobacco juice on the ground next to Rachel's feet. He admired his shot and regarded her with scorn.

"Vengeance is mine, sayeth the Lord, and I will repay." Johnson laughed low, laid a confiding hand on her shoulder.

She flinched. Then he leaned so close, she smelled the onions on his breath. "I'll finish what I began in Richmond. You do remember our dalliance in your barn before Colonel Rourke interrupted us?"

She thrust his hand from her shoulder. Two men rode up and she cranked her head to await the new arrivals. Mr. Walsh from Elm Street, and the other, remained hidden until they cleared a path for him.

Lieutenant Bowman.

Her instincts had been correct. Lucas had it all figured wrong, his most trusted colleague entangled in a den of serpents.

Bowman dismounted, stood next to Johnson. Despite subtle differences their features were the same. Why they could be brothers.

"So you noticed. We're half-brothers, different mothers but rooted from the same pappy," Bowman said. "Our pappy had a predilection for passing on his seed to many women."

"How convenient for the Confederacy…two snakes from different litters," Rachel challenged with a slight smile of defiance and decided to play the fear card. "Tell me, how do you know the Union army is not surrounding this place?"

"Believe me, Miss Pierce. I would know," said Bowman. "Old General Dodge is home sound asleep. You forget I work in the Office of Civilian Spying."

"How could I forget? You were the one who set Lucas up. You were the one giving information to Rebel spies. You are despicable."

"I agree. But we have short time here, Miss Pierce." Bowman's voice cut like a knife through the gathering darkness. "This meeting is for your benefit. To have trapped the Saint is a monumental victory for us. To celebrate our victory, both my half-brother and I will sample your charms before we hang you."

"Of course," she said, her knees shaking.

Lucas' words haunted her, warning her of the perilous game she played. These men were the cream of the Confederacy, the seasoned, hard-bitten bunch who moved furtively like rabid rats that destroyed everything and anyone in their path. Johnson tied her wrists and marched her down to the house, his sword clanging against his thigh with every step.

Rachel heard the shots in the distance and jerked her head around.

"We got 'em, Captain," they yelled from the forest.

"Your young friend, I presume?" Johnson taunted.

"Jimmy!" Rachel choked back a sob. Had they had killed her sweet, adorable protector? Oh, good God, Jimmy didn't deserve to die. She fought the tears that threatened, silenced the scream of agony that tore from her heart. *Her fault.* She was to blame.

The sun plummeted behind the ridge and, with it, her spirits sank. She kicked at Johnson, catching the toe of her foot beneath his heel. Johnson cursed as he stumbled and spun around, his full six-foot frame toppled to the ground and slammed onto packed earth.

One of the men snickered. "Looks to me, Captain, you're going to have your hands full tonight."

Rising, he spat out, "You bitch. I'll teach you to show respect. The kind of respect you'll never forget." He rammed her forward, knocking her to her knees, the heels of her bound hands plowed the earth.

With a tether tied to her, he yanked her up with such force, the ropes whip-sawed her skin. He dragged her after him, and hauled her into the house, and passing a gap-toothed guard, disrupted him from his game of solitaire. Johnson prodded her up the stairs, then thrust her into an enormous room, which by all appearances, seemed to be the entire second floor of the home. Johnson locked the door and turned to her.

"I do so love war," he sneered, his fingers playing on the hilt of his sword. "I really do love this war as it makes my blood run hotter."

Her muscles tensed, remembering how she had humiliated him in front of his men, and the brutality this monster could inflict. He snickered, then set her bonds free. "I like my women to give me a little fight."

Hoofbeats thudded in the distance. She dared to glance out the window, knowing any chance of help would have been with Jimmy's escape. But Jimmy was dead and no one else knew of her whereabouts to come to her aid.

Ragged clouds moved to cover the moon and cloak its brightness. In defense, the moon rose free of its gauzy web and touched the tops of the trees with ghostly silver. A mounting wind keened about the house, then veered to stir the oak outside the window. Now stripped of leaves, its branches clawed the house.

A rider galloped through the trees, a rough silhouette illuminated by the waxing moon.

"My messenger," Johnson furnished as he watched her, his delight at her nervousness evident. "He tells me every fifteen minutes if soldiers advance on us. So be rest assured, I will not be cheated of my time with you." He poured himself a whiskey from a bottle on a table next to a large overstuffed chair and gulped it down in one swallow. He hissed through his teeth. "Ah. Now where were we?"

"We weren't anywhere." She circled the room, inching away from him, aware of any sudden move on his part. She'd fight him with every ounce of her strength. Her fingers brushed a window pane. How easy to throw up the sash and jump?

"I took the liberty of nailing the window shut, just in case you have thoughts to escape. The Saint seems to fly out windows." He kicked up a three-legged stool, toying with her to produce greater fear, a sick game of power.

Stay confident, unafraid, anything to hold his violent inclinations at bay.

"You know what I did to a slave girl who dropped a cream pitcher on my trousers?"

She yawned, feigning boredom. "I can't imagine."

"I raped the bitch over and over to teach her a lesson. She dared to expire on me. Not one of them died that soon. So, I kicked her whole body until my boots were worn and bloody."

He snickered again, and if reptiles could make such an insidious laugh, it would sound just as horrendous.

Rachel shivered. "What does your story have to do with me?" she said, stalling for time. Her gaze darted and she kept moving, always keeping something between them. There had to be a way out of this mess. Her heart panged. Simon was in Washington delivering messages, and she had drugged Lucas. How she wished she had listened to him.

"Once I got me and twelve-year-old girl slave. Itty-bitty thing. How I loved to hear her howl. I played with her for six months. Made her mama watch too. Her mama hollered pretty good too."

With slow deliberate steps, she paced, forcing herself to appear unhurried, despite the pleasure he took regaling her with his sick deeds. Her palms sweated, and she stopped to strike a pose of avid interest. "Go on."

"Up north, I met a real nice woman. Fancy. I plunked myself on her doorstep and refused to move, letting her know I was courting her. She looked like you. They all looked like you."

"All?" She stared at him, the bowels of hell seen in his evil features. "You raped and killed them all?"

"The list is endless. They all looked like you, Rachel. Even the slaves had a hint of you."

Good God! He carried a perverse torch for her. Rachel bit her lip, the salty taste of her blood palpable on her tongue. For the first time, she knew not what to do. *Escape.* Her only alternative. But somewhere outside were thirty Copperheads. Inside, she stood trapped with Johnson between her and the door and the guard in the kitchen. She scanned the room for something she could use as a weapon…a bed, a lantern, and the stool he sat on. Nothing.

She glanced out the window, considered smashing the glass to jump out, then through the cloying darkness, a furtive shadow moved from the tree line to the barn. If this was a cruel joke, if someone decided to torment her further…only, there it was again, just a hint of movement. Her heart slammed into her chest. She'd recognize his form anywhere.

Lucas!

He came for her. Oh, thank God, he came. A bud of hope blossomed inside.

"Captain Johnson, tell me how you learned I was the Saint." She must sound unconcerned…delay…give Lucas time.

"Enough!" He snapped out of his morbid story trance and stalked over to her. He shoved his face directly in front of hers. His eyes gleamed, his lips thinned, then curled up in a sneer. "I want to hear you scream…to beg me."

Lucas stopped next to the barn, hanging back, melting into the evening gloom, waiting for the two guards circling the edifice. The moonlight was on his side, casting long shadows from the house, his own outline melting into the evening silhouettes. He rammed his fist into the first guard, plowing him into the next, dispatching them both. Many of their numbers were meeting in the barn, near three dozen of them.

His gut tightened. He'd seen Johnson drag Rachel into the house. He could only imagine what abuse the monster planned and itched to get his hands on the bastard.

He dashed to the house, stepped onto the porch and edged to the window. One guard reclined next to a potbelly stove. Bending low, Lucas picked up a stone and hurled it at the door. His ruse was a good one. The guard unlocked the door and stuck his head out. Lucas rammed the muzzle of his gun underneath the man's chin.

"Where is she?"

"I don't know."

Lucas shoved the barrel farther up, dislodging the guard's

Adam's apple. The man measured his intent and backed into the house. A horrendous scream curdled Lucas' blood. He swung with his left arm, and with a teeth-jarring crack, the guard toppled.

Lucas raced up the stairs and rammed his full body weight against the door, the wood fracturing from its hinges and smashing against the wall. Seeing Johnson's fist poised above Rachel's lovely face, breath hot as fire burned from Lucas' lungs.

Johnson glared at Lucas, his mouth twisted in surprise and rage. "Where the hell did you come from?" He pulled his saber from its sheathe and held it at Rachel's throat. A trickle of blood ran from the sword point where it jabbed into her soft flesh.

Lucas placed his boot on top of the stool, resting his hand upon his knee He laughed and watched Johnson with a gambler's impassiveness, the cold, steady eye, the carefully controlled voice, but with deadly meaning.

His blood burned fire in his veins. He held himself under tight control until his rage cooled. To see Johnson pierced at the end of his sword would give him singular gratification. This was no man, but a rabid animal that dared to touch his wife. "Will you give me the pleasure, or will the world know you as a coward?"

"I will definitely give you pleasure. I would not think of disappointing you." The stillness lay palpable, incongruent with the violence that festered within the room. Lucas pulled out his sword. "You will learn, Johnson, to leave what is mine alone."

Johnson's glower shifted from Lucas to Rachel. "I'll take care of you after dispatch your lover."

"Despite your air-tight secrecy to leave New York and other northern cities in ashes, your plans have turned into a sieve,"

Lucas taunted then breathed a sigh of relief when Johnson lifted his sword from her neck. There would be hell to pay.

Calm, Johnson moved toward him, an air of madness about him. In the broad room, Lucas made two quick jabs with the point of his sword to provoke the man. Johnson laid back to attack, giving Rachel time to roll across the bed and dart behind him.

Johnson lunged, hoping to catch Lucas off guard. "You are a traitor. A swine. A proper threat would be to stuff your teeth down your throat."

Lucas kicked the stool into Johnson's shins. "Try it anytime," Lucas mocked.

Johnson charged into direct attack. His cut and thrust rose brutal and severe, but Lucas dropped into a casual position and deflected each blow. For too long he'd been away from battle, but the bloodlust returned in rapid force. He cut and thrust and now started to weave the sword into a vicious dance of attacks, reaching deep and long on the inside, drawing blood from Johnson's abdomen.

Johnson was no less skilled. His enemy was resolute and clever, but as their swords clashed over and over, Lucas sensed the weakness in Johnson's arm. Lucas drove on with a quick series of thrusts, the fine steel of both blades clanging together then sliding to the hilt.

Time halted as Lucas stood nose to nose with Johnson, the swords crossed over their heads as every muscle labored. To pull out his gun and end the fight had appeal but then every Copperhead would hear the shot and be fierce to set upon them.

Sweat beaded at Johnson's brow. The victory Johnson

predicted for himself would not be easy for Lucas was battle conditioned. By brute strength, Lucas shoved him off.

Johnson growled, rushed at Lucas. In rebuttal, Lucas' sword flashed fire as he answered Johnson's tireless thrusts. He slashed his enemy's shoulder, and another caught above his knee. Blood stained through Johnson's pants and shirt. No room for error.

By some miracle, a slight breach emerged in Johnson's jacket. Lucas lunged. Johnson fell back in surprise. The fine steel of Lucas' blade pinned through his adversary's black heart. He opened his mouth to speak, but no sound came out. He advanced toward Lucas, stumbled then dropped his sword. He managed to hold his balance, clutching the sword piercing his chest. The coppery scent of his blood infused the air, and his eyes glazed as they stared at Rachel.

"I loved you, but you betrayed me."

Lucas stepped back, withdrawing his sword. Johnson pitched forward, falling to the floor in a loud thud.

"He was a sick monster," Rachel shuddered. "I'm glad you killed him. Now he can harm no more defenseless women."

"I want to put as much distance between the rebels and us as possible." Lucas wiped the blood free from his sword on Johnson's jacket.

Rachel cried out and his head snapped up. Lieutenant Bowman held a gun to Rachel's head. Another Rebel appeared. Lucas raised a brow. "Congressman Martin." He nodded to the notable Washington politician.

"I see you've been busy, killing my half-brother," said Bowman. "But it has gained me an additional prize. I can get rid of you finally, Colonel Rourke."

"The game's up," Lucas smiled. "Your schemes are wasted."

"Whatever are you prattling about?" said Bowman.

"As we speak, Federal detectives are arresting your men in New York, Chicago and Baltimore."

"Impossible. How did you know?" Bowman shoved Rachel farther into the room, keeping his gun trained on her, the realization dawning. "Of course, courtesy of our dear Saint."

"Of course," Lucas answered casually. "Federal Detectives have known about these treasonous acts for some time now. They have been shadowing your men for twenty-four hours a day from the moment they entered the cities."

"My God! It can't be true," cried Congressman Martin. "We are to be exposed. You know what this means?"

"Shut up," said Bowman. "He's bluffing. Our sentries would have warned us long ago of any approaching Union soldiers."

Lucas shrugged. "It's the truth. They are on their way." He hoped his ruse worked.

Bowman carelessly boasted, "No one knows of my involvement. I've been spying for the Confederacy all along and no one was smart enough to figure it. Not even the intelligent Colonel Rourke. The Union is staffed with fools and you, Lucas, are the most gullible of all. How easy to do favors for you, be at your beck and call. How easy to play on your loyalties and set up your abduction from Washington to Richmond. Somehow you escaped. Miss Pierce, our lovely traitor and the Saint which she goes by, obviously lent her assistance."

Lucas stepped forward, palms up. "She's not the Saint. He's a man living in Richmond. I would know." He feared for Rachel more than life itself. He dared a glance at her pale countenance, his sweet, brave Rachel, so vulnerable. A black rage bubbled in his blood.

Bowman snorted. "You are a fool to make me think otherwise. After I properly mourn your corpse in front of General Dodge, he'll promote me to your position. To get rid of the evidence, I'll shoot her, then you."

Lucas reached for the Colt concealed behind him. He leveled it at Bowman. "You'll never live anything down if I shoot you."

The congressman scrambled. Yet Bowman remained a man of swift understanding, an essential attribute of his trade. He'd not succeeded so long under the Union's nose because he was stupid.

"You are full of surprises, Lucas. Your resilience never ceases to amaze me. I couldn't believe the day when you walked into our office after your long sojourn in the south. But for now, I hold the power. You must understand there are many men outside loyal to me and resentful of your crimes against the Confederacy, especially as a born and bred Virginian. As a gentleman, I will let Miss Pierce go if you drop your gun. For it is truly you, Lucas, that I want dead."

"Don't do it, Lucas," Rachel warned.

Bowman cocked back the hammer on his gun, resounding in the deafening silence into a single click. Lucas' jaw tightened.

"The standoff is complete. I hold all the cards," Bowman bragged.

There might be a slim chance Bowman would keep his word and release Rachel. For his part, Lucas wondered why he wasn't shaking.

Death had reached its icy hand out to him before. He knew it would someday touch him.

Was this the day?

"I've decided there are occasions when it is undoubtedly better to lose graciously than to win defiantly." Lucas slid his gun across the floor. "Let her go."

"No," Rachel shouted. Tears fell down her face.

Bowman kicked the gun out of the way. "Not on your life, Colonel Rourke. You know what your fault is, Lucas? Being alive."

Bowman marched Lucas outside and into the barn, greeting his companions, interrupting their meeting to run his new show. "I have not only captured the elusive Saint, but also Colonel Rourke, my illustrious superior. It takes a spy to catch a spy," he sneered. "Let this be a lesson, you must always expect the unexpected from your enemy. Tie them up, and we'll enjoy a cozy bonfire, toasting...I mean roasting our guests."

His companions cheered. "Enjoy your journey to the Netherworld."

"No one likes to hear the prophecy of his own death," said Bowman.

Lucas dismissed the prediction with a grin.

Lucas and Rachel were lashed to a wooden beam. Accelerant was thrown on the hay-strewn floor to hasten the flames. The barn doors were closed, leaving them temporarily to adjust to the darkness.

Lucas saw moonlight filter through the slits in the planking, casting vertical shadows. His eyes fell on munitions boxes. Lucas cursed. The whoosh of fire wended its way through. A match must have been tossed. His ears caught another unusual sound. That of teeth chattering.

"Have you ever been scared?" Rachel whimpered.

They were being burned alive while tied up in a barn surrounded by Copperheads that were going to assassinate President Lincoln. "Yes, plenty of times," admitted Lucas, becoming angrier now that she was so frightened. He remembered her fear of fire when her home burned down, stemming from when she had seen her father's gruesome murder. How he wished he could spare her of this.

"You are not human, Rachel unless you get scared. But these men don't scare me, they are just scum."

"Why aren't you scared?"

He heard the break in her voice and it tore him apart. "Because I'm going to be free in a couple of minutes."

She turned her head toward him, and her mouth dropped open. He shrugged out of the ropes.

"How?" She didn't finish, coughing on the rising smoke.

Lucas completed untying his feet and pulled a knife from his boot. He sprang to cut her ropes from her. "You aren't the only one who has tricks up his sleeve. It's an old Indian maneuver I leaned from my younger brother, Zachary. You put as much air into your lungs and billow out your chest while they are tying you. It gives you enough slack to shrug out of them. These idiots were too dumb to see it."

"It's a brilliant idea. I'll have to remember it."

Lucas smiled. With her fear diminished, he found the glowing admiration in her voice gratifying. He finished cutting her free and pulled her up.

The wood hissed and crackled. Fire rioted up the walls, igniting the hay in the loft. He kept a wary eye on the munitions boxes, watching the fire spread, and felt her trembling beside him. "I wonder where Simon is."

"Simon's here? Then there's hope." Her voice shook.

"No. I sent him on an errand."

"At a time like this."

"Now don't get all balled up with that temper of yours, Rachel."

"When did you realize my suspicions on Bowman were the truth?"

"I had my misgivings long before your suspicions. I just wanted you to give up your fixation to spy. But you wouldn't listen. Now you've got us in real danger. But fools usually need repetition to understand even the simplest of ideas."

"You came for me, Lucas. How?"

"You little idiot. Did you think I'd fall for the drug you put in my brandy? I know you like a book. I took hold of Simon and shook him until I thought his teeth would break. He told me."

"Were you awake the whole time?"

Lucas could see she was truly distressed. He knew what she was getting at, and it gave him pleasure. "Yes. Even though you thought you drugged me, I heard you say you loved me."

She gasped, and he yanked her into his arms and smothered her with a forceful kiss. "That's better. Now you have something else to think about." He grinned. "You can be sure we'll continue this later." She pushed at him.

"Lucas, knowing all that, and what I did to you…why did you come for me? The truth now."

Lucas eyed the flames spreading nearer to the munition boxes. "Because I can't live without you."

"I want better."

"I love you." He held her close. "I'm in love with my wife. In fact, I thought I'd never love a woman the way I do you."

He tugged her to the munition boxes and pried one open with his knife. Just as he expected. Guns. Ammunition. He tossed one to Rachel. "Load quickly. And watch my back. There are a lot of vipers out there, and we're going to make it out of this mess. I don't plan on dying this way."

"How do you plan to die?"

"Old. Very old and with you in bed with me doing all kinds of wicked—"

"How can you think about—"

"You best try, sweetheart, because I promise you, you won't have much time to sleep later."

Smiling, she cocked her gun. "We are in the middle of a burning barn and you're talking about…well you know. You're awfully confident."

Lucas could almost see her blush. "That, too." Her smile was all he needed at the moment. He moved to a wall where the fire had not spread and looked out. The Copperheads had vanished, but Lucas knew they were somewhere out there. He could feel them.

Rachel started sobbing. "Jimmy is dead. They shot him."

Jimmy? Dead? Couldn't think about that now. The smoke grew thick, his eyes stung, and his throat was parched. Lucas kicked through the planking. Fire rushed up with the additional oxygen. "On the count of three. One…two…three." They jumped through a wall of fire into fresh sweet air.

An awful crackling and exploding came from behind them. Lucas held tight to her hand. "Keep on running." He dove with her into a ditch, covering her with his body. A spectacular explosion burst into the air as the fire had found its way to the munition boxes. The whole ground shook and the percussion from the blast deafened them.

Ears ringing, Lucas rose first, shaking his head to get his hearing back. He pulled Rachel up, dodged a bit of soaring barn wreckage on fire that plummeted back to earth.

"Let's get out of here before our Rebel friends decide to check on their handiwork." He tugged her forward. Near the house they were met with a volley of shots. He shoved her back on the porch. Woodchips showered over them. She moved to the other side and both fired on those curious enough to come out of their hiding places and scattered them like quail.

"Hold off for a while, sweetheart." He tossed her more ammunition. "That's the last of it, Rachel, and when we get out of this mess, I want your solemn promise you will not be doing any more spy work. My wife will not put herself in danger."

"I promise, Lucas. I'm tired of war."

Lucas sat satisfied for the moment; her promise was real this time. "I want you to know that I will never impose on you how you ought to be."

"I know that, Lucas."

More rebels advanced and they fired more shots to fend them off. He leaned his head against the house and moaned.

"What's wrong?"

"I have only one bullet left." Lucas saw them getting bolder as the Confederates rounded the house to get a better shot.

Sitting ducks. He shoved Rachel behind him and breathed a prayer.

From the opposite direction, an explosion of shots erupted. Horses galloped in, thundering across the yard, at least a hundred Union men. Never was he so happy to see his men in blue. General Dodge charged at the forefront, the old commander's eyes wild with the zeal for battle. Gunsmoke hung in the air. The Confederates were beaten back and rounded up.

Lucas rose and walked to Dodge. "About time, General. Thought I'd have to fight this war by myself."

"As you can see, we are here, Colonel Rourke. I should court-martial you right now for escaping my guards, but since you alerted me to these murderers, we'll talk about it later. Been too long sitting behind a desk. Feels good to be back in the thick of things. When I received your message from this young man," he pointed to Simon, "well, it took me some time to gather men. I will say I had trouble locating the place in the dark, happened upon Jimmy O'Hara who helped guide us. Saw the explosion, heard the gunfire and hightailed it here."

"Jimmy O'Hara!" Rachel shrieked. "He's alive?"

"Why, yes," General Dodge said, leaning over in his saddle, gazing at Rachel admiringly.

Beneath a tangle of brows, Lucas saw a slash for the general's mouth, then a slight upward tilt of his lips. For the first time since he worked for the old sleuth, Dodge cracked a smile, bursting into a full-blown grin.

The general whispered to her, "I speculated that the Saint might have been a woman...now I know for sure. It is an honor to meet you."

Rachel opened and closed her mouth, but when Jimmy pushed his horse through, she ran to him.

"Very much alive, Miss Pierce," the Irish hooligan boasted.

Lucas frowned at him.

"I mean, Mrs. Rourke," Jimmy amended.

"What do you mean, Mrs. Rourke? Lucas, are you married to this woman?" Dodge sat back in his saddle, his eyes darting from one to the other.

"Yes, sir. It's a long story."

Another smile appeared from the general. "And one I'll be sure to hear. For now, we have other business to attend. Round up the rest of the Rebels!" Dodge commanded and turned a jaundiced eye to the ones already caught. "All such persons engaged in secret acts of hostility will be regarded as spies subject to martial law and penalty of death. If you are identified as enemies of the United States government which is more than likely, you will be immediately brought to trial before a military commission, and if convicted, executed without delay of a single day."

Several of the Rebs paled. Congressman Martin sputtered. Lucas became distracted when Rachel dragged Jimmy from his saddle, placing kisses all over his cheeks.

"You dear, precious, adorable boy. I thought they killed you."

Lucas didn't like the attention Jimmy was receiving, but he felt good.

When Rachel raised her head, an odd look of horror covered her face. "Lucas!"

She bolted from Jimmy, hurling her body at Lucas and knocking him to the ground. A shot was fired from behind. He rolled Rachel beneath him and tossed off a shot in the direction of the rapport. *Bowman.* He nailed the bastard in the leg and he went down. General Dodge's men swiftly surrounded Bowman and placed him in irons.

"Lucas?"

It was a bare whisper. Enough to freeze the blood in his veins. He looked down. Her hand lay on her chest. Blood soaked her dress. She had taken the bullet for him.

"I have to use both of my hands for a moment, love," he said gently, laying her with great care on the ground. Her breathing was stilted, shallow. He had to see the damage.

She gazed at him, trusted him with those large amber eyes of hers.

"I'm not going to die, am I?"

She was so brave. *To die?* No. He choked. "I'm going to rip your dress a bit." She nodded. He flipped out his knife and cut open a swath. Remembering his audience, he cut as little as possible to reveal the wound. He probed into her wound with his fingers. He expelled a breath. The bullet did not hit any vital organs, but the damned thing was lodged in her shoulder muscle. Tears ran down her pale cheeks.

"You have so much courage, Rachel. We've come a long way, haven't we?" He soothed her like a child, but she was sturdier than most men he'd seen on the battlefield. "You're going to have to trust me. I've done this before when I was a cavalry scout. I know it'll hurt a lot. I promise we'll get you the best medical attention as soon as possible."

A flask of brandy was passed to him, and Lucas poured it liberally over the wound.

"You've captured my heart and soul, Rachel, and I could easier lie down and die than be without you. The thought of losing you...if I hadn't made it here on time tonight...it's more than I can bear. You are a part of me...you have been a part of me for so long...since that first night in Richmond...you have completely blindsided me."

"Oh, Lucas. I only want to be with you," she cried.

"My beautiful Rachel. I'll always be with you."

With the tip of his knife he probed for the bullet like a surgeon plying his trade. Her eyes flickered as he tipped it up and out and tossed the ball away. Someone handed him a clean handkerchief and Lucas pressed it in place to stem the flow of blood. Rachel had fainted. Lucas lifted her into his arms. His eyes filled with tears at the thought that he could have lost her forever.

Chapter 31

"The doctor will be down in a few minutes to give orders on your convalescence. But I'm telling you, Rachel, there will be nothing but strict bedrest for you. I have servants hired to do everything," Lucas commanded.

She'd been asleep off and on for the better part of two days. Lucas stayed by her bedside the whole time, and he looked like the walking dead. He hadn't shaved, his clothes were disheveled and dirty, and his dark hair ruffled. He was handsomer than she ever remembered.

She struggled to sit, and her shoulder stung where the bullet had struck. Lucas helped position her. "You worry too much."

"With due cause."

She smiled as Lucas turned his gaze from her to glare at Simon and Jimmy. "I hope you both understand my orders. Loud and clear."

"Yes, sir," they chorused.

Rachel caught them smiling at one another. They had all become good friends.

A pretty black servant woman entered the room, her head bowed. "Pardon me. I must sweep and mop the room. Don't mean to trouble you all," she said.

Her broom clattered to the floor. Her hands rose to her cheeks. A horrendous scream pitched through the air. "Simon! Oh, Lordy, I don't believe my eyes."

"Mama. Is it really you?" Simon jumped up, knocking his chair over in the process. He dashed across the room and ran into her open arms. Both cried like babies, his mother using her apron to dab Simon's eyes, then her own.

"I thought you died in the barn fire, Mama."

"No, baby boy. The people who helped us get away wanted the bounty hunters to think that. I didn't want to go without you, but they'd shoot me if I put everyone in danger. They had a large group to protect and promised they'd help you escape. On a return trip, they approached our old master's plantation. Other slaves say you had run off and were not to be found or thought dead. I thought I'd lost you forever. Oh, God of mercy, thank you. This is a sweet day!"

Rachel glanced to Lucas. His cobalt eyes melted into hers. He was affected as much as she. In her heart, Rachel came to the sudden realization she had played a role in saving those persecuted from slavery. Not all. But some. Simon was wrapped in the gentle cocoon of his mother's embrace when two soldiers appeared at the door and a very tall man entered.

"President Lincoln! This is a surprise, sir." Lucas bolted to attention, followed by Jimmy and Simon.

Simon's mother fainted dead away. Simon knelt on the floor, fanning her face.

"My ill looks do that to the females upon occasion," Lincoln joked. "And how are you, Mrs. Rourke?"

"I'm doing fine, Uncle Abe. It's good to see you again," Rachel said. Lincoln took her hand and gave it a squeeze.

"Uncle Abe?" Lucas stared thunderstruck, aghast at her familiarity with the President.

Rachel laughed. "I expect a little of our history should come to light. President Lincoln and my father were lawyers who rode the circuit together in Illinois. Often, Uncle Abe visited our home."

"I remember Rachel when she was this high." Lincoln raised his hand three feet from the floor. "Used to bounce her on my knee back then. She was a rather serious, introspective child, headstrong in a lot of ways as I recall." Lincoln paused to stroke his beard. "Since then she's been an awful worry for me playing the role of the Saint. If anything had happened to her…I would have felt deeply responsible as her father was one of my dearest and most cherished friends."

Lucas glanced at Rachel. "You told me you had friends in high places, it never occurred to me—"

"I tried to tell you, Lucas."

"I hope I haven't caused a family quarrel," said Lincoln. "I will say this though, Colonel Rourke, if it will rest your mind, as Commander in Chief, I command Rachel to conclude all measure of espionage from here on out. Rachel is not in the south any longer where I could not stop her heroic and indispensable activities. She is in Washington and under my jurisdiction."

"Thank you, Mr. President," said Lucas relieved. "Acquiescence is a new word for Rachel. There were times I recall, she'd rather drink vinegar. But your orders do have a delightful ring. Yet I can't imagine what other revelations will surface today." Lucas exhaled, a long speculative sigh, and Rachel laughed again.

"Uncle Abe, allow me to make introductions," said Rachel. "This is Simon and Jimmy O'Hara. And...did you get my wish list?"

Lincoln chuckled. "When she was younger, it used to be licorice sticks or peppermints, now it's more exacting, but just as affordable, especially in light that she saved my life."

Lincoln sobered. "First, I will relay to you that a nefarious attempt was made last night to sack and burn New York. This disastrous plot, had it succeeded, would have resulted in a frightful sacrifice of human lives and property. Rebel emissaries and agents dogged by our Secret Service operators closed in on every important Rebel agent in New York, Cincinnati, St. Louis, Baltimore, Indianapolis, Portland and Boston. Caches of arms, ammunition and medical supplies were found and confiscated. Plans of Federal buildings, warehouses prison camps, bridges, shipping centers, and arsenals throughout the country, all subject to attack were uncovered. Numerous arrests have been made swiftly and secretly."

"A military tribunal will try the Rebel agents charged with treason against the United States government. I can only speculate on what would have occurred if we didn't have the valuable information Colonel Rourke, Simon, Jimmy, and you, Rachel were helpful to obtain ahead of time." President Lincoln fished around in his pocket. "I can't seem to locate...Major Dodd, do you have what I need?"

"Yes, sir."

Lincoln waited as Major Dodd produced parchments. "First of all," Lincoln glanced around the room until his eyes fell on Simon who had just revived his mother into a standing position.

"Mr. Simon. I am very glad to make your acquaintance. For your bravery and years of service to the United States government, you are awarded this Campaign Medal plus a commission in the United States Military with back pay." Lincoln shook Simon's hand. "Congratulations to you, young man."

"Lord be praised!" said Simon's mother. She fainted again.

"My ill looks must be more overcoming to people than I think." The President expressed another witticism, and then searched the room.

"Mr. James O'Hara. For your bravery and loyal service, you will receive a raised commission from the army under Colonel Rourke, of course, for your vital service to the United States government. Your education will commence immediately with future commission to West Point."

Jimmy preened like a bantam rooster as he shook Lincoln's hand. They all liked President Lincoln, sensing his compassion for all that was fallible in humankind.

"Colonel Lucas Rourke." Lincoln turned his dark cavernous eyes on her husband. "You have my undying gratitude for everything you have done in service to our country. You are now to be recognized for helping us win this war and to keeping the Union together. Because of fine men like you, who are championing what is right, the world will be left a much better place. For recognition of duties rendered, I am promoting you to brigadier general."

"Thank you, sir." Lucas took the President's hand and shook it heartily. Rachel's pride swelled. Lucas was stunned. He had expected heavy reprimand. Instead he was promoted.

"However, *Mrs. Rourke...*" President Lincoln leveled the full intent of his dark gaze. "...will be demoted to civilian status for the remainder of the war. But at this time, I wish to confer upon your person the highest award I can offer—"

"This must be award day," chuckled the doctor as he entered the room and stood at the foot of Rachel's bed.

"Yes, it is, Dr. Jenner," said Lincoln. "I had my personal physician see to you." Lincoln winked, and Rachel's jaw dropped. "How is the patient doing?"

"She is recovering well and in very remarkable condition for a mother to be."

Rachel's eyes widened, her mouth dropped open. "I'm—I'm having a baby?"

The doctor laughed, eyed Lucas and then offered his hand to congratulate him. "It happens from time to time to young married couples. Some call it an affliction, but others call it a time for joy."

Lincoln bent over and kissed her forehead. "You mind what I say from now on...no more intrigue," he whispered in her ear. "There will always be ogres and tyrants in the world. We'll leave the maneuvering for your husband. I want to see my good friend's grandchild born."

Rachel looked around her. They were all here. Everyone important in her life...Jimmy, Simon reunited with his mother, Uncle Abe and most of all Lucas. *Her family.*

Everyone departed to allow the young couple privacy.

Lucas laid a wrapped box on her lap. "I've been wanting to give you this present, and especially now I want you to have it in honor of our child to be born." He sat on the bed next to her and took her hand. "I love you, Rachel."

"Oh, Lucas, I love you, too. And I promise that the Saint is laid to rest. It was risky and scary. The truth is, that everything I fought and struggled for came before earning what is the greatest worth, and that's you."

Rachel opened the gift and a slow, tremulous smile came to her lips as she pulled a Bible from the package…a Bible just like the one her father had given her. "You knew."

Her eyes swimming with tears, she let her gaze rest on her husband. "I could never be happier than I am at this moment." She lifted a hand, laid it on his unshaven jaw.

"Lucas, I'm hungry."

Author's Note

"Power dwells where men think it dwells. It rises as a deception, a shadow on the wall. And an exceptionally small woman can cast an exceptionally large shadow."

Tactical battlefield intelligence was vital to both armies in the field, and in the annals of the War Between the States, women spies emerged the most colorful and notorious, taking great risks in the field of espionage. In the development, of Surrender to Honor numerous elements of real-life people and events were integrated into the novel. Rachel Pierce emerged an amalgamation of Rose Greenhow, Belle Boyd, Elizabeth Van Lew, known as "Crazy Bett", Sarah Emma Edmonds, and Harriet Tubman. Of particular note, was a comparison to the well-educated, African-American Mary Jane Bowser who posed as an illiterate enslaved woman inside the Confederate White House in Richmond, gathering critical intelligence with her photographic memory. Hundreds of women flirted, cajoled, and tricked men into giving up top-secret information. The creativity of female spies was boundless. The elegant Victorian fashions lent these ladies plenty of places to hide contraband and coded messages beneath tight corsets, layers of petticoats and crinoline and stacked coiffures. Under heavy strain, their sacrifice helped win battles, yet if caught faced imprisonment or hanging.

The Office of Civilian Spying is a fictitious name for the Union's decentralized intelligence gathering initiatives. Under Yankee Generals Winfield Scott, George B. McClellan, Ulysses S. Grant, John C. Fremont, Grenville Dodge, and also, President Lincoln, intelligence agendas became the early glimmerings of today's Secret Service and Central Intelligence Agency.

Acknowledgments

Most books wouldn't be written without the help of some special people. I would like to acknowledge Caroline Tolley, my developmental editor and Linda Style, my copy editor, and Scott Moreland, my line editor. Their insight and expertise were indispensable. Hugs also to my spouse, Edward, my right-hand man because without his support, none of my writing would be possible. Also, hugs to my five children, eight grandchildren, Eugene Dollard, Dr. Marcianna Dollard, Nancy Crawford, Brenda Kosinski, Paula Ursoy, Andrew Albury, and posthumously, Loretta Bysiek—your love and comfort surround me.

Many thanks to the gracious support of Western New York Romance Writers Group.

Finally, a special note of gratitude to my readers. You will never know how much your enthusiasm and support enrich my work and my life. You are the best!

About the Author

Best-selling author Elizabeth St. Michel has received multiple awards for her work.

Her first book, *The Winds of Fate*, was a number-one hit on Amazon's list of best sellers and a quarterfinalist for the Amazon Breakthrough Novel Award.

Surrender the Wind, Elizabeth's second novel, received the Holt Medallion and the Reader's Choice Award and was a finalist of the National RONE Award, which honors literary excellence in romance writing.

Sweet Vengeance: Duke of Rutland I won the prestigious International Book Award.

Her fifth book, *Only You: Duke of Rutland Series III,* achieved the American Fiction Award and the "Crowned Heart Award" from *InD'tale Magazine*.

St. Michel lives in New York and the Bahamas.

Dear Readers,

It has given me particular pleasure to write *Surrender to Honor* for you, which introduces General Rourke's younger brother, Colonel Lucas Rourke, head of Civilian Spying for the North. Colonel Rourke is honor bound to uphold the Union and responsible for a vast network of spies. When Confederates abduct him, his only hope is the enigmatic spy who surrenders her heart and soul to save him. Rachel Pierce is the notorious Saint. Witnessing her father's brutal murder by slaveholders, she emerges disciplined in the high art of spying, moving through southern latitudes like a ghost with no trace of her footsteps and defying every one of her enemies without the slightest hint of their knowledge. Caught in a dangerous web of intrigue, they uncover secrets that will prolong the war and cast them both in danger.

There is no greater compliment to me as an author than for my readers to become so involved with the characters that you want me to write more.

That said, I'm happily returning to the Civil War era and the powerful Rourke family of Virginia. As you know, my first installment, *Surrender the Wind,* detailed the journey of legendary Confederate General John Daniel Rourke, the eldest son and his providential meeting of Catherine Fitzgerald from New York during the American Civil War.

My third installment, *Surrender the Storm,* acquaints us with the third brother, famed Confederate Cavalry Colonel Ryan Rourke. Jaded from years at war, he is scornful enough to kidnap a group of nuns from beneath Yankee noses, stealing them to his Confederate camp to nurse his injured men. Yet Colonel Rourke acquired more than he bargained for. The youngest, Sister Grace, dares to challenge him and her provocations are not angelic at all. Why, she possesses a face and sway of hips that would make a monk lust.

In the shadow of fear, Grace Barrett has secrets and joins the Sisters of Charity to veil her identity. And while the beautiful Sister Grace has sworn to keep her vows, this wrong Rebel may be just the right man for her. Yet will Colonel Ryan Rourke's scars make him not only run from the world but from the woman who has the sole ability to heal his soul?

Although I can't tell you much more, I can promise you this: like my last novels, it is written with one goal in mind—to make you experience the laughter, the love, and all the other myriad emotions of its characters. And when it's over to leave you smiling…

P.S. If you would like to receive an emailed newsletter from me, which will keep you informed about my books-in-progress as well as answer some of the questions I'm frequently asked about publishing, please contact me on Facebook, Twitter or webpage at www.elizabethstmichel.com. I would be thrilled to hear from you!

Books by Elizabeth St. Michel

The Winds of Fate

The Surrender Series
Surrender the Wind
Surrender to Honor

Duke of Rutland Series
Sweet Vengeance
Light of My Heart
Only You
Lord of the Wilderness

www.elizabethstmichel.com

Made in United States
Orlando, FL
20 March 2022

15944422R00192